EVERY OTHER INCH A GENTLEMAN

By the same author:

Martin Bonehouse, The Book Guild, 1996

An Ecstasy of Fumbling, The Book Guild, 1998

EVERY OTHER INCH A GENTLEMAN

Mark Stewart-Jones

Book Guild Publishing
Sussex, England

First published in Great Britain in 2007 by
The Book Guild Ltd
Pavilion View
19 New Road
Brighton, BN1 1UF

All characters in this publication are fictitious and any resemblance to real people, alive or dead, is purely coincidental.

Typesetting in New Baskerville by
SetSystems Ltd, Saffron Walden, Essex

Printed in Great Britain by
CPI Antony Rowe

A catalogue record for this book is
available from the British Library

ISBN 978 1 84624 108 6

For C. B. B.

And thanks to I. A. J.

Contents

'There's this bloke . . .'

Shortly before eleven o'clock, a jackdaw settles briefly on the roof of the guest house, perching for a moment or two on the crossbar of the television aerial. This bird's sudden arrival and its hasty departure are not noticed by the gentleman occupying the room by the bathroom on the second floor.

He checks again. Twelve hours and eleven minutes by his watch or twelve hours and eight minutes according to the alarm clock by the bedside.

Something in the jackdaw's beak periodically catches the light of the August morning sun, it is the coloured foil sweet wrapper, discarded earlier in the day on the beach by a small boy with chubby legs.

In some quarters this bird was referred to as *corvus monedula*; others still simply call it a daw. Different names, different times, just like the gentleman on the second floor.

He trusts his watch, purchased from a department store, a very good department store, for seventeen guineas, and not the alarm clock. Although time had betrayed and humiliated him as it betrays all eventually, its slow and meticulous measurement was some slight recompense.

It is a hot day again and already he can smell himself. He will get dressed soon but not just yet, he will await the symmetry of twelve hours precisely.

The sweet wrapper tumbles from the jackdaw's beak as

the bird takes flight and a quarter of a mile away a boy feels the cold sea against his stocky thighs for the first time that day. The sky over the town, over the rows of neat tall salty houses, is blue and seasick with gulls and terns. The jackdaw slips away, a shadow again, its own shadow, a silhouette sailing in search of clouds, in pursuit of its own darkness.

Three of the walls are wallpapered, pink regency stripes with alternating pink and turquoise roses. Hideous, he thinks, like a cissy's pyjamas. Perhaps because of ill-fitting window frames and the resulting damp (why do you always remember things like that?), the wall around the window was simply painted plaster. Magnolia, that was the colour. Whatever it was, it was certainly more pleasing on the eye. Nicotine would have been a better name. Certainly it would have been more accurate in this case. Magnolia isn't the name of a colour, not really, it sounded too much like a country in an Ealing comedy, probably with Alastair Sim in it playing the Archduke of Magnolia.

Magnolia.

Mag-nolia.

Magno-lia

He repeated the word to himself so that its meaning and context evaporated. It was just an abstract sound, the stuff of language rather than language itself. A sequence of noises. Unrecognisable. Magnolia. It was in a song, wasn't it? During or just after the war, he'd heard it. Quite well known. Maybe he had a recording of it. He used to have a gramophone, nice one it was too. Cost a fortune. Something about magnolia. Coloured lady sang it. What's her name? Dead now. Scent of magnolia or was it stench of magnolia? What the hell was all that about? Poplar trees as well. Stench? Doesn't sound right. Was it right?

Somewhere, a little boy piddles in the sea and watches the bubbles, then he turns and looks for his mother.

Somewhere, just audible over the waves he hears somebody calling.

Meanwhile, in the street outside the Seaview Guest House, just below the gentleman's window, a stout red-faced man is whistling. He does so oblivious to the fact that he is about to step on a sweet wrapper. It is going to be another hot day, another stinker, and he wipes the sweat from his forehead with the back of his hand. He continues to whistle the same sequence of notes, a tune he has known for years and years. Today he has certainty, he has clarity. (A piece of coloured foil now attaches itself to the sole of his shoe.) He would sacrifice heaven and life eternal just to taste her mouth again, just to feel the contours of her breasts. He would exchange his soul to experience the dampness between her legs once more! Just for one more chance! Just for the possibility of one more chance! He would deny God, he would repel the devil just to glimpse a real eternity. That was infinity, the infinity of the flesh, infinity made flesh. That was all he would ever need to know and a man who has no doubts will always whistle. So he whistles

This short trilled refrain is heard by the gentleman on the third floor. No, he thinks, not that song, please don't be that song. It can't be, it just sounds like it. He doesn't want it to be that song. He would rather it was the song about the scent of magnolias. But for a second he stops thinking about time and remembers.

He remembers the changes! Key of C major – always his favourite and by far the easiest key for his voice. Down through a nice E minor and resolving on G6th. An easy sequence to remember and a sweetheart to play. Common time too, the boys in any old provincial fleapit couldn't bugger that up! Catch a rim-shot with the first 'out', then again on 'walk'. God, he could do that and sing the bloody song at the same time

I took ***out*** *my little Willy for a* ***walk*** *down Piccadilly.*

People always stop and stare . . . He has heard enough. At twelve hours and three minutes by his watch, he stirs himself from his bed to close the big sash window.

I took ***out*** *my little . . .*

Foxtrot, novelty vocal refrain with piano accompaniment . . .

Ssssschockckckck!

The whistling is heard no more.

Back on the bed, history denied. The past repelled. Sanctuary and silence. Nostalgia is only the yearning for meaning, the desire for a time when we could sense purpose and reason in our lives, when there was an order to things we could understand.

But the gentleman doubted if there had ever been any real meaning in his life. The greatest gift we have erodes away to nothing as we ask of it why? or how?

Hadn't his father said that once?

Or his mother?

Of course not!

He had just thought of it himself but nostalgia is notoriously generous!

According to the Inland Revenue (variously 'bastards', 'a dog with a bone' or 'the scum of the earth') he had just turned sixty-three. An age when a man is quite familiar with the sweet distortions of hindsight but he loathes himself for succumbing once more. A distortion, however well-meaning, is always a lie.

History was facts and he was fine with facts.

He had been born in the summer, that was history, a simple fact. But to claim that it was the most beautiful perfect summer ever was not history, that was a lie. Seeking a kind of comfort, he glances for a moment at a dark metallic object just visible under his pillow and he almost smiles.

It will be tonight, he thinks, and he smiles like a man who is finally certain about something.

Meanwhile, a little boy in ill-fitting draw-string bathing trunks starts crying and will certainly never wish to recall that August Bank Holiday on the north coast of Kent in 1978. The holiday which was going to be so special, because he was going to see lots of whales in the sea and perhaps even mermaids and pirates and submarines and starfish. But all he would remember would be the terrible panic that particular morning when he thought he'd lost his mother and father. He looks everywhere dazzled by the sun and blinded by his tears. His crying becomes louder and louder but all he can taste is salt, salt, salt.

His nose, his mouth, his skin, his eyes, salt, salt, salt, salt and water, salt in water, salt the water, salty water . . .

Eleven hours and fifty-eight minutes.

On second thoughts, he hates the silence, it makes him agitated. He opens the window again and delights in the sound of traffic.

The motor car, like cinema or the aeroplane, was one of those glorious technological landmarks which he believed to be located at that vague point where his generation began and his father's had ended.

His father's life had been in black and white.

His father's life was in sepia.

Or maybe rendered faithfully in oils.

Years ago, back at home in his tiny little back bedroom in Eastbourne, there was always the noise and bustle of the busy main road. All the summers of his childhood, he drifted off to sleep with the drone of lives being lived at a pace that was not his pace floating in through an open window.

Time hadn't been invented then.

(This is why, of course, we waste most of our adult lives trying to recreate or relive our childhoods. Everyone knows that! The holiness of the young is only in their ignorance of time. Time is despised and loathed because to understand it is to know that it will always triumph in the end.)

The first awareness of time is the sensation that it passes too slowly.

Then one day it starts passing too quickly.

He sings to himself.

I took out my little Willy for a walk down Piccadilly . . .

He wants to smile but still he finds it too difficult.

'. . . going off like that!'

'. . . worrying your mother like that!'

He doesn't understand. He is confused and wet and cold.

'. . . going off like that!'

'. . . worrying your mother like that!'

'. . . giving us both kittens!'

He thought that worrying about people was a good thing, it means you must love them. Mummy loves him but Daddy is telling him that it is bad if people worry about you. If I make Mummy worry about me, it must mean it's my fault and does it mean that Mummy doesn't love me properly? She looks cross and in his head she is still shouting at him.

'. . . worrying your mother like that!'

'. . . giving us both kittens!'

Salt again! Everywhere! It fills his nose eyes and mouth as he stands rooted to the spot, unable to move. The only physical sensation he feels is the wet sand between his toes and a sharp sudden breeze which makes the damp tears on his cheek tingle and sting! Then, a taste at the back of the mouth, a horrible taste. Never had he felt so alone, never so scared, never so in need of their love. He wants to be hugged, he wants to be warm, he wants to feel safe again. Only for a minute and he knows he will be fine again.

'. . . going off like that!'

'. . . worrying your mother like that!'

'. . . giving us both kittens!'

He cries and cries, they ran away and left him, they didn't really love him and he *made* them come back, that's what they said! He *made* Mummy worry. She didn't love him, they didn't want him. They had never wanted him, they wanted him to be eaten up by a giant octopus.

'. . . going off like that!'

'. . . worrying your mother like that!'

The Seaview Guest House stood in Royal Terrace at the western end of the seafront, opposite the famous white-washed entrance of the Hayland Rock Hotel. It had been the Paradise Hotel for many years and the gentleman on the second floor by the bathroom can recall it vividly as it used to be. He is quite aware of all the changes that have taken place but refuses to make any judgement.

Differentness.

Now he can well appreciate that!

But *betterness* is a quality that exists only in the past tense and too frequently in the minds of the middle-aged!

Things change and that was all he really needed to understand nowadays.

Love, money and the inexhaustible pursuit of both will always blind us to purpose and meaning.

Thank God!

Eleven hours and fifty-three minutes.

He strokes his chin with an awkward familiarity and

wonders if he should shave now or later. As he does so he is certain that he can hear whistling again. But it's nearer this time

I took out my little Willy for a walk down Piccadilly
People always stop and stare
I took out my little Willy for a walk down Piccadilly
But Willy seems to like it there . . .

He picks up the Webley Mark IV army service revolver that he has secreted under his pillow and running his thumb along its six-inch barrel with near ceremonial reverence he puts it in the pocket of the raincoat that hangs in the wardrobe. Then he stretches himself out on the bed and within minutes he has drifted off to sleep again.

They laughed at him once because he thought sandals were so named because they were usually full of sand. But this had seemed quite sensible to him at the time. He knew that whenever you got sand in your sandals you never got all of it out. Not properly. Some stayed inside for ever and ever. This was something he definitely knew to be true but he didn't want to tell them in case they laughed at him again.

But he liked wearing sandals. (For one thing they had buckles, which he could fasten himself, he didn't even have to ask Mummy to help him.) As they made their way from the beach onto the Promenade, he sits down on a step and puts them on again.

'Come on, we haven't got all day, you know . . .'

He didn't like looking at his feet but he had to when he put his shoes on. His feet weren't very nice, Mummy always said his feet were a nightmare whenever they tried to buy new shoes. They were the wrong shape she used to say but he didn't understand why. They used to put this funny thing under his foot to measure it sometimes and that would make Mummy cross. She would sound angry and ask him why he couldn't be normal like all her friends' little boys.

Auntie Paula said he had footballer's legs but she didn't say that he had footballer's feet. It was always best to keep them covered up, he thought. Then no one would have to see them.

'We haven't got all day, you know . . .'

Daddy doesn't always mean it. Mummy always says that whenever he shouts at him. Daddy doesn't always mean it. But she hasn't said that today so he must mean it.

'We haven't got all day, you know . . .'

They amble back towards their guest house together, but no one says anything. The boy in his sandals stops at intervals and stares at the sky.

He tastes the salt once again as he traces with his tongue the flight of a distant s
w o
o p
i
n
g
seagull.

After dozing for twenty minutes or so, the gentleman on the second floor stirs himself and finally gets out of bed. Lacking any real sense of order in his daily life he'd invented for himself a series of rituals.

To this end, he coughs violently and feels the sputum rising in his throat.

The tune that he hears in his head now is a different one. Nobody stops and stares and nothing smells of magnolia. This one is one of the very early songs, possibly the earliest . . .

He recalls the drawing on the cover of the sheet music, that awful sentimental picture of a girl on a swing with a dog watching her. What on earth were they thinking of? Looked sort of Victorian, looked like an advert for bath salts, Vocal novelty with ukulele accompaniment, copyrighted 1943 throughout the empire and a tanner from Boosey and Hawkes!

In all the places I have ever been
It's the nicest predicament I've ever seen!
I can see your predicament . . .

No, no! This is not good! Sentiment was not required then! And it is certainly not required now. Especially not now!

He coughs again and finally to his satisfaction produces into his hand something of vaguely satisfying colour and consistency.

Roughly ever since his fiftieth birthday, he had been hearing in his morning coughing spasms the desperate hacking of an elderly man. Resigned to this, he opens a packet of Gold Leaf and lights the first one of the day. Fifty was when he was suddenly as old as he remembered his father being when he was an old man.

No amount of experience can prepare you for that!

He looks at the water stain on the sleeve of his pyjama jacket and then scanning his memory fairly randomly for images of past erotic conquests he finds himself recalling . . .

In all the places I have ever been
It's the nicest predicament I've ever seen!

No, not now!

Then, finally . . .

Catherine!

Oh Catherine!

He had met Catherine a long time ago, when he must have been twenty-one or twenty-two, certainly no older. Memory tends to favour details, that is its one major flaw, its great tragedy; after forty years or more, is that it recalls little else aside from details. There was no sense of Catherine any more, no essence remained. Any more than the words of an old tune or the picture on the cover of a long-forgotten song sheet. Nothing of any value.

Just details.

Sadly, a series of unconnected facts now constitute the whole idea of Catherine and his time with her.

Catherine talked a lot. That was another detail he remembered. But so little else remained. In the great vastness of the vastly vast eternal it was the only evidence that they had once made that great connection. A sadness. But recalling someone with slight sadness, he tells himself, is not the same as recalling someone with regret.

I can see your predicament
I can see your predicament . . .

Eleven hours and twenty-seven minutes.

Meanwhile in another room on the second floor, the large room with three single beds, at the far end of the corridor, a woman in a headscarf and sunglasses is rummaging through a suitcase looking for a cardigan. She is observed by a small boy in sandals, who sits cross-legged on the bed next to her.

'Don't sit like that, you'll snag the counterpane,' she tells him.

Snagging the counterpane sounded very serious and important and he must be careful not to do it. Snagging the counterpane was very naughty. It was a grown-up thing probably. He didn't know what snagging the counterpane meant but he liked the words very much. It sounded a bit like an aeroplane. Perhaps he should know what it means, perhaps he has been told lots of times. He wonders if he has just forgotten. Snagging the counterpane? Smagging the counterpame? Perhaps he just can't remember, perhaps that is why they're cross with him again and why they keep shouting.

'Come on, for goodness' sake . . .'

'It's in here somewhere . . . I know it is . . .'

'Perhaps you forget to pack it . . .'

'Look . . . I didn't forget to pack it . . . as a matter of interest . . . it's bloody well in here somewhere. I'll tell you something for nothing, you're not making it any easier for me standing over me and breathing down my bloody neck!'

'Sandra!' He furrows his brow and tilts his head towards the boy.

'What?' She turns around. 'Look, are you ever going to actually listen to anything your mother says? Tell me now. How many times do I have to tell you not to sit like that!' She lashes out with her hand and catches him just below the knee.

He puts his hand over his mouth and bites into the fleshy part of his palm.

It tastes salty.

The gentleman is now vertical again and staring at his reflection as he relieves himself with sadly unanticipated ferocity into the sink below. The sibilant hissssssssssss and pisssssssss and the slight unsteadiness on the feet followed by the rising familiar pungent stench. He gazes with greater intent at the mirror and his thoughts amble for a diverting moment in a vaguely scientific fashion. With the ageing process, was there a general reduction in the elasticity of facial muscles? Was this science? Fact? The evidence looked right back at him in silent confirmation. These familiar becoming-less-familiar-every-day features could once express love, rage, fear, anger, hope and sadness with relative ease. Nowadays they seemed to be fixed permanently in this single expression – the one that conveyed only a deep and profound disappointment.

He continues to gaze at his reflection.

He wasn't so good with smell.

A little boy had once developed a love of books and a greater love of second-hand bookshops partly because of the smell. The smell of dusty shelves and old pages always reminded him of the smell of his first children's annual, a Christmas present and, as far as he could recall, the first book that had actually belonged to him.

In the centre pages of the annual there were four illustrations showing the four seasons, each with a little rhyme underneath describing the picture. It is something he would never forget. This was how he imagined life to be! Each season is so perfect, so desirable there would be so much to experience again and again. There would always be something to look forward to. He'd heard that a lot. It was obviously important. Something to look forward to.

His favourite picture was the one of Winter, where the father sits reading his paper in an armchair. He lounges by the fire with all the family around him, while through the window there are some children building a snowman. Everyone is smiling and laughing. This daddy is a kind daddy. He smokes a pipe but his mouth still rises upwards at the corners in a slight smile. He wears a pullover and looks content. How he wanted him to be his daddy! How he wished he could have just walked into that picture and joined them all by the fire.

'Now, a fellow goes out for a walk . . .'

Midday.

Eleven hours precisely, he notes with a certain quiet satisfaction as he makes his way downstairs.

In the hallway a lady adrift in her undetermined middle years in the middle of another Bank Holiday polishes the dresser, considers ailing hanging baskets and wonders about her lunch.

Her name is Dorothy Burton, the proprietor of the Seaview Guest House.

'Afternoon, Mr Seyton.'

With some effort, he gives her one of his ten-by-eight dimples-and-teeth cordially-yours Moe Seyton smiles. 'Hello there, Mrs B.'

'Missed breakfast time again, I see' she says darkly and fixes him with a vague stare, which might be read as either hostile or maternal in intent.

He nods amiably. 'I'm afraid so.'

He has been missing breakfast time for forty years.

Breakfast time was something that belonged to that other world, the world in which he strolled as the perpetual tourist, the eternal immigrant. It meant something entirely different to him.

Bedtime, night-time, lunch-time . . .

He is quickly dragged from his reveries by . . .

'Oooh very nice . . . very smart!'

She is clasping the lapel of his navy-blue blazer between her thumb and forefinger. 'Now that is what we used to call a right nice bit of cloth. Beautifully finished too, isn't it?'

'Er . . . thank you.'

Another ten by eight cordially and for a second or two he looks uneasily at her hands. They are honest hands, manly hands, manual, had it tough hands, day-in day-out all the hours God sends hands, all right for some, you name it hands.

With practice, your face will lie for you, but your hands will always betray you!

He turns away and brushes something off his sleeve. There must have been men without number, he reflects, that were once driven to the point of madness by just the thought of these hands. There was a time when these hands were glimpsed in the waking dreams of youth softly caressing, stroking, scratching, teasing, unbuttoning . . . loving . . . Ah yes, but where were these men today? he wonders.

As indeed does she.

Jack Milton, before he went soft, used to do the best bit about guest houses and landladies that he'd ever heard, far better than anything of Max's. It was such a brilliant bit, gag after gag and hardly a pause for breath. He did a week with him once in Hastings, years back and had never seen an act with that sort of pace. He was flying! Christ, you didn't want to laugh in case you missed something and that made you want to laugh even more!

For what his opinion was worth, Milton remained one of the few real geniuses in the whole business and now he's either dead, retired or doing the holiday camps.

But there is nothing comely or ample or 'accommodating' about Dorothy Burton, she would never tap upon his door at midnight and demand to be let in.

There are no travelling salesmen locked in her wardrobe screaming to be let out.

Or dead milkmen on the doorstep.

Have you seen my horse?

Mrs B. had worried and fussed herself free of her gender a great many years ago.

Somewhere there might be lusts and passions. But here there are only aches and pains and rain and cocoa.

Gets me right here it does.

Finally, she loosens her grip upon his lapel and he discreetly edges towards the door.

'Don't work too hard now, do you hear me?'

'Well, you know what they say . . .'

But he will never learn what they say as he has already pushed open the door and is now hurrying down the front steps onto the street. A brass band somewhere plays one of those tunes that only brass bands know and the pavement glows like white gold bleached in the noon sun. Then the brass band stops playing and he fancies he can hear applause.

He pauses for a moment and glances down at his lapel as if half expecting to find evidence of its recent encounter with Mrs B. before setting off towards the seafront.

Meanwhile, directly above him, a little boy watches him from an open window on the second floor. He thinks that the man has a sad face but he isn't really sad. He must be happy nearly all the time because he has such a happy walk. The happiest walk in the whole wide world. His daddy doesn't have a happy walk, he has a really cross walk.

'Look, Mummy.'

'Look Mummy what?'

'It's that man who didn't wake up this morning. The lazybones. Remember?'

'What?'

'That man.' The little boy points at the man below him in the street.

'Look, Andrew, not now please. Mummy is very busy. Why didn't you go for a walk with Daddy when he asked you?'

The little boy doesn't reply. When he went back to school after the summer he would have to learn lots and lots of new things but some things he knew well enough already. Some things you don't have to learn, some things are always in your head.

He looks out of the window at the man again and follows his progress until he reaches the corner of the street. Then the man stops suddenly as if startled and glances back towards the Seaview. The little boy waves but the man doesn't see him.

But he was still the happy man with the happy walk.

Bye-bye, Lazybones.

One day . . .

'Andrew, I am not telling you again. Come away from that window now this minute! Do you hear me?'

The little boy turns towards his mother and smiling with a bravery that only children know about, says softly, 'Sorry, Mummy.'

At that moment, without warning, the brass band of the Thanet and Medway Rotary Club commences playing for the fourth time that day 'I Do Like to Be Beside the Seaside'. The opening cadenza drifts along the Promenade, across the beach, eastwards along the seafront where it passes a gentleman in a blue blazer, up the slight incline of an adjacent road and in through an open window of the Seaview.

A pair of pale slender arms immediately close the window, while a pair of moist eyes blink, blink, blink, blink . . .

Once upon a time there was a little boy who invented

words. He invented words for all those things he didn't know the proper word for. He thought that one day when he was grown-up there would be words for everything in the whole world and then he wouldn't have to use BLADDI-BLAP to describe that feeling in your tummy when you know you are about to cry and when your breathing goes a bit funny and it's too late to stop even if someone makes you laugh.

But he had just learned to stop crying instead.

One day when he was walking back home from school for his lunch, he got caught in a sudden freak storm. The sky darkened and suddenly he found himself brought to a standstill by the violent gushing winds and torrential rain. He didn't cry. Even when he saw motorists stopping their cars or when he watched everyone running for the nearest available cover.

Rain and hail lashed his cheeks and the backs of his legs like great bunches of wet nettles but he kept walking. He didn't cry and for a moment, his was the only figure to be seen moving in that storm torn landscape. Still he didn't cry. Then a car slowed and stopped beside him. The driver pushed open the passenger door. He couldn't hear what the driver said and through the driving rain he could not recognise the driver or the car. But it was not warnings about strangers that prevented him from getting into the car. He continued his solitary ordeal for a totally different reason.

Because it was the sort of thing he thought Jesus would do.

Oh, it don't half make your eyes water . . .

After fifty, a man can not venture very far in any direction without colliding with something that recalls a wasted possibility!

That afternoon he had barely ventured twenty yards! It

was the sudden encounter with a vague melodic suggestion he could hear in 'I Do Like to Be Beside the Seaside'

They might have been right, that was the awful thing. Maybe the arrangement was too American, 'too hot', that was what they used to say in those days. But they always hated him anyway and were usually just looking for excuses. They always kept him down, kept him right at the very bottom of the bill. All because he wouldn't play their game, wouldn't be their trained monkey.

I'm doing a bit of what I shouldn't oughtta
Oh, it don't half make your eyes water . . .

Yes, of course, that was when it all changed. That season in 1947. It was going to be a good one. No, it was going to be the best one ever! The world had moved on, things were changing, the industry was changing. Variety was dead, they said, awaiting its post-mortem and quiet funeral – radio and film, that was the future for comedy. We all knew that but there were still a lot of acts getting their start as front-cloth comics. It was the best grounding there was. Even now, virtually all the comedians on TV (some good – some not so good) all of them started in variety doing ten or twenty minutes a night. God, he had worked with most of them!

Nineteen forty-seven was the year it was all going to happen. It was a hell of a bill too, he was lucky to even be on it! Especially with his reputation!

Oh, it don't half make your eyes water . . .

He was in his thirties then, not by much but he was still a young man although he'd put in the mileage all right! For that season, he had really tried to clean everything up and he was doing a whole new act, new songs and some great bits. Yeah, it was cheeky, of course it was cheeky, that was what they liked, maybe it was even a bit blue in places but not like his usual act! There was nothing to get too worked up over. Nothing to upset grandma or the kiddies too much, after all, you had to do matinées on a Saturday.

Oh, it don't half make your eyes water . . .

This was going to be the running gag and the title of the closing song. (Catchy song it was too, one of the better ones, nice little melody over the chorus, far better than 'I Took out My Little Willy'.) He was also doing 'Playing at Home with Mabel' and 'I Can't Quite Put My Finger on It', which were good tunes too with nice little arrangements. He knew he had put together a really strong act and he looked the part too. Hair greased back, the old George Raft, touch of pancake, new suit from Moss Bros and shoes from that cissies' shop off Regent Street. Every night halfway up the bill stuck in between Jack Jackson, who wore a chef's uniform and uselessly juggled kitchen utensils and The Suttons, 'Husband and Wife Eccentric Dance Act' (Wilson, Keppel and Betty less a Wilson or a Keppel) and they were pretty useless too (although Mrs Sutton had fantastic tits). Trinder was in there too somewhere and some Yank singer.

He really couldn't fail.

The fact he did might therefore be cruelly considered a sort of achievement.

With diminishing conviction he blamed fate, bad timing and circumstance for this. But found little solace or comfort. It is worse than a broken heart – you might recover from a broken heart. 1947 was the year it all changed all right, it was the year it all started to go wrong. And no, he had never really recovered, had he?

Too vividly, he recalls . . .

It don't half make your eyes water! . . .

I said it don't half make your eyes water, lady! . . .

I said . . .

That was it! Night after night after night! And he recalls the hideous silence, that hideous emptiness, that void in front of him. Thirty-one years have passed but there are things that will never pass.

Twice in his life he had felt such a silence of isolation and rejection, those nights at the Alhambra in the summer of 47 and many years before when he was a child lying in his cot. He could still remember this so clearly, as he was lying there he would hear a door closing, perhaps it was his bedroom door but he couldn't be sure about this, and then he would wait. Hardly daring to breathe, he would be waiting for the sound of his mother's footsteps. If he heard the sound of footsteps it meant that she was coming to him, to kiss him, to hold him, to read him a story, to be with him. He would know again her warmth, her love, her touch, her smell. If he heard nothing it meant that she was going away, it was only downstairs but it might as well have been Africa. She had gone and left him.

But he has no wish to remember this.

Oh, it don't half make your eyes water . . .

It is a cruel God that allows you just enough idle time to doubt his existence.

With a flurry of rising notes, the brass band concludes their rendition and Moe Seyton finds himself once more on the seafront at Margate on August Bank Holiday. With an involuntary sigh, he looks at his watch and does another quick calculation in his head.

Ten hours and fifty-one minutes.

He wanders along the crowded Promenade, through the molten mass of brightly coloured aimlessness, so vulgar in their brief pleasures and stupefying diversions. He might be amongst them but he would never be of them. Avoiding eyes that betray such wretched intent and low delights, he glances idly at the windows of giftshops and cafés as the brass band starts playing a rousing version of 'Little White Bull'.

He passes the clock tower and continues towards the harbour. He would have to eat sooner or later and it is this vague notion which occupies his thoughts as he walks. Whilst studying a menu, he catches his reflection in the window of the Harbour Café and Grill. He pauses for a few moments.

Cod and chips with peas, two sausages, eggs and chips. Not chips again . . . Perhaps Mrs B. was right, the blazer did look good. Why shouldn't it? Yes, with the open-necked shirt, light cotton trousers and tan brogues, you could pass for a bank manager perhaps. He was once told by a young female acquaintance that he was a rather handsome devil and he has, for many years, taken a perverse delight in this expression. But he was presentable in a vague avuncular way, with his long straight nose and a fairly even set of teeth. Sausages and mash with onion gravy and peas . . . One pound twenty-five. A civil servant then, certainly someone respectable.

Don't be ridiculous, you look like nothing of the sort. You look like a bookie on the make, you silly bugger! Snake and pigmy pie and chips . . . One pound forty. And stop looking at yourself! For God's sake, you want people to think you've arranged to meet a tart? Minced beef and onion pie and chips . . . Or that you're some big cissy or something! Sausage roll with chips and peas, a quid. Walk away! Now!

In a minute, in a minute. Apple tart with ice cream, apple tart with cream, apple tart with custard . . . Why should taking care over your appearance be such a bad thing anyway? Maybe you just need to have a more sombre-coloured scarf around the neck or something? Strawberry gateau and today's selection from the sweet trolley . . . or something . . .

Or something . . .

Checking his watch he walks swiftly through the glass-panelled door and into the interior of the Harbour Café and Grill.

Ten hours and forty-eight minutes . . .

Barney Langton, having walked the whole length of the Promenade for a second time, pauses at a kiosk to buy a bucket and spade for his son. Then, on a whim, he decides to buy himself an ice cream. No wait, have you got one of those what do they call them drink on a stick things you know an orange one please yes that would be fine thank you very much. But he is not hungry and it is cold and tastes vaguely of metal and cleaning materials. It is discarded almost immediately.

This was not what he had imagined.

He was standing roughly (it was hard to know exactly) where there had once been a hugely unconvincing Dalek, in front of which children posed for the cheerless camera and the skinny man with wild hair and hands and eyes that had seen far too much. It had been too easy. Too cinematic. As he had pictured himself hands in windy trouser pockets, alone and strolling with white waves a-rolling.

But his senses were elsewhere that afternoon. And besides

it wasn't raining and the place was about as far from deserted as it could be – a thought flashed through his mind. God, even in his fantasies he was always

alone.

No, it wasn't working. Despite growing up in Wingham, a small village east of Canterbury no more than a Claud Butler with drop handlebars ride from where there were once Daleks, and not seeing the place for almost a decade, he was thinking about something else.

Something very different.

He ambles once more amongst flashing flesh and shadows in no particular direction. He is simply grateful for the chance to be on his own for a while. To delight and wallow once again (without interruption) in the shameful bliss of the previous evening.

Would he repeat the experience? Today? Tonight? Christ, now even?

An excitement so great that it feels more like fear or panic rushes through him. Once he had sought redemption in love, he felt it would save him, rescue him, cleanse him, forgive him.

Then he sought redemption in art.

But there was no truth in either.

Man is not redeemed, he is simply entertained.

Come in make yourself at home, enjoy yourself, please.

Have a neat life and a tidy death!

And close the door on your way out.

Then the Frenchman starts singing once more.

Ju-ker box . . . ju-ker box . . .

Of course, he can excuse himself for his actions. After all, if nothing else it was a kind of entertainment. (Was he to be excluded from that too?) Anyone in his position would have done the same thing. Besides it is probably a healthy thing to do now and again. Through temptation, we reveal ourselves, we catch a glimpse of our true natures.

So, he succumbed.

So what?

Regret would not ease his conscience.

And in the guilt there might well be found something warm, dark and secret.

And, by the way while we're on the subject, wasn't this supposed to be a holiday? Put it all behind us a little break we could do with a little break couldn't we try and forget about it there's nothing we can do about it now couple of days away do us good take the boy to the seaside lets go to Margate for a couple of days before the start of the new term, you could do with a break you said so yourself as long as we are a bit careful with the old money and don't go too mad . . .

But that is what she doesn't understand.

We all need a little madness now and again.

If only to stop us going mad . . .

Clack Clack Clack Clack.

I'm not mad. I'll prove it to anyone, listen to me.

The seaside only makes sense to the very young or the very old.

The rest of us haven't got a clue!

Perhaps they share some vague primal notion that all life came from the sea and that one day it would return once more.

Rare and delightful therefore, he thinks, to be both too old and too young! In fact, approaching his thirty-second birthday, he feels with some justification to be fairly accurately located at some central point between the two.

Once more he forces himself to gaze down at the beach below at the people cavorting with restraint, decency and famous Kentish reserve on tame municipal sands. A single bead of perspiration slowly traverses the arc of his eyebrow. At such times as these, how could anyone not enjoy such a splendid sense of exclusion? Spare me please the accusation!

By his pleasures alone this man was judged not of our kind!

Guilty, your honour. Take me away!

One thing that should be quite obvious to anyone, the English feel deeply uncomfortable with exposure of any kind. Anyone can see this! This is why, he concludes, we all look so utterly ridiculous at the seaside. We always somehow manage to look *accidentally* undressed, as if our exposed state has resulted entirely from the recent theft of all our clothes.

A sudden flicker of doubt passes through his mind but Barney Langton now considers himself an onlooker rather than a participant.

An Exile in Swineland . . .

Then, with a flatulent flourish of pomp and pomps and womps and pomps, the brass band opens its rendition of a Sousa march but the Frenchman is still singing in Barney's head.

Ju-ker box . . . ju-ker box . . .

But the other words do not come so easily now, adrift in the day after and lost in the cruel afternoon sun.

Clack Clack Clack Clack.

Having squeezed himself into a window seat at the Harbour Café and Grill, Moe Seyton orders sausage and mash with onion gravy. The restaurant is hot and stale and his nostrils flare slightly. His arrival has been closely observed by a customer seated at a corner table.

Moe gazes blankly out of the window and listens to the sounds around him. Steel on china, on china, over china, oh vagina, his thoughts rise and float upon the breakneck rhythms of a hundred hurried lunches.

Clack . . . Clack . . . Clack . . . Clack.

Onions, he thinks, never a good idea, they'll be repeating on him all day probably. His gaze falls on the salt cellar set on the table in front of him. White plastic with the word 'SALT' on one side and 'SEZ' on the other. The ketchup bottle is lacking its label. Brown sauce with bangers, leave the onion gravy.

He senses movement somewhere behind him. Moe Seyton closes his eyes and tries to think about Catherine . . . sausages . . . blazers . . . Dorothy Burton . . .

The sun passes behind a cloud, a child somewhere is drawing a picture of an octopus.

Dorothy Burton now naked aside from his cravat which she has tied around her neck, drapes herself across the eiderdown and licks her lips.

Mrs Burton doesn't normally do this sort of thing with her guests. 'Is it terribly wrong of me?' she asks in a squeaky little girl's voice. 'Do you think I need to be taught a lesson . . .'

'So, these two guys are at the seaside . . .'

'Good evening, gents, and I have to say how delighted I am to have been asked back to your delightful . . . er . . *premises* here tonight.

'Anyway, it's nice to see that so many of you have been allowed out for the night. What about that stripper then, gents? Wasn't she something? The lovely Gigi! Wow, what a girl! I was just talking to her backstage but I had to leave quickly because something came up! Seriously, gents, phew, talk about three's a crowd!

'So what's everyone drinking here tonight? What have we got over here then? What's that beer you all drink down here? That old Spitfire, is it? Am I right? Talking of drinking. My wife never drinks, doesn't even drink tea or coffee anymore. All she drinks is milk, no word of a lie, breakfast, dinner, tea, all day long. She drinks gallons of the stuff. It's true. So, I says to her the other day, "Here, Doris, if you drink much more milk you are gonna turn into a c . . ."

'But I was too late . . .

'Last week, guess what? Happened again, didn't it? Wife comes home early from the bingo, catches me in bed with the au pair, doesn't she? Beautiful she is too. Swedish, blonde, you know what I mean? So there I am, I've got my head between her legs. I've just got started and the wife walks in. So she says to me, "Here if you carry on doing that for long enough you'll turn into a c . . ."

'And she's bloody right and all!

'I'm getting a divorce, did I tell you? Do you want to know why? I'll tell you. Relations. Simple as that. Relations. She wants them for dinner and I want them instead of dinner!

'Well, before we go too much further I think we should address the subject. You know what I'm talking about, gents. I heard all them rumours, I have. I know what they say about me and I am pretty sure some of the good gentlemen here tonight would like to know if they're true. Not all of you, some of you don't even know what I'm talking about do ya? Well, you'll just have to occupy yourselves for a few minutes. I don't mind, talk amongst yourselves if you want. You, sir, I'd rather you didn't do that if you don't mind! Someone will have to clear it up! Where was I? Yes, tonight on this stage I'm going to lay all the rumours to rest once and for all! Nah, don't panic, sir. I'm not doing that! If I do that we'll all get pinched! No, no I'm just going to tell you a true story. You see since the last time I was here, I've got myself a new girlfriend now. Lovely girl she is, long blonde hair, huge, you know . . . potential. Anyway she works in this little fag kiosk on Waterloo Station. And do you know what she keeps saying to me? Oh for pity's sake, Moe, haven't you got anything smaller?

'It's true. But she doesn't travel with me, so since I've been down here I've got myself a new girlfriend. Gawd, you should see her! No kidding, a right old burglar's dog she is. 'Ere look, geezer down the front here smiling! Smiling all over his face he is! What's the matter mate, you know her do you? Taking her out later he is. Good luck mate! Yer gonna need it!

'Where was I? Oh yeah. This old cow says to me, right, we were having a bit of kiss and cuddle down on the beach there, like. She goes "Oi, Moe!" "Yeah," I says. Bit shocked like. Coz she's got my name right and it's like the only fucking sensible thing she's said all evening. "Moe," she says, "Don't think you're gonna get your wicked way with me." Can you believe the cheek on this? "You're not getting it!" "Yes I am," I says. "How d'you figure that then?" she says. "Easy," I says "Mind over matter." "Mind over matter?" she says, "How do you do that then?" "Dead easy, missus. I don't mind and you don't fucking matter!"

'Please yourself. Quiet tonight, isn't it? Don't let me keep you up. Didn't this used to be a club once? If they'd told me I was booked into fucking Madame Tussards I would have stayed at home!'

And it was precisely in this manner that Mr Moe Seyton, the Last of the Great Front Cloth Comics, renowned Composer of Risqué Songs and Comedian for Gentlemen Only had opened his act at the Grosvenor Place Oddfellows Club and Lodge the previous evening.

A Silvine drawing book, four Pro Arte crayons (two broken), a Biro refill, a pencil case and a selection of pencils are strewn across the counterpane of the double bed. The boy is bored of ships, ships weren't like trains, you could never get bored of drawing trains. In trains you could see the driver and he always drew the driver with a happy face. But on a ship where does the driver sit?

'Mummy?'

'What now?'

'In a ship. When it's going. Where does the driver sit?'

'I have no idea.'

'How do you make it turn when it's going?'

'Andrew, please not now. Mummy is not feeling very well at the moment. Why don't you draw me another starfish. You can show Daddy when he comes back, can't you?'

'Why are you not feeling well?'

The boy leaps from the bed, rushes towards his mother and throws his arms around her waist. 'Don't be ill,

Mummy,' he whispers to the blue flowers and the pink flowers with the green bits sticking out. For a moment he nestles his face in the folds of the skirt. She smells of washing and soap and doing the ironing on a Monday. Always familiar smells, all the nice smells he knew. Daddy always smelled of funny things, of outside and away, of things he didn't like, things from his work probably.

Sandra Langton is not having a good day.

Maybe she would make an appointment with Doctor Singh when they got home. See if she could get some more of those other tablets. The first ones. They definitely worked, she could see that now. Some of the young mums on the estate had a problem with Doctor Singh and they were always saying such terrible things about him. How they couldn't stand for him to touch them and that he was a foreigner and dirty. She had even heard a rumour that he wasn't a proper doctor, that he'd studied in India and they didn't do things properly there. But Sandra had always found him to be a very kind and understanding man. She always felt that she could tell him anything and it was good to have a doctor like that. Might not be that anyway, she might just be early – now that would be a relief. Thought having the boy in a bed in the same room would be enough. How wrong was she about that?

She ruffles her son's hair. Needs washing should have done it last night needs cutting too. 'Mummy is feeling a bit tired today that's all. Nothing for you to worry about. I'll be fine in a minute, I promise . . .'

. . . Pah pah pah-pah paaaaah pah pah-pah!

At that moment Thanet and Medway Rotary Club Brass Band launch into a spirited rendition of 'Onward Christian Soldiers'. The boy holds his mother even tighter but says nothing.

Pah pah pah pah-pah pah . . .

He doesn't like this song. They have to sing it every

morning in school. He didn't like a lot of the songs they had to sing when they had their prayers. They always seemed to be about battles and wars and marching as to war. And standing up and fighting and always about fighting. He used to get in a big muddle. They always used to get told off for fighting in school but every morning they had to sing about it. The boy hated fighting and the big boys in top class were always making him fight. Sometimes he used to cry.

Maybe it was OK for Jesus to fight because he lived a very long time ago in the olden days.

But every time he had to sing about fighting it always made him think of the boys from top class.

The boy's father is now starting the long walk back to the Seaview Guest House. They would be wondering what had happened to him. He said he'd be back for lunch but he still wasn't hungry. He hadn't been hungry all day and he hadn't touched his breakfast.

Juke-er box, juke-er . . . The Frenchman's voice fades as the cross of Jesus hurtles itself past the sentries of the senses.

But he couldn't stop thinking about that hair. He didn't want to. In fact he is actually terrified of the image fading from his mind. He had noticed the previous evening, *in the still of their moment,* a single fine solitary hair growing from a freckle at a point on the subtle slope where her neck curved to meet her shoulder. Maybe no one had ever noticed it before, perhaps she had never even seen it herself, he was the first, he was the great discoverer. Numbed by its beauty, he had gazed at it for a period of time he could not even approximate. It was utterly perfect, a miracle of genetics and chance, of fate and biology, a million zillion years of evolution distilled into a single tiny half-inch fragment.

It made her both human and somehow beyond human

A simple celebration of the Creator's art.

Not a committed atheist any more (everything becomes

harder with age – even disbelief), no longer one of Nietzsche's gentlemen.

Just a short, anxious, uncertain man who has recently been reminded that there is still so much unimagined beauty in the world!

One who has started to secretly suspect that atheism is, when you really thought about, a dogma as unyielding and closed-minded as any despised and mocked orthodox religious belief! All the same fixed parameters! And an uncertain man will always smile at a new uncertainty.

Barney Langton dawdles, glances dutifully yet vaguely at the entrance to D
R
E
A
M
L
A
N
D

He considers a five-minute detour and then promptly decides against it. He hated fun fairs, hated the singularly depressing idea that people willingly herded themselves into small fenced-off areas in order to have 'fun'. But this wasn't real fun. This was municipal fun, corporate fun, committee fun . . .

We find that nowadays it is a sad fact that the public need their enjoyment to be regulated.

Hitler would have built fun fairs everywhere if he'd won the war!

He turns away and slowly walks up the hill towards the station and watches a train in the distance.

Trains didn't always mean flight and escape anymore. Sometimes they meant capture and return. Then for no reason he begins to think about Ten Number Six and the

Exchange & Mart Man. He hadn't thought about him for many years and there was probably a good reason for this.

As a teenager, as he returned in the early evening from a Saturday in London, he would always see Ten Number Six and the *Exchange & Mart* Man. The train from Waterloo passed through Faversham, negotiating a short elevated section before it reached the station, and fleetingly from this particular viewpoint, the flattened perspective of the streets and houses invested the landscape with the quality of a child's drawing. A two-dimensional panorama of parallel lines and right angles, the houses and streets the same shade of grey. But not a colour – an absence of colour. An unintentional, inadvertent accidental grey.

(Like the gunmetal grey walls of his every tomorrow morning.)

But there he was!

From that lofty vantage point you would be certain to see him. Although Ten Number Six and the *Exchange & Mart* Man wasn't a really a *him*, he was actually a species. Ten Number Six and the *Exchange & Mart* Man walked to the corner shop every Saturday evening in his slippers to buy his eponymous articles. Ten Number Six and the *Exchange & Mart* Man was aged between twenty and seventy, was dull, stupid and ordinary, had a dull job, a stupid wife and lived in an ordinary house with dull furniture and stupid records. But in a life once filled with such glorious uncertainty, he knew that he was never going to be Ten Number Six and the *Exchange & Mart* Man. He would never sink to such depths. He would soar and fly – such dull airless streets shall not contain him.

Then one day you find yourself walking back to a guest house in Margate carrying a bucket and spade. Your mind is occupied and you have little awareness of your surroundings. You watch a train in the distance and someone watches you.

And you know you have just become Bucket and Spade Man.

Somewhere it is always six o'clock on a Saturday afternoon in Faversham. And there is Ten Number Six and the *Exchange & Mart* Man casting his long shadow on the silent street, as he lumbers gracelessly towards home

At The Harbour Café and Grill, somebody has just started singing. In fairness he is doing so with reasonable discretion.

With a chubby forefinger, the man from the corner table is now tapping Moe's shoulder while he continues *sotto voce* in his ear.

> *But I think it very odd*
> *that he calls it praising God*
> *So get up off your knees Sister Eloise . . .*

Moe turns and offers the man an indulgent half-smile.
Not now, please.
"Nobby Newton, I presume?'
Oh God, not now.

People are looking, please.

'You should do some of those old ones again, always went down well. I tell you I nearly died when I heard it. Saw you do it at a show once in Lewisham or was it Tooting? Back in the fifties this was mind. No it was Lewisham definitely. Don't know how you got away with stuff like that. I really don't. I was doing me National Service at the time and we went, a great load of us, me and all me mates. Well bloody saucy it was. We all of us thought you were gonna get yourself pinched at any minute! You got nicked a couple times around then, didn't you?'

Moe responds to the question with a slight shrug of the shoulders. He remains seated, smiles a little harder, avoids direct eye contact and inclines his head to the vacant seat opposite. 'Why don't you just sit yourself down, Sam?'

Sam Taylor, down on the seafront for the afternoon on a bit of business but not all business, eh?, is in his early fifties and appears flustered hot and agitated. As he negotiates his not-inconsiderableness between chair and table edge, Moe notices that the man's belt is undone and the waistband of his trousers unfastened.

Mr Taylor wears browns and fawns and yellows, harvest festival plough the fields and scatter, faded beige and aged, subtle stains and muted magnolias.

A large ill-at-ease man with a complexion that tended towards either the sanguine or perhaps the simply furious. While heavy eyelids and slightly bulging eyes usually left Moe with the impression of a man who had squeezed himself into a skin that was a size too small.

'I'll never know why you always come here for your lunch, the food is disgusting. Anyway tell me, how did it go last night? Sorry I didn't make it. Something sort of came up in the last minute. You know how it is in this racket.'

Moe rolls his eyes heavenward and recalls with some shame his Devious Cough Mixture bit.

Devious Cough Mixture? You got that down here on the coast yet? S'all the rage up in the smoke, I'm tellin you. Bloody missus is always going on about it, says all her friends don't talk about nothing else anymore. They can't get enough of it, she says. You sure you haven't heard of it? Perhaps it's called Wily Expectorant down here. Them bloody woman down our way can't get enough of the stuff. Wife says their husbands give it to 'em. But the daft cow don't know what she's on about. Can't even remember the bloody name half the time – no word of a lie. She says to me the other day, "Ere, Moe, when you gonna give me some of that Cunning Linctus? She'll be bloody lucky, I'm telling you. Told her if she wants to get involved with that stuff, she can get someone else to provide it. Coz you've got to be firm haven't you, fellas?

Sam Taylor is frowning sympathetically. 'That bad eh? You should give them a couple of those old songs, you know. "Sister Eloise", it's a bloody classic, I'm telling you. Did I tell you I managed to track down a copy recently? Antique fair in Maidstone. Don't imagine there are too many of those kicking around nowadays, eh? Ten-inch 78. "Nobby and His Hobby" was the A side, wasn't it? "Sister Eloise" on the other? Bit scratched like but it plays OK. Bloke who sold it to me said it was an interesting curio. You know how they talk these blokes. Do you mind, I said to him, he happens to be a friend of mine!'

Sam Taylor laughs. In doing so he opens his mouth slightly wider than was absolutely necessary and displays a quite impressive collection of gold crowns.

He reaches across the table and with cautious informality he taps Moe on the elbow. 'Nah, I'm just having a joke.'

Moe says nothing but in his mind he pictures bangers and mash with onion gravy.

Ten hours and forty minutes.

A shadow passes across the table as a man outside walks quickly past the window. A glimpse of a face, a green shirt, and a bucket and spade. Why are they taking so long with my dinner?

His stomach announces its hunger.

No clock anywhere. That can't be right, can't see one anywhere. Onward. Aquamarine and turquoise, a bit of wood-effect panelling here and there, a painting of a café in summer with umbrellas over the tables. Not by anybody famous. Garish bright colours. Why isn't there a clock here? Onward. Not a real painting, just a print or something. Spanish or French. Never know why but you can always tell, can't you? Maybe it's the light. Onward. No clock, can't believe that. Onward, onward. Onward Christian Soldiers? Odd choice that. What can they be thinking of? More aquamarine, a plastic starfish and another painting, obviously the other one of the pair. Similar scene, a bar with a stripy canopy. Red and white . . .

Then he looks again at Sam Taylor who is still singing quietly to himself.

Which is the tricky bit? The bangers? The mash? Forget about the onion gravy if you have to, just make up some Bisto. I don't mind, really I don't. Remind me what a frying pan looks like, point me at the larder and I'll do it myself. Jack Milton again. Why is it taking so long?

'Tell you Moe, there's a lot of nostalgia for that old stuff nowadays. It's like it's all gone full circle or something. I still reckon you could get yourself four, even six times your current wedge if you went out under the name of Nobby Newton again. Not these crappy clubs either. I mean how many years have you been coming down here doing the bloody Oddfellows? It's beneath you, I'm telling you. You'll get no coverage there. Believe me I've tried. Boss doesn't want to know. If it's between you and the knobbly knees contest or the donkey derby then you haven't got a hope. You need to be working somewhere decent for a change. Get yourself some little local pick-up band, pay them next to nothing. A dozen of those old songs, bit of banter, you got yourself a great little act. That's an event, that's news! It's one hell of a comeback story, give me an exclusive and I'll guarantee you a double-page spread, competitions, reviews, the works. Then I'll punt the story round the smoke and I'm telling you there's no way they'll be able to resist! No offence, Em, but half of them probably think you're dead anyway.'

In common with many people of his profession, it takes a lot to make Moe Seyton laugh and this is the closest he has come in a long while.

'All I'm saying is that it's a fantastic opportunity, that's all . . .'

Sam Taylor had over the years acquired something of a reputation for his dogged persistence. It was not without some justification and he could quite genuinely boast (and he did so not infrequently) that many years ago, fresh out of school he had made *more than a respectable salary* as a door-to-door salesman. *Persistence, sincerity, persistence, sincerity, persistence* . . . that was always the way in those days.

Keep them talking.

Rule number one. Silence is not the salesman's friend.

Course it's all changed now . . .

'. . . You'd be on your way again in no time.'

'Thanks, Sam, and I appreciate what you're saying but I'm not really looking for that *sort* of exposure. Not any more.'

'I know, I know.' Sam Taylor glances about him and then leans across the table as though about to impart a great secret. *Persistence, sincerity*. 'But will you just *think* about it?'

'OK, I'll think about it.'

Today Moe Seton is happy to tolerate his friend's flamboyant overtures as there is a favour he will request of Sam before the day is out. A favour for which he would seem amply qualified. Of this favour and its precise nature Sam remains at present completely ignorant. There will be a right time but this is not it. What Moe really wants at this moment is his lunch. He glances down at his watch and takes a quiet delight in his intentions.

Ten hours and thirty-seven minutes.

Sam wipes his mouth with the back of his hand. 'It's such a tragedy that you're not working as Nobby anymore. Tommy, Jimmy, Jack and Maxie, you were right up there with the best of them, right. I know at the time people said . . . well, they said you went just that little bit too far sometimes. Bound to get you in trouble. But times have changed, audiences are much more . . . receptive nowadays.'

Moe shrugs his shoulders but declines to reply. He has had to listen to the same comment for over thirty years. Today, he has a few plans of his own.

'Sorry 'bout that. Got your order mixed up with table seven.'

The woman's voice is dull and devoid of all emotion.

'Thank you very much,' says Moe Seyton without looking up. He scrutinises the plate in front of him for a few moments as though it required an answer.

Then shaking his napkin with a flourish and watched closely by Sam Taylor, he tucks into Cornish pasty and chips.

A man who once went just that little bit too far.

1915–1978

Rest in peace.

'Thank you for my bucket and spade Daddy, Daddy, look at my picture. I've done a starfish and look I wrote underneath it, see. It says, "To Daddy, love Andrew." Do you like it?

Please say you do. You do like it don't you? I've given him a big smiley face, look. He's very happy because he's on holiday. Like us. Mummy says she's poorly but she's not *really* poorly so we can still go out, can't we? You said we could and I haven't been naughty, have I? Not really naughty. Not like before I haven't when I made you cross. But I said sorry, didn't I? I want to go on a boat one day, can we go on a boat one day, please say we can. We can go somewhere a long long long long *long* way away. And Daddy, when you're the driver of a big boat on the sea how do you make it turn? Mummy says she doesn't know but that was when she said she was poorly as well. I said they must have a big steering wheel or something. When you're on a boat what happens if you bump into a whale? I don't want to bump into a whale. I drew a picture of a whale but my blue pencil broke and so I had to make it brown. They're ever so big, aren't they, that's why they have to live in the sea because they're too fat to live anywhere else. That's what I told Mummy but she said I was being silly but I wasn't being silly, Daddy, was I? And Daddy? . . . Um, do seagulls come from the North Pole, do they, Daddy? Because in school Mrs Harvey says that lots of the animals that live in the North Pole are white. So do seagulls come from the North Pole? Because that's a long way away too, isn't it? I got red pen on my leg . . . look! Mummy says it will come off in the bath but it won't, will it? It will be there for always, won't it? For ever and ever and ever. When I was little I had pen on my arm and that went away but that wasn't a proper pen, was it? Can we go out soon please? Please Daddy. You promised we could go out, you did, you did. And you said if I was good I could have an ice cream, Please, Daddy, I haven't been naughty, I promise. Look at your starfish, please, Daddy. It will make you happy always. He will always be smiling for you and you'll remember our holiday for always and always. Please take it . . .'

‘Thanks, Andy. It’s a wonderful picture. He’s lovely isn’t he? So where is Mummy then?’

‘She went to the toilet again. She’s always going to the toilet. Why is she always going to the toilet?’

Barney Langton fixes his eyes on his starfish. ‘Well, she must . . . need to, I suppose. Perhaps she has been drinking too much tea. Lots and lots and lots of tea, what do you reckon?’

‘I don’t know . . .’

‘Come on, find your sandals and when Mummy comes back . . .’

At that very moment the door behind him opens and closes.

Sandra Langton, a small embroidered handkerchief covering her nose and mouth, steps delicately back into the room.

‘You’re back then?’ she asks without removing the handkerchief.

‘I thought we could all go out and get some lunch, what do you think? Sorry I’m a bit late, I just sort of lost track of time. I’ll bet you’re both starving now, aren’t you?’

‘I suppose so.’

Father and son watch her in silence as she wanders over towards the dressing table.

With the index finger of her free hand she traces the outline of the floral motif on the handle of her hairbrush. She looks at herself in the mirror and demands once more of her reflection meaning and solutions.

She had always wanted a dressing table of her own, a bit like this one, but a white one like the ones she remembered from films. With gold handles and three mirrors. It would all be gleaming and sparkling and she would sit at it every morning for hours just making herself beautiful, more beautiful than ever! She had once really believed that things like that just arrived in your life as you grew up and became a big lady, like husbands and babies . . . Beneath her handkerchief, she bites her bottom lip a little harder. It never happened. A small bathroom cabinet, a chest of drawers and a shaving mirror on the windowsill. That was it nowadays. Of course she didn't need a dressing table but that was hardly the point was it? The adult will always betray the child. She read that somewhere once – thought it was something to do with being a bad mother! She understood far more nowadays. Do like this wallpaper I must say. Regency they called it, it looked really nice, bet it would look really good in the lounge, really brighten the place up, no doubt about it but Barney wouldn't even hear of it. Likes it all plain. Maybe she would take Maggie's advice and get herself a little job now Andrew was in school and that . . . Oh Jesus . . . only a couple of hours a day, in a shop perhaps. The stationer's next to the bank wanted a girl a couple of weeks ago . . . Save a bit of money and then maybe . . . who knows . . . perhaps find herself a little dressing table.

She shakes herself free of her reveries. Right then, cardigan, handbag . . . But wasn't it partly true that most of the things in life that you really desire, you really crave, are always the impractical things, the luxuries, life's glorious inessentials . . . always seemed to be in her experience . . . sunglasses, purse . . . *must* find an open chemist this afternoon . . . the bare basics, the absolute minimum but always the odd luxury . . . that was the secret, that was the key to it, that's what Maggie says anyway . . .

'Right, I'm ready,' she says finally in cold lifeless tones. 'Let's be off then. Although I don't know why we're bothering, everywhere will be packed by now.'

Dorothy Burton is filling the sugar bowls in the breakfast room when she hears footsteps on the stairs. This is followed by the sound of the door to the front porch being opened.

Sugar bowl in hand, she hastens to the bay window. Peeping through the net curtains, she watches the Langtons as they leave for the afternoon. Family in 203. Didn't hand their key in again, must say something about that. Not that the Seaview has as many rules as some, but nonetheless rules are rules. Funny couple. London, somewhere. Said he was a teacher, teaches French I think he said, at one of those new modern secondary schools with a thousand pupils or something. Doesn't look like a teacher though. Heard them coming and going all hours last night, goodness knows what time it was and she's ever so pale. Poor dear, looks a bit under the weather possibly. Little lad seems happy enough, mind. Must remember to say something about the key . . .

They walk quickly away from the Seaview and around the corner. Andrew is walking between his parents holding onto their hands. Daddy's hand is warm and sticky like his but Mummy's hand feels a bit cold.

They walk the length of the Promenade and are forced to conclude that Sandra's gloomy prognosis was not an inaccurate one. Eventually they pause outside the Harbour Café and Grill, where Barney reads the menu.

'What did I tell you?' asks Sandra turning away. 'They're all packed out. Lets find a chip shop. I really can't imagine what you were expecting at this time of day? It was a ridiculous idea.'

In silence, Mr Langton responds husbandly to what he recognises to be the underlying implications of this remark. 'Wait a minute, there's a table here right in front of us. These two old blokes are just leaving . . . come on quickly before someone else gets there . . .'

Barney and Andrew rush towards the entrance leaving Sandra to follow them at her own pace. In their haste, they almost collide with the two gentlemen leaving the restaurant.

‘Ooops, sorry.’

The taller of the two men looks at Barney and then at Andrew and smiles.

‘I knew him, I knew that man, I did’ Andrew whispers to his mother as they take the seat in the window. ‘He’s Mister Lazybones.’

‘You mustn’t be rude about people like that. Just tell your father what you want to eat.’

Sometimes you know why you start crying and other times it just happens. Even when you’re being really extra super brave.

Well beyond the gaze of weekenders, revellers, cavorters, panhandlers, punks and paddlers on a secluded and sheltered sandy bank between Palm Bay and Long Nose Spit, at latitude 51° 23′ 31.06″ North, longitude 1° 25′ 02.81″ East, Jessica Warne lays stretched out semi-naked in the midday sun. Her clothes are strewn in random careless piles about her, yet despite her back being exposed to the sun all morning her skin remains pale.

Never the world’s neatest young woman (as her mother never wearied of reminding her), one would have however imagined she might have treated such new garments with slightly more respect. The new Day-Glo pink T-shirt had been in her possession for less than forty-eight hours. God, her dad had absolutely hated it and told her bluntly that no daughter of his was going punk while living under his roof. But that hadn’t put her off. She thought it was really cool and that was all that mattered.

But Jessica Warne (Jess to her mother, Jessie to her friends) wasn’t really punk, not like a proper one, not really, not like some of those girls you saw in Canterbury. It wasn’t like she wore a bin liner and had a safety pin in her cheek, was it? Yeah, the Boomtown Rats were OK, but they weren't really punk were they, same as the Tom Robinson Band. They looked a bit punky but they didn't play proper punk music. Blondie didn't play punk at all, she thought. They used to but not any more. Blondie were brilliant and the doubts had remained – maybe she should have bought that record on Saturday.

Every time she went shopping in Canterbury it was the same, Ray's Records and Miss Selfridge were practically next door to each other. It wasn't fair. Her life was becoming bogged down in difficult choices! Yes, she knew she already had 'Picture This' on a seven-inch single but this was a limited edition twelve-inch on coloured vinyl! Might even be quite valuable in years to come. But then again it was such a cool T-shirt and the footless tights were epic. So she had sat where they normally sat, on what they fondly termed 'Their Bench', the one next to Dolcis and considered her options.

Miss Selfridge had won only by default on this particular occasion because a creepy vile man had sat down next to her on the bench (suddenly, it did not feel like Their Bench at all) and started talking to her. He might have followed her into Ray's Records but was unlikely to do so if she made a run for Miss Selfridge.

She had always liked shopping with Loretta (Donna Summer, The Eagles, Fleetwood Mac) and sometimes with Claire (Cliff Richard, Diana Ross) but it had been nice to go on her own for once. Nice to do things at her own pace.

She'd had an unhurried milky coffee in the Wimpy, had a look at all the astrology books in Smith's and seen all the posh, snooty furniture in Habitat before even setting foot in Miss Selfridge. But then as she pushed open those heavy glass doors, there was that tingling again, that slightly nervous rush of something, just like there always was. Or maybe it was even stronger because she was alone. It was a brilliant feeling – it was like when you're a kid and you're just about to kiss a boy for the first time and you feel all giddy and you want it to happen but you want to save it up as well.

Maybe, on reflection, it had probably all worked out for the best. Loretta was just always so cool about everything but Claire would have hated the top, loathed it, probably had forty fits over it. Claire hated anything that was even slightly punk and was always going on about how all the Herne Bay boys were going up the town looking for punks to fight. But Claire (Cliff Richard!!!) was like that, a bit strait-laced in her ways, not boring exactly but more of a coward and she never liked anything too out of the ordinary.

It was like that time they first found that tiny little sheltered cove down by Botany Bay, when they had all gone topless for the first time. By the time they'd managed to convince Claire that no one could see her the sun had gone in. That was typical of Claire. But if you thought about it, as long as you had some privacy it seemed a very natural thing to do. Besides when you go abroad everyone does it and you feel really conspicuous if you don't.

Jessica Warne had been abroad twice and had informed her friends that she may like to live in another country one day. She had never developed the notion beyond that, but it had hinted at something that had gnawed away at her for a while now.

She knew, no she was certain, convinced beyond all doubt that one day she would live in Anti-Cliftonville – wherever that was.

But she liked to consider herself a realist and she knew that for the time being it would have to remain simply an unfulfilled possibility. Just one in a life that will shortly be considered in bleak moments to have been little beyond a series of unfulfilled possibilities.

At latitude 51° 23′ 31.06″ North, longitude 1° 25′ 02.81″ East, Jessica Warne remains motionless, oblivious to the water lapping around her toes, the gentle breeze that blows occasionally over the small of her back and the sand which now matts her hair.

But Jessica Warne will not remain unobserved for very much longer. She will shortly be exposed to the scrutiny of one Malcolm Tanner, an accomplished waterskier and member of the Foreness Marine and Aquatic Club.

At the moment he catches this first fateful glimpse of Jessica Warne, she has been dead for well over twelve hours.

Cornish pasty and chips (the latter a little on the unpleasant side and perhaps Sam had been right, but the former wasn't bad) had been consumed in an almost reverential silence. During this brief respite Moe reflected upon the precise nature of the requested favour that he will reveal to Sam in due course.

But the hour of revelation is not yet upon them.

Now, as they stand together on the pavement outside the Harbour Cafe and Grill, Moe turns towards Sam and smiles amiably. Reflecting upon the events of the day, he now experiences, quite unexpectedly, a fleeting moment of delighted contentment.

Sam returns the smile for, as will shortly be revealed, Moe is not the only one working towards a particular agenda this afternoon.

Dogged rather than driven, determined rather than inspired, from the boyish door-to-door salesman to his current job as Deputy Editor (events, sports and features) of the *Thanet Gazette*, Sam Taylor's career choices seemed to acknowledge a certain ruthless sense of purpose. Everything was instinct, he said, between survival and extinction there is only instinct.

Call it living by your wits, following your nose, it's all the same at the end of the day. Some of the younger guys on the paper respected him, he knew that, they looked up to him. But you can't learn that – you're born with it. Or not. Simple as that. It's a gift. Whether weighing up the merits of a story or a potential customer oh yes I'll say it's a good drying day *today*, you're right there but what about yesterday say what you like you can't depend on the flipping English weather can you I mean it was absolutely p . . . p . . . persistently raining yesterday wasn't it eh eh you see what I mean there you're smiling aren't you . . . It's all the same. Gut instinct.

Greatest judge of all.

This wasn't the first time that he'd pitched the comeback idea to Moe. He'd made an almost identical suggestion a year ago when Moe had last worked the Oddfellows. But that day it had been more a subtle implication, a you're an intelligent chap you work it out yourself sort of hint. Today he had been direct and uncompromising. Not that he'd met with any more success, but it was still early days.

Moe didn't like talking about the Nobby Newton years, never did much. He was a hard bloke to fathom sometimes. Nobby was a legend, pure and simple and there had never been anything like it, not before or since. Sam never saw him at his prime but only caught a couple of shows in London during the early fifties, even so he was still a remarkable performer.

When you really thought about it, he was always operating well within the perimeters of the classic double entendre but nobody ever pushed those boundaries quite as hard as Nobby Newton. But sometimes though he really did go just that little bit too far. Maybe more than a little . . .

God, but that was thrill of seeing him!

Sam had met his hero for the first time in 1963, just after Moe had ceased working under his more infamous alias. It would be presumptuous to refer to him as a good friend but they would always meet up whenever he was in the area.

But every time he saw Moe he saw Nobby.

He couldn't help it. If you'd been there you would understand.

At the time, he was such a unique performer – you never knew if he'd suddenly say something really rude and outrageous and it was like it could happen at any minute. Any second now he was going to lose it completely! He was like a coiled spring on stage, a time bomb and that sense of danger and anticipation never left you for a second. There was this great unspoken association – he was *daring* and by simply watching or listening to him you became daring too.

Of course as his reputation grew so did the folklore around him. There were always stories in circulation, like the one about what he was supposed to have said at Blackpool in 1949 (it involved the then Princess Elizabeth) and how a policeman had walked on to the stage of the Lyceum and announced that he was making an arrest. OK, it might have been a plant (Sam was always dubious), but come on, it was great theatre!

He'd even heard it rumoured that this man standing a matter of a foot or so away had been the original lyricist of that *other* unofficial wartime anthem. The one about Hitler having one ball, sung to the tune of 'Colonel Bogey'. Everyone knew the song and if you thought about it, it stood to reason that somebody had to have composed it. Nobby was the perfect candidate. Some times the story would take a more specific turn. He'd first sung it at the Hackney Empire, then the audience rioted, or joined in, or beat him up, depending on which variant you hear. It really didn't matter if the author had been Nobby or not (frankly it was unlikely) the point was the story circulated and a great many could find no reason to doubt it.

Similarly, that apocryphal story that Max Miller was *supposed* to have told. Everyone knows the story. But Max would never have told a gag like that, never in a million years. No, that story was originally attributed to Nobby, and it was said that many people would attest that the gag was a regular part of his act. Of all the stories, Sam could believe this one easily – he'd heard him tell many similar stories.

Never cheeky or endearing like Max, or aggressive like Trinder, Nobby was slightly distant, aloof and didn't seem to want to engage with his audience. Max would work from the footlights, leaning forward chummily as though refusing to acknowledge the boundaries between performer and audience. It was a smart move. The audience could identify with this man, he might dress a bit flash but he was just like them, he spoke to them and for them. Nobby used to tell his audience that it didn't matter to him one fig if they laughed or not – they were still paying his wages.

But he was feared by the Establishment and loathed by critics, one of whom once famously wrote that 'variety has not yet produced a Mozart or a Shakespeare but in Mr Newton it has surely spawned a Devil.' He had been subsequently damned and banished to the outskirts of variety. Yet the man was a true original and his resulting obscurity had been the harshest judgement of all – albeit one that was inevitable. Nowadays when people shed their tears over the demise of variety, nobody wept for Nobby Newton.

In the past year or so, he has read a couple of new books about the history of variety, watched a few things on TV about the evolution of comedy and never was the name Nobby Newton even mentioned.

No, not obscure.

Worse than that.

Erased!

If you went up against authority in those days you paid the price, nowadays you'd be some sort of fucking hero, you'd get more column inches than the Pope . . . wait a minute . . . wait a minute . . . Samuel Taylor, I love you – you are, my son, without doubt, a fucking genius . . .

'Well then . . .'

Sam claps his large fleshy hands together. 'Right then, you ready?'

This is not at all the response Moe had been expecting. 'Er . . . well . . .'

'Good. Come on then, there's something I have to show you. You don't know Margate very well, do you?'

Moe shakes his head gravely and looks at his watch.

Ten hours and ten minutes.

When he looks up again he is startled to see two police cars with screeching tyres and sirens speeding eastwards along the seafront towards Cliftonville.

'Something's up,' says Sam Taylor lighting a cigarette and demonstrating what he would probably delight in terming his Great Instinct.

Moe waits for the afternoon to calm down again before he speaks. 'Look, Sam, I really should be making tracks soon. But actually I was just about . . .'

Sam Taylor places his hand on the taller man's shoulder. 'Honestly, this won't take long, you'll be back again in no time. Come on.'

Persistence. Sincerity.

They walk slowly back up the High Street towards Cecil Square. As though resigning himself to his fate, Moe Seyton stops for a moment and removes from the inside pocket of his blazer, an oblong tortoiseshell case. The case is lined and in a bold swirl across the lid are the words Wotton's of Bond Street. He slowly takes from the case a pair of sunglasses very recently purchased from Boots the Chemist and places them on his nose.

Then he glances skywards and drifts away for a moment in

endless
perpetual
astonishing
blueness.

'Young boy says to his mummy . . .'

Q. *Can I have* ***just*** *ice cream?*
A. No. Perhaps afterwards. And only if you're a good boy.

Q. *Why can't I have* ***just*** *ice cream on its own?*
A. Because you can't and because I say so. Choose something else.

Q. *Can I have Spam then? I like Spam.*
A. No, they don't do Spam, you can have sausages instead.

Q. *Why don't they have Spam?*
A. Because they have sausages instead and sausages are much nicer.

Q. *Why have they got a starfish on the wall over there?*
A. I have no idea.

Q. *Are they real starfish?*
A. I don't imagine so. Don't bite your nails, please.

Q. *Do starfish bite?*
A. No, I don't think so.

Q. *Not ever ever ever?*
A. Never.

Barney has chosen to take no part in this or the following conversation. From his seat at the window he watches instead the people drifting back and forth along the harbour and considers the moment. Sauntering aimlessly amongst the crowds and in and out of memory, he recalls for no reason a conversation from the last week of the summer term.

Rupert Hopgood, who had been failing on a daily basis for the past decade to inspire the slightest enthusiasm for the subject of English, while Barney applied to himself to similar ends attempting to teach French in the room opposite, had opened the subject in the staffroom one morning. They had been going through the list of set texts for the following year when suddenly Rupert had demanded to know if Barney would rather go to bed with Emma Bovary or Molly Bloom. He was most persistent. *You have to tell me, you have to tell me, now Langton, now this minute. Molly or Emma, Molly or Emma? Are you an Emmaman or a Mollyman?* As far as Rupert was concerned you simply had to be one or the other. You could, Rupert had insisted, always tell a great deal about a person from their choice and Barney could quite easily believe this. In fact he had managed to avoid giving him a direct answer all that morning.

It actually crossed his mind that it might have been a trick question, one of those silly psychological tests – Rupert was like that sometimes. Was a desire for Emma a suggestion of sexually inadequacy, or homosexuality even? Did Molly represent the Oedipus complex or something to do with being breastfed?

Q. *Mummy, how many legs have starfish got? Is it five?*
A. You've already asked me that twice.

Q. *It's not six, is it? Not like me? Because I'm six, aren't I?*
A. Yes, Andrew.

Of course you were choosing between *ideas* of women weren't you? Male fantasies. Extremes, archetypes. The delicate or the earthy, complicated or uncomplicated. One perhaps we fondly imagine to need rescuing (a dependent), the other one was to be . . . well, enjoyed (an equal).

Dispelling any notion of deviousness on his part, Rupert had actually quite openly confessed to being an Emmaman until his thirties but a Mollyman ever since. (The age was possibly significant but possibly not.)

If really pushed Barney would have leant towards La Bovary (Would he be allowed to see Molly on the quiet? Absolutely not!) He couldn't help himself, he really couldn't and he shouldn't feel that he had to apologise for it! Loyalty to his chosen profession? Perhaps he just felt that there was something marginally more exotic about the French than the Irish. He still felt that way too. They exude a certain . . . *Juke-er box, juke-er box* . . . Suddenly he had started to think about the hair on her shoulder again.

Q. *Can I go in the sea again later on?*
A. We'll see.

What if she was to walk by now, thought Barney. See him here sitting at the window waiting for his lunch surrounded by all this endless dullness. She would laugh at him.

A cruel nasty mocking laugh.

Juke-er box, juke-er box.

God, perhaps she was right to laugh.

Q. *Starfish are real but mermaids aren't real are they?*
A. That's right.

Q. *If I'm really good, mummy, can I go in the sea again?*
A. Don't bite your nails. I won't tell you again.

But she would understand. She wouldn't laugh. She would sympathise. The crowds would vanish, disappear somewhere, who would even care?

God, let a tidal wave take them! Those flustering, blustering, summer-dumbed masses, gone for ever and ever amen. Never mourned never missed never even given a thought.

And then very faintly he would hear *Juke-er box, juke-er box* and she would be standing there alone on the opposite side of the road.

She will be smiling at him.

Q. *Well, can we?*
A. I said we'll see, didn't I?

Q. *Will you come with me again?*
A. I don't know. Take your elbows off the table

Clack Clack Clack Clack. Gradually getting louder. Now with a single finger she beckons him. He would have to go with her, there was no alternative and wherever she might lead him in future he would have to follow. It would be his fate, his destiny.

Simple.

You see when God finally reveals himself to us, he does occasionally choose a most ungodly means of doing so!

Q. *But why were there no starfishes in the sea here?*
A. I have no idea.

Q. *Do whales eat starfish, Mummy?*
A. No, whales don't eat starfish.

Q. *Why are sausages much nicer?*
A. BECAUSE I SAY THEY ARE!

Suddenly without warning, Sandra Langton feels a strong stabbing pain in her abdomen. She really shouldn't have raised her voice like that. Poor Andrew, it isn't his fault. It never is and she knows she isn't being very . . . The pain grows more intense. If questioned on the subject she might have likened the sensation to someone pressing a fist into her. Pressing pressing *pressing*. The agony contorts her face, forcing her eyes to close and her mouth to open.

For a moment or two she does not breathe . . .

She is a little girl she wants her daddy she wants it to stop she doesn't deserve this she knows that this is not fair she mustn't blame herself she shouldn't feel that she is being punished she must not blame herself she promised him that she wouldn't blame herself he was terribly kind and he had such lovely soft hands and there was his wristwatch too brown leather strap expensive-looking as well she remembers it clearly she always liked a nice wristwatch on a man she mustn't blame herself she didn't do anything wrong she must never forget that . . . owwww . . . she wasn't strong enough she probably just wasn't strong enough that's all there was something wrong with her they didn't say anything but she knew she could sense something happening inside her she wants her daddy she wants him there next to her holding her and forgiving her telling her that it really and truly was not her fault that she must not blame herself and that *these things happen* she must never forget and one day she will learn that there is no sense to things one day . . . one day . . . one . . .

The pain passes as suddenly as it had arrived.

. . . *these things happen* . . .

She takes a deep breath.

'Are you OK?'

'Mummy? Mummy . . .'

. . . *these things happen* . . .

Sandra looks at the boy and smiles. 'I'm . . . all right. I just had a bit of a funny pain in my tummy that was all. It's gone now.'

Barney whispers across the table. 'Is there anything I can get you? Do you need anything?

'No, it's passed now. I'll be fine again in a minute. Maybe I'll feel better when I've eaten something.'

'Yes, you're probably right.'

And with that Barney lapses into silence once more. The Frenchman too was quiet for once. In fact all he could hear was:

Q. *Will you have sausages too, Mummy?*
A. I don't know. Perhaps.

Q. *Will you eat my peas for me?*
A. I might. Or maybe I'll just eat you all up instead!

Q. *What's warm and smells of piss?*
A. Piss.

Or a tramp in a sauna . . . Calcutta . . . Joan of Arc . . . or every phone box in Margate in August!

And in this fashion did Moe Seyton (jokes for *all* tastes and persuasions, traditional and in the Modern Style) pass the time as he waited for Sam Taylor to finish making his call.

'. . . Listen, Colin, I'm not asking you, son, I'm telling you . . . no, no, I appreciate that it's a Bank Holiday but it will have to wait, won't it? Call your mate at Fort Hill nick and see if he's got anything . . . What? Well, it seemed pretty major from where I was standing . . . Look, just do it, will you! . . . Then get on your moped and get over there . . . For God's sake, Colin, I don't know, just use your eyes . . . What now? . . . Oh God, I don't know . . . Well go and buy some, it can't be that difficult, can it? . . . Then go and hijack someone's lawnmower and fucking siphon some if you have to! Just get yourself over there . . . Look, I'll see you back at the office in half an hour or so and Colin, Colin . . . Don't fuck up again. I'm hanging up now.'

Meanwhile Moe reads the names of the shops, ponders how the uninitiated might interpret 'A FINE SELECTION OF NOVELTIES AND AMUSEMENTS', gazes at the sky and wonders about nothing in particular. Why did Bank Holiday Mondays always, even now, still *feel* like Bank Holiday Mondays – particularly in the early afternoon around this time. Don't know how it works, couldn't even begin to explain it. But you could take away all the people, all the cars, strip the streets of everything and yet if you dropped me down here now from outer space, I could still tell you it was a Bank Holiday Monday. How does this happen? You can always spot a Sunday evening without trying all that hard too!

The phone box braces itself, shudders and ejects Sam Taylor, who promptly removes a handkerchief from his trouser pocket and wipes his forehead with it. He then lights another cigarette from the smouldering butt of his John Player Special. 'Sorry about that, Em. Jesus, I sweats like a pig in this heat, first hint of the sun and I'm dripping.'

For the first time that day, for reasons he could not begin to fathom, Moe suddenly feels a great wave of warmth towards his friend. A smile spreads across his face and remains in place as he speaks.

'Stop the press, eh?'

'Maybe, we'll see. Probably not. Not if that bloody Colin has anything to do with it.'

'Who?'

'Doesn't matter.' With some effort, Sam manages to put his handkerchief back in his pocket. 'You know what they say, you pay peanuts – you get monkeys. Well, I must be paying bog roll or something because, honest to God, I keep getting wankers!'

Moe's grin broadens slightly. 'I like that. I haven't heard that before.' For the second time in five minutes he is astonished to find himself thinking like a comedian. This happens so rarely nowadays that he is uncertain how he should respond.

'Anyway, we can forget all about it for a while. You and I are going for a walk.'

'A walk?'

'Come on, it won't take too long.'

Moe lights a Gold Leaf and checks his watch.

Nine hours and twenty-seven minutes.

As they turn into Queen Street, Mr Taylor turns to Mr Seyton. 'I will definitely try and make it down the Oddfellows tonight if I can.'

'Oh, I do hope so' says Moe. 'Might be something a bit special tonight.'

'In what way?'

Moe smiles but declines to answer. Not now, not now, wait just a little longer . . .

'Anyway, what's the door policy there nowadays?'

'There isn't one. Not anymore. Just a sign that says "Tonight – Gentlemen Only". Couple of years back, if I remember rightly, you had to be a . . . er . . . member.' The word, which had been rendered obsolete in its usual context through years of comedic abuse, was difficult for him.

In fact his member was incredibly hard! (Rim-shot and cymbal crash.)

'What sort of time?'

'I'm on about ten. It's their usual Bank Holiday Stag Weekend. There's a couple of strippers. Actually, one of them left her records at home last night. Silly girl. She had to do her entire act without music. However, I have to say, in its own way, it was a most arresting performance. A Vision Satyric-On!'

Sam says nothing but furrows his brow in exaggerated bemusement.

Moe offers an understanding smile. 'I'm sorry. Perils of the profession, Sam. Back when I was working regularly, I never got to see much television. All I ever managed to catch was *Children's Hour. Animal Magic, Mr Pastry, Blue Peter,* that sort of thing. Nowadays I've got a little portable in the caravan but I never watch it. Actually, I'm not even sure it works any more.'

Sam grips his upper lip between his teeth. Sometimes he didn't care to be reminded. Perils of the profession? Oh yes, we all know about the perils of the profession, don't we? But what about the penalties? Like the one you get for stepping over the mark just once too often, for going that little bit too far? Justice must be seen to be done! Of course and nowadays the man they once called 'The Naughtiest Mouth in the South' lives alone in a small, reasonably maintained two-berthed caravan on a site just outside Portsmouth.

The man who had paid the price and been sentenced to Bank Holiday Stag Weekends!

It was tragic beyond words.

He could cry . . .

Suddenly, the sound of a distant police-car siren agitates the still surface of the afternoon.

Something was definitely up.

Sam is still walking fractionally ahead of Moe as they negotiate the incline of the hill. The exertion leaves him slightly breathless and he pauses for a moment while a berating, mocking voice in his head serenades him with a traditional chorus:

ciggies and booze ciggies and booze
[Simple self-chastisement coupled with all
the usual noble intentions.]
must cut down I
must cut down I
should cut down

'Are you OK?'

Sam nods. Now is the time, he thinks. Now or never and before he can debate the matter any further he hears himself taking part in the following exchange:

Sam: *[breathless]* Wife and I took my father to Brighton once. Must have been twenty years ago at least. [*shakes head*] Wasn't long before he died actually, now I think about it. [*fondly*] I tell you, the old boy hated the seaside, absolutely hated it, and I can only assume the whole jaunt was Beryl's idea. Certainly wasn't mine. But he didn't get out much and it was a chance to go for a run in the car, which was still quite new at the time, I suppose. Anyway, the day was a disaster as I recall. The weather wasn't too fabulous and Dad just complained the whole time, [*adopts accent*] the car journey made him sick, the beer was off, his fish and chips had too much vinegar or not enough vinegar. [*own voice*] So, it's the middle of the afternoon and basically, I suppose, we've all just had enough, so we decide to head back to the car, which is parked up some quiet side road. [*dramatically, as though reading aloud a children's story*] Suddenly, we turn a corner and there's these three big Teddy Boys walking towards us. Really sharp-looking guys. Drapes, bootlace ties, brothel creepers the full works. Then in the time it takes to blink I see Dad rushing over towards them. Big grin on his face and by the far the most animated he's been all bloody day. I look at Beryl and I'm thinking Jesus, the silly old fool is gonna get himself chivved any moment. So he walks up to them and says [*slowly*] 'Hell-o', just like that he said it, no word of a lie. [*slowly and deliberately*] 'Hell-o . . . Good-der Arf-ter-noon'. I've no idea what he's up to. Anyway, the three Teds wander off muttering something and we get in the car and head for home. He's not saying anything much, he's just sitting in the back of the car grinning to himself. Eventually, curiosity just gets the better of me and I ask him what the hell was all that Hell-o business about. Well, he says, you've got to make them all welcome nowadays. Make who welcome? Everyone from all over, he says, it's a time of peace. We must open our doors to all of them and we must respect their cultures and customs. Suddenly, I get it. Silly bugger actually thinks he's been talking to three people in national costume! Can you believe it?

Moe: That's a great story, Sam. [*frowns*] Is it true?

Sam: [*indignant*] Of course it's true! Yeah, [*reflective*] that was my father for you. I never dared tell him the truth, there didn't seem any point. So he died believing himself to be this great English diplomat. [*starts walking*]

Moe: [*following*] I'm sure there's no harm in that.

Sam: True enough. I can only be grateful he didn't live long enough to see his first punks. God knows what he would have made of them. Doesn't bear thinking about. Probably instantly volunteer to take them to his leader!

Moe: [*chuckles politely*] Probably.

Sam: [*suddenly animated*] Funnily enough, that's just reminded me of something I've been meaning to ask.

Moe: [*cautiously, with a strong hint of cynicism*] Really?

Sam: Yeah. It's just something I've been thinking about recently. I was wondering what you thought of all these punks nowadays. I presume you have them where you are – they're all over the place. You see, I just wanted to know if you had an opinion.

Moe: [*shakes head slightly, appears puzzled by the question*] Not really, not that I am aware of. [*shrugs*] I'm sorry. It's just not something I've ever given much thought to.

Sam: You see, it strikes me that there's a lot of common ground between all this punk stuff and Nobby Newton. [*animated, as though fearing an interruption*] Look, just hear me out, will you? They're all going up against authority and in their own way they're using outrage as way of challenging things. Sound familiar? I just think there's a whole new audience out there just waiting for Nobby Newton. You could make a fantastic comeback, I'm telling you! They would love what you did, what you stood for, you'd be a hero to these people. To a whole generation. You could go out as the oldest punk in the business: Nobby Newton – England's first punk rocker. You could maybe wear a bit of the gear, not enough to look stupid, naturally. But just think you could do some of the old songs as punk songs, bring them right up to date. I tell you, Em, they'd love you. What was that one again? The other side of 'Sister Eloise'? 'Nobby and His Hobby'. Classic. Would have made a great signature tune. [*emphatically*] Would *still* make a great signature tune! *(sings)*

Moe: [*quietly, as though to himself*] I don't think so somehow, I really don't think so.

Sam: [*frustrated*] But Moe, it's just sitting there waiting for you, you'll only be claiming what's rightfully yours for fuck's sake! This is your time now, [*emotional*] I just know it, I can feel it.

Moe: [*calmly but firm*] Come on, it was long time ago, Sam. Too long. Things are so different now, the patter, the timing, it just wouldn't work. They wouldn't get it any more, I'd be like one of those Teddy boys! Comedy evolves and like anything that evolves, some things survive while some things become extinct. [*slowly with feeling*] And sometimes you just have to let things go . . .

MORAL:
It is only the foolish man who underestimates the comforts of darkness!

Q. *Why can't I have an ice cream now?*
A. Because you should wait for your dinner to go down.

The *why* which followed this reply is long and plaintive but is met only with a slight raising of eyebrows. In the ageless and wordless language of mothers, the gentlest reprimand is implied.

And understood.

The boy will not discover this lunchtime how long it takes a dinner to go down or what starfish eat.

The Harbour Café and Grill serve what is arguably the worst coffee in England, probably Europe and quite possibly in the entire universe. Barney Langton takes another wretched sip and finds an almost perverse pleasure in the lingering metallic aftertaste. It is like drinking a cup full of five pences. Yet his palette now also detects a slight hint of soil, of something earthy and gritty. The surface of his tongue feels as though it has been recently coated in a layer of warm dust.

The perfect poison for an adulterer!

He feels his tongue pass across the back of his teeth as he

plays with the word in his mouth. Sweeter and stronger than any coffee he had ever tasted, he savours the term and its associations. Adulterer. It sounds historic and important, heroic even, a word dragged from Dickens or Hardy. Not normally the sort of expression applied to unhappy French teachers. Naturally, he would defend himself in tones befitting such an occasion.

Ah, yes but if I am to be punished for my weaknesses, then am I not simply being punished for my humanity!

They were certain to let him off.

Three cheers for weakness and humanity!

He smiles as he remembers that Molly and Emma were both adulterers and he takes another delicious mouthful of small change.

Sandra notices the smile. 'You feeling all right?'

Where once there might have been concern now he could sense only the vaguest curiosity.

'Fine.'

'You've hardly touched your plaice.'

'To be honest I'm not hungry at the moment. I think I'm probably just too hot.'

Sandra looks at her husband. You could never tell. Even when he told the truth he always managed to make it sound suspicious.

'SCCHTHWWWWWUUUUUUSCHHHH!'

'Please, Andrew, be a good boy for mummy. Just drink your squash from the cup. Don't use the straw, eh? Just this once'

'Why?'

'Just do as you're told. There's a good boy.'

The adulterer observes but says nothing.

Had anyone else spotted this connection? Think of modernism, think of jazz and Cubism. Think of New Orleans and Montmartre, Picasso and Jelly Roll Morton, Storyville and *Les Demoiselles d'Avignon.* And ask yourself where precisely did the twentieth century begin? And you must answer that it grew out of the red-light districts, it first flourished amongst the brothels and cat houses.

The adulterer takes an unparalleled delight in this discovery.

Isn't that just fabulous! Whores and artists!

You could argue that the two most significant cultural events this century took place roughly simultaneously on opposite sides of the Atlantic. Thousands of miles apart and yet they shared a single common source of inspiration. And what a source! No longer State or Church but Whorehouse! This inspiration was a liberation and how could it be otherwise? It was vital and vulgar, alive and joyous – dynamic and LOUD!

In an old European city, they made their paintings dance while in the New World men were putting bright colours into their music!

And now ask yourself again, what is the connection?

He would ask Rupert about this at the start of term. That would shut him up!

He smiles to himself and then feels his wife's gaze settle upon him. Her face has been washed free of all its innocence, he thinks, not like Andrew's. One day soon he will tell him the story – he would understand.

It would go like this.

Once upon a time there was old giant called Barney. He was a nice, kind giant not a nasty one and he lived in a dark, airless dusty little room – a room that had no windows and no doors and it was so terribly dark that he did not even know if he could still see. And I think secretly that Barney believed that he had gone blind. Because the room had no doors or windows, Barney was never able to go out. The room was horrible and boring and Barney had nothing to do. But because he'd never left the room he could see no reason not to be happy. Then one day somewhere in the darkness a shaft of light suddenly appeared! It was just a vertical crack in the darkness, an opening – a door maybe and it let in a light so bright and white and pure and good that it took Barney's breath away. Oh goody, he thinks, at least I am not blind any more because I can see this lovely bright shaft of light! This makes him happy for the whole day and he goes to bed in a really happy mood. But then a funny thing happens, even though he's really tired he just can't get to sleep. He just lies there thinking. Do you know what he is thinking about? About that shaft of light, that's what. What if it really was a light shining from behind a door? Maybe he could find a way of opening the door and then he could leave his horrible room forever. But Barney is scared what might be on the other side. What do you think is on the other side? Barney is frightened and so he closes his eyes and pretends that everything in the room is exactly the same – there never was a light and he never saw it. He makes himself blind to it. In doing so he makes himself blind again. He tries to forget it but somehow the more the tries not to think about it the more it comes back into his mind. So he goes down on his big giant knees and he prays for the first time in his life. Dear God, he says, I promise that I will be a good giant. I will learn to live with the longing, with the doubt and with the misery but please God just keep me safe from glimpsing POSSIBILITY!

Leigh Greenglass tosses the remains of his cheese and chutney roll into the ornamental flower-bed.

Mr Greenglass is forty-four and not enjoying his day away from the depot. He should have stayed indoors. Why bother coming out? A stupid idea. Must be going soft in the bloody head.

You could say whatever you like about living in bloody Margate, it's OK – not the best place in the world maybe but not the worst neither. But the fact remains that there is something seriously depressing about spending your life watching other folk having their holidays in front of you, right? I mean, be fair now, the last thing we need right at this moment is to see scores of people enjoying themselves! Like these two old blokes here crossing the road coming towards me, fat bloke and a tall chap in a blazer, not a sodding care in the world! On holiday, probably, left all their troubles at home!

Don't mind folk being happy, that's their business; it is just all that bloody enthusiasm all the time! Like bloody children the lot of them. Must go to the fair, must see the sea . . .

Leigh Greenglass walks back towards the centre of town and begins thinking about something else.

Mr and Mrs Greenglass have sexual intercourse most Saturday nights and special occasions like Bank Holidays and so tonight at some time around 10.30 as he enters her he will think about Diana Dors again.

He always thinks about Diana Dors nowadays.

Leigh Greenglass does not particularly care about Ms Dors and, if questioned on the subject, would have to admit to spending very little of his time considering the matter. To be honest he is uncertain if he actually finds her all that attractive.

But now, Mrs Greenglass 42, mother of three, packer of lunches, keeper of souvenirs and budgerigars . . .

Now that was a different matter entirely!

Mrs Greenglass absolutely loathed Diana Dors!

God, always going on about her she was nowadays.

Diana Dors this, Diana Dors that . . . a right old bloody racket.

So tonight it will not be the breasts of Nelly Greenglass beneath his hands nor her nipples beneath his fingers but Diana's. It will not be her neck, her arms, her legs, her belly or her sex, it will not be her mouth he tastes tonight. Not auburn gone grey – in need of a set so soon after the last flipping time as well makes you blooming wonder – but blonde and dazzling and voluminous.

Then with a locked door no hurry take your time like what you see smile, she will look at him the way they do in those films they show at the club.

A big pearly-lipped happy smile from Diana again tonight.

To be honest, Leigh Greenglass welcomes the change.

Last year it was Dusty Springfield.

Nelly Greenglass, 42, mother of three, sweeper of stairs, keeper of secrets, promises and photograph albums, had always hated Dusty Springfield.

Leigh Greenglass now crosses Union Crescent and as he does so he passes the two gentlemen he saw a few moments ago who are crossing the road in the opposite direction. The tall men is looking at his watch while he hears the fat man saying . . .

'. . . Will be used for all sorts soon, not just concerts. All manner of stuff . . . pantos, conferences. You name it.'

Then, as if his argument required a moment of cinematic drama, Sam stops walking and stands perfectly still as though suddenly taking in for the first time the splendour and magnificence of the Theatre Royal.

'Isn't it something? Built in the eighteenth century, they tell me . . .'

Moe vaguely considers the building, a distinguished Georgian structure with that slightly over-inflated sense of its own importance. From his particular angle it reminded Moe of an old sanatorium

Sam is still talking. '. . . Maybe get a couple of groups on the bill with you, most of these punk groups aren't able to play anywhere round here. There's this group, CASTRO GTX, local lads, they look like they're from another planet but the singer's dad works in our ad department. You could be a sort of compère for the night. Introduce the groups and then do the closing slot. Like I said, maybe do a new punk arrangement of a couple of songs with the group. Drape a big banner from the windows up there saying "THE RETURN OF NOBBY NEWTON" or something. Quid fifty to get in and all the press you need . . .'

Maybe it was proximity of the sea that made him think of sanatoriums.

'. . . Tell you, boyo, it would just be the beginning. You could sound a bit repentant maybe, the world loves a repentant sinner. Almost as much as it loves learning of the sins over which he is repentant . . .'

No, it definitely had a vaguely medical air about it.

'I reckon we could have it all fixed up by Christmas, a New Year's Eve bash, maybe . . .'

'You know' said Moe quietly but abruptly. 'You know who you sound like?'

'Don't know.' Sam's slightly harsh tone suggests that he is not delighted to be taken away so soon from his chosen topic of conversation.

'You sound like Kaiser Sullivan – he used to frequently drag me down the Strand and up the Charing Cross Road pointing theatres out to me. "I could book you there if you'd *just tone it down a bit,* that's all I'm saying." Used to happen with truly hideous regularity.'

'Kaiser who?'

'Oh I do apologise, I thought the name might be familiar. Kaiser Sullivan was quite a well-known theatrical agent in his day. The Bandit Queen of Shaftesbury Avenue we used to call him. I was on his books for years and years. When Kaiser was good he was one of the best and for a time he was running some really top acts. Ray Fowler, The Ainsleys, Ted Barclay, even Victor Arnold for a while. And he had a lot of faith in me at the start but . . . you know how it is, over the years things got a bit sour. For one thing I thought he was taking on far too many acts. We fell out over money usually and we finally went our separate ways back in the summer of . . . '54, I think it was.'

'Kaiser?'

'He wasn't really called Kaiser of course, that was just a nickname he'd picked up from somewhere years ago. Years before I knew him. Everyone called him Kaiser but his real name was Howard Q. Sullivan. Actually, it's funny but the thing I think I will always remember most about Kaiser is what used to happen whenever he told people his real name. Naturally, they would often ask "what's the Q for?" And he would always tell them right back, quick as a flash, "the guy with the funniest fucking jokes!" '

Sam takes a moment to unravel the subtleties of this anecdote but chuckles politely while he is doing so. Then he clears his throat again. 'Well, I'm in good company I suppose. Is he still around?'

'No, I'm afraid not. Unfortunately, the Kaiser had certain . . . what would you call them . . . certain flaws, certain *inclinations*, shall we say. As a result, he kept some fairly dubious company out of work. Everyone knew about it but what he did in private was his own business. Anyway it all came to an end a couple of years ago when they pulled him out of the Thames just east of Putney Bridge. I read about it, said he was found with a rope around his neck, been in the water for a week, they reckoned. Oh, there was a big Golders Green funeral the following week but I never went. We'd not spoken for years and it didn't seem right. I just sent some flowers anonymously. I still think about him even now.' Moe smiles and with wavering certainty reassures himself that this is historical and factual. Then with no warning it swoops down upon him like the holy blessed bird of sainted memory – an expression he recalls from three decades past.

Less Soho and more Brighton.

'Jesus.'

'Pardon?'

Moe smiles. 'Sorry, I was thinking . . . I was miles away. Kaiser had this phrase he would always use. He'd tell me that I needed to be "less Soho and more Brighton".'

'Eh?'

'It was his way of telling me I needed to tone down my act. *Just tone it down a bit,* he'd say. "Less Soho and more Brighton" meant that I should be cheeky or suggestive rather than overt and offensive. He was always telling me that.'

'Did you listen?'

'Not really. There were too many comics treading the same path. It was a very competitive business and they were all after the same jobs. I thought by being a bit different, there'd be less competition.'

There is something in this man now as he speaks that Sam feels he is seeing for the first time. Regret was perhaps too strong a word but he does detect a certain vacillating conviction.

Doubt?

It made him look old – but it makes everyone look old.

Moe continues. 'He even suggested going out under the name of Neddy Newbury. Be a bit racy, a bit saucy. *Just tone it down a bit.* Generally speaking, there was always a market for the smutty blue material but the business got scared. Club owners didn't really want the police there every night pinching the star turn, it's not exactly good for prestige, as they say. So, "less Soho and more Brighton"! But it wasn't me, I just couldn't work like that. Besides after Max, there were so many acts that could do it better than I could. Guys like Jack Milton, who was head and shoulders above the rest. That man had a way of mistiming gags that was just sheer artistry to behold.'

Sam Taylor nods. Agrees and disagrees. Then with a vague sadness, he recalls that great eight-bar middle section. It was a variation on a Fats Waller bridge, like the classic one in 'Honeysuckle Rose'. It was quite a risk to take in a song like that, it shouldn't have worked, but, credit where it's due, it slotted in perfectly.

Some people like to smoke
Some people like to joke
Seems everyone has got a hobby . . .

'And so here we are, and one day it comes to this. A Bank Holiday weekend in sunny Margate!' Moe looks at his watch and then at the dishwater sea in the distance.

'Kaiser, you were right! This business is just the way you said it was. It's ruthless and it forgives no one.'

. . . Some people ride a bike
And some prefer to hike
But no one's got a hobby like Nobby!

Nine hours and six bloody minutes.

'One day this old lady is walking down the road . . .'

DISCO
SHIT
PUNK AND HEAVY

Due to this being inscribed in what was usually a fairly public location, it is within moments amended to

DISCO
RUBBI SH**XX**
PUNK AND HEAVY

Colin Featherhead then, on the corner of the blotting paper just below his slightly modified criticism, draws another version of the Featherhead Deluxe. It shared with the Featherhead Custom many of its revolutionary features. The thirty-six frets would naturally be standard on all the models. But the Deluxe boasted eight pick-ups, compared to the Custom's six, which gave it the widest range of sounds of any guitar ever manufactured. It was also the loudest.

But it was the unmistakable contours of the bodywork, the angles and particularly the strategically placed holes that were such a radical departure away from the traditional lines of Gibsons or Fenders. Single-handedly, Colin Featherhead had revolutionised the whole idea of guitar design.

The version which he was currently drawing came in black or red. Naturally, it was priced higher than the

Custom and with a fitted case it would set you back £12,000. Joe Walsh had bought five and the bloke from the Sex Pistols was now using it as his main guitar.

He was enjoying himself. Sometimes there are things you do when you are on your own that you do just because you're on your own!

Underneath his drawing, Colin Featherhead writes 'SEX PISTOLS'.

Then in the opposite corner of the blotting paper he writes 'SHAM 69' and 'AC/DC'.

Then he writes 'TED NUGENT'.

I LIVE FOR LUCIFER
I LIVE FOR LUCY FUR
FOUR LUCY FOUR
4LUCY4

Then he writes in a slower and steadier hand . . .

JESSICA WARNE
JESSICA WARNE
JESSICA WA . . .
JESSICA WARNS
JESSICA WARMS
JESSICA WORMS

He has a low, rattling laugh. A particularly distinctive rattle – one that reminded the unfortunate listener of bars, chains and padlocks.

Sadly, there has never been any joy or warmth in this young man's laughter. In fact, there is something deeply unsettling about it. Colin Featherhead laughed like a person who wasn't accustomed to laughing. Rather than cruel or mocking, which was often the assumption, his laughter was simply unaccomplished.

He starts to draw the outline of a naked woman.

There are currently no less than seven files on Colin Steven Featherhead scattered about the various departments of Thanet County Council and virtually all of them refer to his father's suicide in 1964, when Colin was five. The most recent of these documents, currently residing in a locked drawer in the offices of the Social Services, also alludes to 'possible anti-social tendencies' and a 'thwarted need to form good male bonds'.

He laughs again and draws a pair of exaggerated nipples.

Poor Jessica.

She had a great body, and now that is all she is (pubic hair), just a body, its funny she was *somebody* with *some body* on her and now she was just *some body* (armpit hair) nothing else just a body when you're dead you're just a body she used to have tits and a fanny and an arse but now she is just dead it is all taken away from her (mouth with cigarette) when I die people won't ever think that I got a cock and balls I'll just be Dead Colin's body (cigarette smoke spiralling out to form the initials J.W.) I wouldn't mind if someone wanted to look at me it wouldn't matter to me I wouldn't think it was disgusting it's not disgusting anyway I don't think so anyway she wasn't that shy when she was . . .

Suddenly the main door below him slams shut and echoing up the stairwell he hears . . .

'COL-IN! . . . COL-IN! Jesus, how many more times do you have to be told?' There are angry heavy feet now. Steady. Regular in slow old black and white cartoon time up the wheezy wooden staircase. 'Are you listening to me, boyo? Don't park your stupid bloody moped on the pavement, leave it in the bloody road. What's the matter with you? Why don't you ever listen to people?'

The young man quickly removes the top sheet of blotting paper, screws it into tight ball and drops it into a nearby bin.

Moments later, with a furious flourish and a shortness of

breath, a red-faced Sam Taylor throws open the glass-panelled door and steps into . . .

'. . . the smell of fish and fucking chips or something?' He wrinkles his nose in dramatic disdain. 'Open a bloody window, Colin, for God's sake. It smells like one of Ghandi's flip flops in here.'

The editorial offices of the *Thanet Gazette* occupy a half a dozen rooms on a couple of floors above the branch of Interflora at the southern end of the High Street. They are drab and deeply unlovely premises and as Moe follows Sam through the door his first impressions will be of the old-fashioned phones, a broken venetian blind and the vague sickly aroma of roses.

'Hurry up, lad, I can hardly breathe.'

Rather than be an awkward witness to an altercation in which he wishes to take no part, Moe casts his eyes downward. Thus he adds to his initial impressions an awareness of the similarity between brown marble-effect linoleum and dried blood.

Eight hours and fifty-one minutes.

Sam Taylor removes his jacket and does so with a delicacy that could be misinterpreted as modesty. But is sadly only the grim awareness of his own obesity and the damp patches under the arms of his shirt. He sits on the corner of a desk and of the six possible options he chooses the one from which a sheet of blotting paper has recently been torn.

He manoeuvres himself into a fairly upright position and crosses his arms – this he does almost automatically in fear of revealing

o
( )
o
(   )
o
(   )

'So, boyo, how did you get on then?'

'What do you mean like?'

'Your little trip earlier on, remember? The reason why we're both here. Jesus Christ!'

'Oh yeah. That. Yeah. Good.' He finally succeeds in opening the window.

'So, enlighten me. What was it all about?'

'A girl it was. She were dead. Police weren't saying much, very funny about it they were. Kept telling me there were no information at present. But most of the people I spoke to said they'd heard it were no accident.'

'Meaning?'

'You know. Like she was killed like.'

'Really?' Sam places his hand over his mouth and beneath the great raw sausages of his fingers he smiles to himself. It was hugely satisfying on what had otherwise been a fairly frustrating afternoon to discover that the old instincts were as good as ever. He looks over his shoulder towards Moe who hovers in the doorway. 'You can come in, you know.'

Moe steps into the room while Sam waves his hand absently to and fro above his head. 'Colin, this is Moe Seyton, a friend of mine. And Moe this is Colin, the office monkey. Brought to you by kind and gracious permission of the East Kent Business Incentive.'

'I'm a junior reporter, actually,' says Colin airily.

Moe manages a smile but keeps his distance. 'Pleased to meet you.'

'Anyway, tell some more about this girl. I mean, you say "girl", do you mean that she was a child, a teenager, a young woman? Do we have a name yet?

From the pocket of his denim jacket, Colin carefully removes a piece of crumpled paper which he then flattens and pretends to read. There was no reason for him to do this but he thought he might be creating the right impression in front of the visitor.

'Girl's name is er . . . was er . . . Jessica . . . Jessica Warne. She was seventeen. Lived over Cliftonville way. Went to Margate Comp. Used to go out with a right twat called Dave . . .'

Sam frowns. 'I'm impressed. I thought you said they were holding back information.'

Colin smiles awkwardly. 'Er . . . well, they are. I just got the name from someone. But I know her, see?'

Now, at this remark, Sam Taylor's famous instincts begin to grumble and rumble deep within him like some ancient and mysterious precognitive contrivance. Suddenly, a feeling of vague suspense and anticipation is rushing through him. He holds his breath and stares at Colin with eyes that no longer need to blink. 'Really?'

The young man shrugs his shoulders as he perches himself on the corner of the desk opposite Sam. 'Not that well, like. She was the year below me in school. Used to see her sometimes, you know, hanging around. Mario's Fish Bar, used to see her there with her mates. This was a few years ago, mind you. She wasn't as rough as some of them you see around the place. She was into star signs and horoscopes. All that stuff. Reckons she could read palms and tell peoples fortunes but she wasn't spooky or nothing . . .'

'Good-looking, was she?'

With his seaside sly saltwater grin, Sam glances chummily towards Moe but fails to make eye contact. 'Won't be two ticks,' he says as he reaches across a desk and grabs a telephone.

But his friend doesn't reply, absorbed as he is gazing absently out of the window at the people in the street below. For no particular reason, he has started observing the progress of a Mrs Rosemary Davies as she makes her way towards the bus station.

Wearing her best powder-blue lightweight shower Mac, Mrs Davies is walking with her customary sense of urgency and purpose. She carries on her arm a sturdy ivory-coloured mock-crocodile handbag which contains the following items:

One rain bonnet
One brown leather purse containing £4.87
One pension book
An appointment card for Canterbury General Hospital
One quilted make-up case (empty)
One stainless-steel lighter
Five Murray mints (wrapped)
One Murray mint (unwrapped).

For Mrs Davies (when all is said and done) inventory will ultimately function as autobiography. Yet nowadays she is becoming increasingly troubled by the notion that nowadays when a person dies, he or she seems to be very little beyond a series of *lists.*

Two Sunny Smiles photos
One wooden clothes peg
Unopened packet of Benson and Hedges (20)
One folded magazine article of a knitting pattern
One tartan-patterned glasses case containing an Opal Fruit (lime).

Often these are official. Wills, audits, medical reports, but this is what we all leave behind. Bundles of paper. *For* us but not *of* us.

Only on our behalf.

The human condition is such that we leave no trace of our humanity.

One keyring (keys absent)
One ladies watch (no strap)
One roll of cotton (dark brown)
One cotton ladies handkerchief (flower motif).

Dates. That was the other thing. Lists and dates. After you die people seem to find it easier to remember you as a date. Often they recall the day you died. That was a curious custom, if you thought about it. To recall a life by marking the day when it ended and a loved one by the single event that caused the most pain. Mrs Davies has been thinking about that a lot recently. She arrives at the bus station and checks her watch again. Eight minutes, nine minutes to be safe, better make it ten.

Eight elastic bands
One small jar Vicks Vapour rub
One 5″ × 3″ colour photograph of a dog, possibly a terrier
One 5″ × 3″ colour photograph of a group at a wedding reception
One Post Office Savings book.
One A5 brown envelope containing twenty ten-pound notes.

Having timed her walk, she then checks the bus timetable and calculates that she must leave her house by twenty past nine tomorrow morning.

It is very important that she gets the early bus for tomorrow morning Mrs Davies will be going to Ricemans in Canterbury. She is going to buy her deathbed.

She had been fairly firm with the consultant but not in an overtly aggressive way and she was sure he understood. She'd put her point across calmly and was careful to stress that it was something to which she'd given a great deal of thought. She was sure he had been impressed with that. He had been frank and matter of fact with her and it seemed that he was encouraging her in a way to do likewise.

Months, he'd said, possibly even a year, but she was finding it increasingly difficult nowadays to think of time in such precise terms. Everything is now simply Things That Happen, Things That Happened or Things That Might Happen. Or, more frequently, Things That Might Not Happen.

She'd concluded her request to the consultant by explaining that she wanted the bits and pieces that she knew around her, the things that she loved. While the care provided by the hospital was undoubtedly top class, there is the comfort that only comes with familiarity.

So it was decided, and while the appointment concluded with talk of district nurses, Social Services and Meals on Wheels, Mrs Davies was already making plans. She made a great number of plans over the next couple of days. Fairly high on her list was the bed. She wanted to do things properly, remain sensible and not give in to any silliness. For one thing she had not the slightest intention of ending her days on an awful old wooden-framed bed with its ancient mattress. She would often say that she hadn't had a decent night's sleep in ages and she was telling the truth.

She would draw some money out of the Post Office and would buy a new bed. Get the bus into Canterbury and get one delivered. Go to Ricemans, they always had nice things in there. In these plans too she had found comfort, she'd found some order, some control again – a tiny beam of light in all the shadows and confusion. A hint of clarity.

She'd make sure it was a good one too, a nice modern one and she'd ask Sam to take away the old one, he said he's still got that old roof-rack. Stick it on the tip or something. Sam is always good with things like that.

Before she returns home later this afternoon she will enter a shop at the bottom of the High Street selling 'A FINE SELECTION OF NOVELTIES AND AMUSEMENTS'. Mrs Rosemary Davies has one further task that she has scheduled for this afternoon.

Although Mrs Davies takes no further part in the events currently unfolding at the offices of the *Thanet Gazette*, it is worth noting that the Sam with the roof rack is Sam Taylor who is at present unaware of the medical condition of his ex-wife's favourite auntie. And she once saw Nobby Newton on a bill at Bristol Colston Hall. Although she has no particular memory of the event, perhaps, if prompted, she might still possibly remember Nobby saying *'Widow's mite? Widow's mite? Well, after the war and that and all they've been through, you can't blame 'em really!'* if only for the sustained jeering that followed. They also share the same birthday.

Then there are those two photographs in her handbag. The terrier (very recently deceased) was called Chips. He died as a result of injuries sustained in a road accident. While nobody actually witnessed the incident it was assumed that he had run out in front of a car. But this was not actually the case. Chips had actually collided with a moped. One that was ridden by Colin Featherhead, who nowadays still avoids the road at the bottom of the hill with the bad lighting.

Then, if we were to study closely the photograph of the wedding party we would see a smiling Mrs Davies raising her glass at the centre of the picture. To her immediate left is a young girl looking slightly awkward in her bridesmaid attire. The girl is Jessica Warne.

The telephone in the little house halfway down the road

at the bottom of the hill has been ringing for several minutes. Meanwhile Mrs Davies is paying for her crucifix.

She holds out her palm and waits for her change.

Describe the pain. Describe the pain.

Shut up. Please. Why did there always seem to be someone asking her to describe the pain? Doctors, mothers and stupid flipping husbands like him. Please just shut up. Why was it always so important? She doesn't want to describe the pain, she doesn't even want to think about it. Shut up. Just leave her alone.

Sandra? *Can* you describe the pain?

No, not this time she couldn't but they always made you feel stupid. Was it a dull pain? Or a stabbing pain? She didn't know. She wasn't stupid, she just didn't know. She just wanted it to stop.

She only knew that it was deep inside her and it was private and it really didn't concern anyone else and it was punishing her because it didn't understand. And it didn't care. But it was her problem, her agony. Hers. Something that belonged to her and her alone. And that was how she wanted it.

She would suffer but she would be as brave as the boy in the Bible . . .

Couldn't they give you something for it?

Describe the pain.

Then they'll give you something for it.

Shut up. It will pass in a moment . . .

It.

Will.

Pass.

A great shoal of brightly coloured fish with rubies and emeralds on the wings of extinct giant butterflies which are really sparklers on a windy bonfire night at the boundaries of this great and terrible universe which become lanterns on a tree in a garden by the sea and a lighthouse down below and far away . . .

When Sandra Langton finally opens her eyes again she is standing on the pavement outside the Harbour Café and Grill in the dazzling afternoon sun. She takes her hand away from her stomach and realising that she is stooping slightly, she straightens up. She notices the worried look on her son's face.

'Ooooh ouch,' she says with a smile.

Andrew says nothing and starts to run towards his mother. Barney quickly grabs the boy by his arm. 'Steady on, just a second there. Let's give Mummy just a couple of minutes . . .'

'But I want to . . .'

'When I say in a minute, Andrew, I mean in a minute.' And suddenly he was the despised and stuffy old French teacher once more.

'I'm OK now.' Sandra's tone suggested that the matter should be of little consequence to either of them.

'Are you sure?'

She nods vaguely at this as though she could barely remember what they were talking about.

'Did you bring that prescription out with you? We'll go and sort it out now.'

Sandra maintains her airy detachment 'Um . . . I think it's in the suitcase. I'm sure I saw it . . .'

'Doesn't matter. We'll take a slow walk back to the hotel. Maybe you can put your feet up for ten minutes. Andrew and I will go and get it for you. Won't we?'

The boy nods emphatically.

He doesn't like this.

HE. FEELS. HIS. BREATH. ING.

START TO.

COME.

IN SHORT. BURSTS.

'Come on, Andy, now, don't be upset. Don't start crying. Mummy says she's OK. We'll go and get her some medicine and she'll be fine.

The boy sniffs his assent.

Sandra looks from her husband to her son and back again. You had to hand it to Barney, she thinks, he could still do a fairly convincing job. But now she knows more and concern wasn't the same as understanding which wasn't the same as affection and concern was easy. Well, it was easy for Barney. As they start to walk away from the Harbour Café she feels the corners of her mouth contort into a shy secret smile.

You're not the only one with secrets, you know?

This is true.

Sandra Langton does indeed have secrets. She drinks a little during the day, wine mainly but now and then the odd gin and tonic. Occasionally she pilfers a lipstick from Boots and she owns a particular battery-operated item for her personal use that she keeps wrapped up in a towel at the back of the airing cupboard.

She also writes poems and has done so for a number of years. These she keeps hidden between the pages of her cookery books, assuming, quite rightly, that this was one place guaranteed to be safe from prying spousey eyes.

Her poems were private, *hers*, as in *belonging to her*, and she wanted them protected from the inevitable mockery – he was a teacher after all. He would probably smile to himself, correct the grammar, scribble suggestions in the margin and give her the old C+ must try harder.

There is a further good reason for this concealment as her husband is also the subject of a number of her verses, along with childhood, weather, death and gardens. In fact he features in her most recent effort completed a few days ago (currently residing within the pages of *Cooking on a Shoestring*, Chapter 8 – Flans and Soufflés).

1971

One Friday night I went on a date
I left home in a hurry I couldn't be late
All through the night it played on my mind
That in my haste I'd left something behind
Then I met the man with a knowing smile
And I forgot all my worries after a while

A surname, a baby, a house and Cortina
A TV, a stereo and a vacuum cleaner
But also the worry, the hopeless despair
Loneliness, fear – my life elsewhere
So I look back to that night and now I can see
The something I left behind was ME

Apart from Sandra only two people know about her poems. Her mother, who keeps an eight-line verse about her garden in her bedside drawer and secretly believes it to be either not very good or 'Modern' or failing that possibly in the Japanese style.

The other person was Tom's mother. Tom is a small pale boy who used to go to Andrew's playgroup. Sandra had really liked Tom's mother and was desperate that one day they would become friends. Tom's mother had gingery hennaed hair and wore brightly coloured clothes. She was brave and wore badges and still believed in things. In Croydon, this was enough to gain her a certain local notoriety bordering on celebrity.

Nowadays, whenever Sandra's friends and acquaintances announced (usually without being asked) that they were so *happy*, *fulfilled* or *settled*, she was never sure if she actually believed them. She wouldn't go as far as to say they were telling blatant lies exactly but it sounded like it they were describing what they wanted to feel, what they felt they should be feeling. Or that *happy* was just a word and they only needed to modify their silly old childish definition a bit. This was simple. Far easier than *changer la vie. Changer le mot!* Her friends just applied *happy* to situations, no better and often more dismal than her own and thereafter the word acquired a new and infinitely more mature meaning! Everyone is *happy* and the whole process can be repeated an infinite number of times.

Not a lie but a cheat, a bit of a conjuring trick and of course you could always do the same with any number of words: 'supportive' or 'caring' or 'kind'.

Similarly, when Tom's mother's confessed, as she did frequently, that her life was boring and quite dull, Sandra always suspected that this wasn't the entire truth and that she was probably only saying it to be pleasant.

But for many months, they would chat idly when they dropped off and collected the boys and after that morning, when Tom's mother had whispered to her that Tom had been an accident, their little chats evolved onto another level. One afternoon as they touched on more cultural and creative matters, i.e. (and Tom's mother was always saying things like 'i.e.', 'and I quote' and 'open brackets close brackets' – it actually got on your nerves after a bit) the complete lack of a decent piano teacher in the whole of their locality for Tom, Sandra mentioned that she hoped Andrew would grow up and 'write poems like I do'. But Tom's mother didn't ask to read them, didn't suggest that they met up later at her house, share a bottle of wine and talk about poetry and important stuff. In fact, Tom's mother barely said anything at all. Her only comment was 'Nice to have a hobby when they're this age, isn't it?'

This was the way it always was.

Sadly, Tom's mother never wanted a lift, had already done her shopping, wasn't walking that way, didn't have time for a coffee and never really saw herself as a Tupperware person.

But thanks for asking.

So nowadays she hardly thinks about Tom's mother.

She has become sealed inside one of those small missiles of vague regret that Sandra Langton likes to bounce off the bedroom ceiling for her entertainment during those endless sleepless small hours.

Now she watches Barney and Andrew, hand in hand, as they walk a yard or so in front of her on the narrow pavement. God, he'd even started walking like his father nowadays. She inhales deeply. Not *happy* or unhappy, dear Sandra, just superfluous, a breeding device and a malfunctioning, broken down one at that . . .

She wants to smile at this but her face is exhausted.

Instead she gains a momentary comfort in the contemplation of the slight extra girth that her husband is now carrying around his waist. A year ago she might have said something but what was the point?

Yet there remained that odd sauntering confidence in his walk, she thinks. She used to like that. Not as vulgar or blatant as a swagger, there was still a certain ambling *awareness* about it. Actually, she had always felt, there was a certain feminine quality to it – in the way the hips and shoulders rose and dipped. It also used to show off his bum to good effect.

Still did probably, if she ever thought about it.

It was a sunny Bank Holiday afternoon in August and they'd come away for their first holiday in years and she knew she loved him but she just had trouble remembering why. When he said 'I love you' nowadays he always did so with a particular emphasis. Like I *love* you. It always sounded as though it should be followed by a little row of dots, like he was taking a breather or had been interrupted. Or it suggested that he hadn't finished his sentence, like the really important bit was just coming, like he was about to say *however* or *but* . . .

She suspected that one day he might finally get around to completing his sentence.

She also suspected that *love* was just another one of those words with an impermanent definition.

Fingers.

This one jabs its clear intentions by pointing towards the door and then tapping a wristwatch.

The response to this is the simple raising of a solitary chubby digit.

This latter action is once again accompanied by a slow shaking of the head and in fact the entire exchange has now been played out three times with little or no variation.

Moe had presumed that this single finger was intended to mean one minute but now he was beginning to wonder. One hour? The duration of one man's life? Sam Taylor is still on the phone, talking predominantly in *uh-huhs* and *I sees*, to someone connected with the local police station. Moe is rather keen to leave but remains mainly out of politeness.

Meanwhile the fingers of Young Mister Featherhead are engaged in a rather different activity and he is currently sitting in the cubicle of the ground-floor toilet wanking. He can be found in there (not that any sane person would wish to find him) at least once every day absorbed in this pursuit. He blames the hot weather. In the winter, however, he maintains that it's been proven to be good for the circulation. In the world inhabited by Colin, the notion that there was more to life than self-abuse was mere idle speculation, a quaint theoretical supposition.

Valiantly insalubrious in his masturbatory habits, Young Mr F. recognises no restriction, no censor or no taboo in his imagination and this afternoon he is thinking about

Jessica Warne. This is because he wants to know what it is like doing it about someone who is dead.

Actually, it is much the same, he has deduced five or so minutes later as the *prrt-prrrt-prrrrt-prrrrrrrrt* of a moped engine signals his final departure from the building.

Moe Seyton looks up from the *Yellow Pages* he has started reading and watches the youth in the leather jacket weave his way unsteadily out into the traffic. A young man who has just started to think about the revised 0–60 acceleration statistics for the Featherhead 750, as he vanishes from view behind a soft drinks van.

Eight hours and thirty-six minutes

His phone called concluded, the ambitious Deputy Editor claps his hands together and exhales loudly.

'Blimey, Moe,' he says approaching his friend and shaking his head. 'Might be a big one, this. The word is that there's definitely evidence of a struggle of some kind, bruising and what have you. We managed to get that much off them and Colin was right. Possibly for the only time in his life. They are treating it as suspicious, officially that is. Off the record they're calling it a murder.'

Moe closes the *Yellow Pages* and pushes it away from him. 'Oh dear, that's terrible.'

'You wouldn't understand, boyo. People in Margate don't go around getting themselves *killed.* Doesn't happen. Not killed like that anyway. They get killed by accident, they get electrocuted by their lawnmowers, they fall down stairs, or in a house fire, a car wreck, one or two hypothermias every winter, we even have the odd drowning now and again. Isolated, tragic bloody things. Like that storm we had back in January, the one that destroyed the pier. But that was like an act of God or . . . *nature.* Not like this. Somebody killed this girl. Somebody who is out there now walking around the place just like you and I.'

Moe frowns in sympathy but says nothing. For the first time that day something related to panic passes across his features. A man into whose day has just been forced a dreadful uncertainty

'I'm sorry Moe, but I'm going to have to scoot. I'm supposed to be meeting er . . . *someone* at the infirmary.' Sam grabs his jacket and ushers Moe towards the door. 'I'll tell you what, if this doesn't get me off the bloody sports desk nothing will!' With customary over-familiarity he pats Moe on the arm. 'Hey, just think I might never again have to write *Despite this early setback, Margate FC continued to fight back and produced some good chances early in the second half. Unfortunately,* . . . and so on and bloody so forth . . .'

When they are downstairs and back on the street again Sam and Moe shake hands. This strikes both men as an oddly formal gesture yet suitably indicative of their particular friendship, suggesting as it did codes and terms that had yet to be defined.

The afternoon sun immediately starts to colour Sam's cheeks and forehead. 'I am so sorry about this.'

'So, what are the actual chances of you being at the club later?' asks Moe, his voice oddly agitated.

'I don't know, very, very doubtful, I expect. In fact, count me out, Em. I just can't know how this will play out and I've just got to go with it. Sorry and all that.'

'I understand.' Moe smiles and takes a tentative step backwards. 'Oh and good luck with your story. Hope it bears fruit.'

'Cheers.'

Sam walks away quickly while Moe gazes at the pavement and silently mouths a word that in truth he rarely uses offstage.

A tear slides down her cheek as Sandra Langton shifts once again onto her side and closes her eyes. Clasping a pillow to her stomach, she raises her knees gradually until she finds a position that offers some relief. Then alone, tiny and marooned in the centre of the vast meadow of eiderdown, she allows herself to drift away on the muted sounds of a summer afternoon. The gentle traces of always. She hears distant traffic and seagulls, a dog barking followed by the sound of a door closing and two familiar voices.

'How can you tell?'

'Didn't you know? *All* dogs are he.'

'No they're not.'

'Yes they are. All dogs are he, all cats are she, all the beautiful women are French and all the good men are taken. The rest are just bastards.'

'. . . Pardon . . .'

'Pay attention!'

'Where are we going again?'

'I told you we're going to find a chemist that's open to get Mummy's medicine . . .'

A car horn sounds three short blasts after which the familiar voices are heard no more.

Then, gently and almost without thinking, she runs her hand through her hair just above her temple. What Daddy used to do when she was poorly like that time with the measles, when she was hot and couldn't sleep and Daddy's gone a-hunting, and with this thought, she surrenders herself to the darkness once more.

Her body leaks another cruel watery droplet that trickles and tickles under her arm.

It feels like a tear, she thinks.

'A little lad walks up to an old man . . .'

This Was How They Met: At about half past three, Moe Seyton allows himself a brief respite from his walk back to the Seaview. Rather than risk a mapless short cut through the backstreets, he has retraced his route back towards the seafront. He is jostling his way through the late afternoon throng along the Promenade when he notices an unoccupied bench in the Marine Gardens. Taking this to be some sort of visionary sign of celestial interference, he chooses not to take up arms against fate but weaves his way over and sits down. Meanwhile, returning from the chemists, the Langtons are taking a short cut through the Gardens and Andrew, having complained for ten minutes about the sand in his sandal is pulling on his father's arm. Barney indicates a nearby bench and suggests they go and sit down for a few moments and attend to the problem. A shadow passes across Moe's face as two florally inclined, lily-of-the-valleyed, sun-troubled, breeze-bothered middle-aged ladies choose to halt their nicelittlestrollbeforetea for a few brief seconds directly in front of him.

This Was What He Overheard: The taller of the two ladies, who is alternatively reading and fanning herself with a small leaflet entitled 'Getting Out and About in Ramsgate, Broadstairs and Margate' expresses disbelief that anyone would name a beach Hackemdown Point. It doesn't, she concludes in East Anglian tones, exactly make one want to rush there exactly, does it? Her companion wondered if it might have something to do with Vikings. She often caught herself thinking about Vikings.

This Was What He Was Looking At: Hundreds of people, hundreds of happy people, hundreds of people who were happier than he was. Happier than he had ever been or will ever be. Joyous frolicking little specs. Ah, but what a gift it had once been to a composer of risqué songs to have the word frolics at his disposal. In common with limerick writers the English-speaking world over, he mourned its slow gradual departure from general use. And to his left a kiosk with a queue, a clock tower and the infinite sea and the sky. Then his gaze happens upon the perspiration stain under the arm of the nylon dress worn by the lady with the leaflet.

This Was What He Was Thinking About: Seven hours and twenty-six minutes . . . And now Sam is out of the picture, what was he going to do? Where on earth was he going to find his witness now? A single solitary witness, a trusted dependable reliable witness and one at very short notice! Sam was ideal for the job, everything about him, so much so that he had never considered for a moment that there might be the slightest need for an alternative. Stupid! He had just allowed himself to be dragged around Margate for two hours for nothing! A contingency witness was required. Urgently. Desperately. He needs to find someone but where does one even begin to look for such a thing? God, he'd known Sam for years, decades in fact. It had been all leading up to this. Maybe it was too late? No, he couldn't let himself think like that. But all those plans! It couldn't happen! Somebody please send a witness! Now! Before it's too late! Please. Mild panic. *Did this sound like a person praying?* In his desperation was he now drifting into areas where he was thinking in terms of faith and belief? That by these means alone, his contingency witness would be delivered unto him? Oh dear. Well, if these are the current realities . . . any time around about now would be absolutely fine . . . But this wasn't all that was troubling him. Could he be absolutely certain that he'd remembered to relocate that little *item* from under his pillow? Didn't want anyone turning that up when they did his room. Of course he did, it's in the pocket of his raincoat. Never thought she would be the type to wear nylon. Or perspire. Never trusted nylon, always thought that somehow only artificial desires, and passions lurked beneath artificial fibres. Fakers, deceivers like Catherine. God, he was really going to have to stop thinking about Catherine. That was twice today. Maybe he would have a bit of a fumble around when he got back to the guest house. That would sort him out. But would it? And that was another thing too depressing for words – that nagging doubt that nowadays masturbation somehow managed to qualify as a kind of nostalgia. (Ironic really for someone who had always regarded nostalgia as a kind of masturbation). A fantasy about the past. That longing to relive and recapture. A single man takes his onanistic interludes very seriously indeed and that something so pure could become tainted in this fashion was most alarming! What was that bit? Died on me. Not long ago, a year or so at most. Bought a handful of gags from that chap in Eastbourne, young fellow, not bad, a couple worked quite well but not that one. It's coming back . . . *Get out of practice don't you, fellas? Geezer I know, been a couple of years on his own now. Got into certain . . . shall we say . . . Bad Habits, if you know what I mean, gents? Says he's scared of women now, won't go to bed with them anymore. Scared? I asked him, What do you mean scared? It's true and all. Reckons he'll shoot his load, fall asleep and wake up with his new lady friend folded in half and stuffed under the mattress. Not a great way to woo, as they say* . . . Could have worked. Maybe it needed detail. Maybe 'Bad Habits' wasn't specific enough, too general. If he woke up and the lady has gone but then he hears a muffling sound . . . No that was getting too visual, too involved, too cartoony. Best forgotten. God, the sun is bloody bright today. Kaiser used to say that you take opposition to convention in this trade. Not intentionally but you work at night and sleep in the day and before long it is simply a case of your rituals no longer being compatible with the rest of the world's rituals. You never ask for this but you are the inadvertent outsider and can't seem to function any other way. But the funny thing about it is you don't hate or even envy you simply develop the ability to exclude yourself. You become, sort of . . . *exiled.* Sunlight. Bedtime. Holidays. He had only equivalents and translations. His simulacra. Christmas. Religion. Never found it easy to talk about religion, one of the hazards of the job. Religion was banned. You could do twenty-five minutes about sex but never God. Like to meet the bloke who came up with that one . . . *stay off politics and religion, stay off politics and religion.* Perhaps this is why he had managed to end up with so few fixed ideas on the subject. *Stay off politics and religion* . . . But if you wanted to believe in something what was wrong with a belief in a sense of order, of justice and fairness? (Maybe better than believing that some great benevolent force would drop a witness into your life when you most needed it. *Because* you most needed it.) OK, a man's faith should be his own business but most people's idea of God is usually that he is wise and fair-minded and lacks all of our silly flaws and imperfections. Someone who is better than us, capable of that great great . . . goodness . . . that we can sense still exists somewhere in each and every one of us. Perhaps he is no more than that – but isn't that enough? *stay off politics and religion* . . . Regardless of cathedrals and temples, God always seemed like a sound enough idea. Then again, Neptune was probably a great idea as well – but no one had ever seemed to be that bothered whether you believed in Neptune or not. But whatever your take on all this, you could not avoid belief. Good evening everyone. I was just wondering, ladies and gentleman, what does an atheist have on his insurance form instead of act of God? Act of superstition and hearsay? *stay off politics and religion . . .* Even disbelief is a belief, if you thought about it – your faith being the unshakeable conviction that something unproven either way is nothing beyond superstition and nonsense. (In this his views, although he is unaware of it, are strikingly similar to those of Barney Langton.) Retirement. Marriage. Families. Children. Children? Children? No please don't sit down, please don't sit down . . . please just walk past, just walk past, please go away . . . please . . . there's a good boy . . . just . . .

This Was What He Was Asked: 'Do you get sand in your shoes too? I do. It's because I got holes in my sandals. Look. That's how the sand gets inside . . . See?'

Andrew points to the petal-pattern design of ventilation holes. 'All the sand gets in here and here.'

Moe says nothing but looks at the man who is now standing besides the boy. The man is smiling amiably but a little nervously. Reasonably assuming that this is the boy's father, Moe returns his smile and then turns away.

A brown leather Start-rite sandal is now brought into regular rhythmic contact with a wooden bench as an accompaniment to the following refrain:

Sand, sand, sand,
I hate this sand,
I hate this sand,

Sand, sand, sand,
Sand, sand, . . .

'Sand?' offers Moe with a shrug, without turning around.

The boy laughs.

'Come on now Andrew, leave the gentleman alone, there's a good lad.' Barney then looks a little closer at the rather smartly dressed man in the blazer and discovers something in his appearance and general demeanour that hints at a possible military background. 'I'm sorry,' he says through a quavering smile. 'I hope he's not bothering you.'

'He's fine,' says Moe with a wink and an indulgent nod of the head.

Then he turns towards the boy and in a voice that betrays a lifetime's habit of addressing children as though they were unintelligent adults, he says 'you know you'd better be careful, young man. You wouldn't want to get on the wrong side of the Sand Police, now would you?'

'Who?'

Moe makes fleeting eye contact with Barney who offers a bland, non-committal smile. 'Surely you must have heard of the Margate Sand Police?'

'No.'

'Well, it's *their* job to make sure nobody tries to steal the beach, you see? People just like you smuggle bits of it away every year. In their shoes and socks and towels, they take little bits of the beach home with them. A little pile here and a handful there, it's been going on for years. The authorities started to worry that one day there'll be no beach left so they called for the Sand Police. You must have heard of the Sand Police, right? They find out where you live and they come to your house in the middle of the night with flashing lights and sirens and their sniffer sand dogs they make you give back all the bits of the beach you've taken away.'

He turns to his father. 'Is that true, Daddy?'

But before Barney can reply and in a voice that was more recognisably his own once more, Moe says, 'No it's not true I was just pulling your leg.'

'Really?'

'Of course.'

The boy smiles like all boys smile when they are six and uncertain and the world is still too big and unknowable. He starts banging his sandal against the bench once more but he doesn't feel like singing.

'Are you intending to do that all afternoon?' asks his father as he sits down next to him.

But Andrew doesn't answer him. Instead he turns once again towards the older man. 'Well, I know all about *you,*' he says in flat, serious tones.

Moe is slightly alarmed at this unexpected and sudden shift in the proceedings. 'Do you?'

'I do.'

'And what do you know, exactly?'

'Well . . .' Andrew ceases his percussive interjections and in a manner that suggests a recent reunion after a long and painful absence he clasps his sandal to his chest.

'I know . . .' The boy is speaking tentatively and cautiously now as if testing the temperature of each individual word. 'I know . . . THAT . . . you . . . that you . . . that YOU are . . . that you are . . . naughty sometimes . . . you are a NAUGHTYMAN . . .'

His father's eyes widen in sudden admonition 'And-rew!' he says, in a voice that he forces out from between his teeth.

'What?'

The boy places his sandal on his knee and decides if you look at a sandal from here and do this with your eyes it looks a bit like a dodgem car.

'You mustn't be rude to people.' He looks at the gentleman and tries an apologetic smile. 'I'm sorry about . . . !

Moe glances at his watch. Seven hours and twenty-one minutes. Time to be magnanimous. 'No, no, no, you have nothing to apologise for. I'm sure he's just having a bit of fun. Is that right?'

There is no reply. The dodgem car progresses up and down the boy's thigh in silence until it gets to here and then it looks like a speedboat.

Moe repeats his question, whilst savouring a little its slightly ironic aspect. 'So tell me then, young fellow, why am I such a naughty man?'

'Because . . .' Going faster now to avoid a giant octopus and the Loch Ness Monster. Speedboats can go much faster than sea monsters, anyone knows that. 'Because you . . . don't . . . eat . . . your . . . breakfast . . .'

At this point in their exchange a young lady, who is struggling with two large and evidently heavy suitcases, stops in front of the bench. She sets the cases down for a moment and stares at Moe, Barney and Andrew in a manner regarded as hoity-toity, disdainful and scary respectively. Then, showing off a rather noble jaw line and profile she turns her head towards the Promenade. She inhales loudly, somehow manages to transform it into a sigh, picks up her cases and quickly walks away.

They watch her depart then Moe quickly steers them back towards the matter at hand. 'So, I don't eat my breakfast then, do I?'

Andrew shakes his head.

Feeling that some brief clarification might be appropriate, Barney explains that his family is also staying at the Seaview and Andrew had been asking questions over breakfast about the unoccupied table nearby.

'I see,' says Moe. 'And you think it's naughty not to eat breakfast, do you?'

Andrew wonders if he should be more worried by sea monsters, and gazes out towards the North Sea. He really wants to know but he doesn't want to know at the same time then something inside goes a bit wobbly or did they only have them in the old days and in far-away countries?

'Pardon?' he says eventually.

'I just was wondering . . .' Moe's face tries unsuccessfully to evict the smile that has just arrived without his permission. '. . . Wondering why you think it's naughty not to eat breakfast.'

Andrew begins to swing his legs. 'Because you are still in bed and that means you must be asleep and when I'm in bed at breakfast time I get told off for being lazy.'

'Do you?'

'Did you know it's *The Most Important Meal of the Day*?'

'You don't say?'

'Yes I do. You must always always remember: *It's a Long Time to Lunch.*'

Moe grins at the boy in a fairly affable manner but can think of nothing further to say.

Meanwhile the person who could justifiably claim sole responsibility for her son's nutritional evangelism is reaching into the internal zippered compartment of her handbag. She retrieves her small appointments diary and finding a particularly uneventful week around the beginning of March, she writes in pencil:

A Mouth to Feed

They said I'd feel discomfort, they said I'd feel pain
What they didn't tell me was that I'd never be the same
They took something precious,
Took away something pure
And left in their place the agonies
Which I now endure

They said I'd feel discomfort, they said I'd feel pain
But they never thought to ask me if it had a name

It? She reflects upon her hasty choice of pronoun and Sandra Langton discovers that she doesn't really feel like writing anything further at the moment. She closes her eyes again.

Exactly one hundred years ago, almost to this precise hour, a gentleman was arrested on the Promenade at Margate. In actual fact the incident took place at a point no more than a matter of yards away from the bench where Moe, Barney and Andrew are currently sitting.

A constable by the name of Trenley Parkwood had been dispatched on that fateful day to 'observe and monitor' a fair-sized crowd gathering along the sea-front. He would later recount the events of the afternoon many times and while he would elaborate and embellish a little he always remained faithful in these accounts to his initial impression of the scene. 'It looked peaceful enough but we have to follow very strict rules about panhandling. It was quite an odd little gathering . . .'

And so it was.

The incident would subsequently be reported in the *Kentish Chronicle* under the headline 'Extraordinary Occurrence in Margate' and there was an article in the *Daily Telegraph* the following week; 'A Seaside Curiosity' ran to a couple of dozen lines on page 11. Both articles generated a deluge of letters and the subject was keenly debated for a while.

A bearded man in a light-coloured suit and a straw boater, who would claim to be an American doctor and to have studied in Paris, Berlin and Vienna had set up a small booth on the Promenade. The booth was brightly painted and adorned with pictures of pyramids and ancient temples and attached to its upper edge amongst the flags of all the nations of the Empire was a colourful banner that danced and flapped in the light afternoon breeze. It read

Apothecareum Athenean
'The Greatest Secret Of The Ancient World'
Free Lecture

The doctor was sitting in front of his booth, writing in a small ledger book. With the warm late-afternoon sun on his face he smiled to himself, lost, content and seemingly oblivious to the first handful of the curious who had already gathered. To be truthful, they had been drawn to the booth not by the promise of the free lecture but by the donkey that was tethered to one of the wooden uprights of the booth. The animal seemed fairly oblivious to its surroundings but as it was usually to be found down on the beach giving rides or pulling a two-person cart it was evidently relaxed amongst small crowds.

The donkey had been hired by the doctor for an hour, the price he was charged for this was never revealed by the donkey handler, who would subsequently speak very rarely of that afternoon's events. Although it was recorded that the donkey was 'one of the best he'd had' and that it was called Chalkie.

When about twenty or so people had gathered around his booth the doctor snapped his book shut, leapt to his feet and with a stiff almost ceremonial solemnity offered Chalkie a carrot. He removed his spectacles with a practised flourish and surveyed the scene. It was at this point that several witnesses later recalled how they were made aware of a sudden silence. Even the breeze seemed to drop.

He studied the faces before him and smiled as if he was half-expecting to see someone familiar. Then he spoke. Now the strange thing was that people could remember almost word for word what he said but no one could recall anything about his voice. There was no mention of a particular accent or pitch or even if he was loud or soft-spoken.

'Good afternoon, ladies and gentlemen and thank you for gifting me with a MOMENT of your most valuable time on this most GLORIOUS of afternoons. In return I can only offer you IN ALL HUMILITY this short lecture. For this afternoon I will unlock for you the GREATEST secret of the Ancients, a secret, ladies and gentlemen, lost for centuries. A SECRET believed buried with the pharaohs of Egypt, the emperors of Rome and the greatest wise men of Greece. For this AFTERNOON I will reveal to you the mysteries of the Apothecareum Athenean.'

The doctor gestured with his open palm periodically but in the main his performance tended towards the understated. His whole approach was clerical rather than theatrical.

The crowd meanwhile had continued to gather in front of him. People had started jostling to get a better view.

'BUT I do not ask you, good people of Margate, to trust my word alone. That will not be necessary and indeed it would be wrong of me to CRAVE such an indulgence. For although I shall prove my claims BEYOND A SHADOW OF DOUBT, I can also produce signed, I repeat signed and INDEED sworn testimonials from members of various European royal families. SO If there is any man or woman who doubts my INTEGRITY or my VERACITY then I will invite them to step forward and read for HIM or HERSELF these letters which I keep SAFE upon my person.'

Then, from the rear of the crowd, a young man standing with a group of his friends shouted out something personal and vulgar.

The doctor's response was instantaneous.

'Sir, you will I hope, IN TIME, learn the virtue of PATIENCE.'

For a few moments, the doctor said nothing. He might have been waiting for a further response from the young man but it was possible he was simply choosing the right moment.

'Yet his urgency is understandable for is he not about to DISCOVER one of the greatest secrets of MANKIND? What I speak of this afternoon is the most marvellous discovery of our time. A great LOST treasure, the GREATEST wonder of the age. Ladies and gentlemen, I will now unveil for you the lost science of the Apothecareum Anthenean.'

The doctor strolled over to Chalkie and patted him on the back.

'This afternoon I will DEMONSTRATE to you the power of the ANCIENTS. A power that can be yours from this day FORWARD.'

At that moment he removed a small vial from his jacket pocket and held it up in full view of the crowd.

'THIS . . . ladies and gentlemen. THIS is the POWER of which I speak, the Power of the ANCIENTS.'

At this point in his discourse and with gestures of scorn and derision, a handful of people pulled away from the group, but there remained an impressive enough number with their eyes firmly fixed on the doctor. Once again the young man at the rear shouted something but this time he was urged to be silent by those around him.

It was roughly at this point that Constable Parkwood neared the scene. He approached carefully so that he was not observed by the doctor.

'THIS is the greatest secret of ALL. The ULTIMATE formula. The ancients were practitioners of this great NOW FORGOTTEN science. They guarded the secrets of their trade with their lives and very few WRITTEN records have survived. Yet DISCOVERED in the Holy Land this past decade, a couple of FRAGMENTS dating from before the birth of JESUS reveal for the first time the secret SCIENTIFIC and CHEMICAL formula. FORTUNATELY due to my close personal friendships with a well-respected professor at OXFORD University, I have been allowed, nay, I have been granted the GREAT PRIVILEGE to study these formulas. This will be the true wonder of the MODERN AGE. Available only from MYSELF for a MOST REASONABLE SUM and yours to TAKE HOME this FINE afternoon.'

The doctor removed the stopper from the vial and drank its contents in hearty gulps.

'WE stand at the doorway of a GREAT new AGE, ladies and gentlemen. TODAY, you have the OPPORTUNITY to become pioneers, the envy of your families and FRIENDS. WHO amongst you has the INSIGHT to share this VISION? WHO is BRAVE ENOUGH . . . yes, I say BRAVE ENOUGH to taste the GREATEST POWER in all the WORLD? I offer you the chance to purchase AT NOT UNREASONABLE COST this secret FORMULA, a ONCE-IN-A-LIFETIME opportunity to share in the gift of the very greatest LOST science of all.'

What happened next happened so quickly that many onlookers were confused by what they saw. In full view of the crowd who were 'party to no trick or deception', the doctor stood directly in front of the donkey and placed his hands on either side of its head. At this point recollections began to differ wildly. He stared into the beast's eyes and spoke a few words which 'sounded like Latin' or 'probably Chinese'. There was sound likened in the *Kentish Chronicle* to 'waves' or a 'distant locomotive' and the donkey 'started to grow dark', it seemed to 'shimmer like the beating of a butterfly's wing' or 'agitate as ripples on the surface of a pond'.

At this point testimonies became significantly less disparate.

'Then the beast was no longer there.'

'He made it vanish before our eyes.'

'It was there one minute and gone the next.'

'It was like smoke or clouds.'

In the dazed panic and confusion that followed, Constable Parkwood pushed himself into the throng. Acting 'quickly and decisively and with admirable presence of mind' and sensing 'the threat of riotous behaviour', he grabbed the doctor by the arm and led him swiftly away, partly for his own safety.

The doctor would later be charged and fined for panhandling and public order offences. He said very little during his incarceration, in fact he had refused to give his name at first, boasting that it would be of little purpose as he would forever be known as the Man Who Made the Donkey Disappear in Margate.

His identity had only been established by a number of letters that he kept about his person. They were a most curious collection, the one in French thanked the recipient for his interest in the fire brigade, another reminded him that libel was an offence under German law while the one in Spanish seemed to concern itself with penal reform. But the addressee on these and all the other letters was the same:

Moe Seyton Esq.

'Right, a big bloke and a skinny bloke . . .'

At 15.47 and 35 seconds British Summer Time, a cloud passes in front of the sun for the first time in well over an hour. Taking this as some vague metaphysical prompt, Barney Langton decides the time has come to return to the Seaview once more. Simultaneously, the older gentleman is deciding upon the best course of action and reaches into his pocket with the intention of locating some coins.

A man who lacks *purpose*, it is said, will create *routines*.

Moe would own up to the latter theoretical possibility but would be outraged at the suggestion of former. But, nevertheless, Moe had developed over time a set pattern to his days that he liked to follow.

Barney stands up and rubs the small of his back with one hand, the other hand he holds out to Andrew. 'Come on, we'd better go and see if your mummy is awake again after her little nap.'

'Why?'

'Please, Andrew. I'm not in the mood.'

'But I want to stay here . . .'

'Come on now, I'm not putting up with any silliness . . .'

'Excuse me. I have an idea . . .'

In the silence that follows his remark, Moe surveys a handful of change and does a quick calculation. 'As this young man has so wisely pointed out the error of my ways,

I'll be sure to bear his advice in mind in the future. So, to show my appreciation why don't the pair of you have an ice cream on me?' He holds his hand out and offers the coins to the boy. 'Here you go, it's OK, go on, take it.'

'Can we, Dad, can we?

'Er, thank you very much,' offers Barney nervously, wondering if a stark refusal might cause offence. 'That's very kind of you.'

A genuine smile of relief passes across Moe's face as he finds himself being led towards the ice-cream kiosk by a young boy who he has only known for ten minutes or so and that boy's father.

'Do you know Margate then?' asks Barney for want of something to say.

'Oh no, I'm just down here um . . . on business . . . shall we say?'

'I see.'

'And you?'

'No, we're just on holiday. We live in Croydon . . .'

Croy-don, Croy-don, Croy-don comes the small chant from Barney's immediate left.

'. . . But I did grow up around here. Little village about six miles or so over that way.' He points vaguely in a couple of directions.

'Actually, you see that café over there by the shop with the beach balls in front? That one . . .' He points with greater accuracy this time. 'I was duffed up there once. Seriously. By a boy in my class at school.'

It was not often you heard someone being nostalgic about a beating and Moe would have to concede that this might actually be a first.

'Malcolm Hammond, a fourth former like me, beat me up because I wouldn't give him any of my chips. He was with the other Malcolm . . . Malcolm . . . Tanner was it? Might have been. Anyway the two Malcolms were fairly inseparable and were always knocking around together. They used to sit together in school. One was tall and fat and the other skinny. The teachers used to call them Grand Mal and Petit Mal. Sadly, much as it besmirches my honour it was actually Petit Mal who duffed me up that night!'

'That is unfortunate. Did you extract a bloody revenge?' Moe smiles with benign indifference (an expression first perfected by background peasants in Flemish religious paintings) and assumes, quite correctly, that as long as his companion continued talking he would not be required to take any further part in the conversation.

But prompted by Moe's question, Barney Langton now recalls an incident that he has forgotten for almost two decades.

To Barney, memory is a necessary indulgence, like love or music – but it served no discernible purpose other than encouraging a sort of soggy regret. It was selective but disordered – like pebbles on a great vast beach that stretched from horizon to horizon. One or two catch your eye for no reason, or you might pick a couple up from time to time but usually you just walked over them, oblivious and unconnected. But, like the perpetual child exploring some new environment, sometimes you are suddenly pulled towards something, something altogether random. It's a bit like that. Like Andrew used to. Still does sometimes.

It's always childhood, isn't it?

Always the same child . . .

We are all different now but once upon a time we were all the same child! We have all grown and developed from a series of almost identical moments of ignorance and wonder!

But by connecting with what we once did we are only vainly trying to connect with something we once were . . .

Why? Well, because we were happier, better, more fulfilled and hopeful versions of ourselves . . .

Details and sensations, shape, form, order . . . and when he speaks again his voice is excited, agitated even, as though unaccustomed to enthusiasm.

'I actually got him into trouble once, Petit Mal that is. I didn't mean to . . . but it was the strangest thing. He sat directly behind me during English. We had a fierce English teacher, a lady, middle-aged . . . Miss Armitage was her name. But one Monday morning we were doing some work on punctuation, like we always did on a Monday. It was very boring and I wasn't really paying much attention. The lessons were basically her booming voice but a hushed reverential silence apart from that. But during this particular lesson somebody made a noise or scraped a chair or something and she went absolutely mad. *Who did that and nobody leaves this room until the person responsible owns up and don't think you're getting away with it and if the guilty party does not stand up now the whole class will have detention for the rest of the week.* Nothing. No response whatsoever. Silence again. She paces around the class staring at all of us individually. The tension is unbearable. Everyone in the class is rigid with fear, no one dares to even look at her *Who did it? I will find out,* she keeps saying. Then suddenly, out of the blue I'm standing up admitting to her that I had scraped my chair. She naturally goes absolutely bonkers at me and gives me detention but the strange thing is I didn't actually do it! Maybe, it was the only thing I could do to lift that awful tension. But, thinking about it now, I really do think that I confessed because the whole incident was being played out like the scene in a book. Maybe from a chapter in *Tom Brown's Schooldays,* or *Oliver Twist . . . Tom Sawyer.* That sort of thing. It was like that one pivotal event that starts a great adventure, a turning point in a story. I desperately wanted that in my life. I think I was just trying to make something happen. I wanted to be surrounded by events and circumstances. Maybe a bit of intrigue . . . Anyway, while she's telling me off, someone in the class mutters something under their breath and I quickly look over my shoulder to see if it was Petit Mal. Before I know it he's standing up too and being given a detention. So it was a sort of revenge, I suppose . . .'

Barney stops talking for a moment and looks at Andrew and then at the older man. He shrugs his shoulders. 'Er . . . I don't know why I'm telling you all this.'

'Because I . . . well, it's a nice story,' says Moe, who having just been reminded of several almost identical incidents in his own past, has just concluded he has found his perfect witness.

Then he glances at the heavens and mouths a silent *thank you.*

Loud sing hosanna.

Carrying two large suitcases and making slow but steady progress towards the bus stop outside the railway station, Penny Hammond dismisses from her mind any lingering resentment towards the two blokes and that little kid that she has just seen down on the Promenade. But they could have offered her a seat, couldn't they? It wouldn't have killed them now, would it? If only for a minute but no, they couldn't even do that, could they. *(But Penny Hammond would just like to say at this point that they're all the same nowadays, young and old alike, makes no flipping difference.)*

Penny Hammond is twenty-seven and doesn't like men very much at the moment.

She used to like men a long time ago. Or she thought she did. She liked dads and uncles and her friends' dads and the way they drove cars and weren't scared of ghosts. And how their clothes smelled when they picked you up but the fabric was rough when you put your face into it. (They always carried you when you were tired.) How they always seemed to know people to stop and talk to whenever you went out. And they could always open bottles and cans. And their watches didn't have all the numbers on them just 3, 6, 9 and 12. And that was very clever and grown up, you know. And their handkerchiefs were really big and you could use them on a doll's bed. And they didn't mind or get cross with you. And they were strong and they knew about things like tummy aches and sometimes they were kind. And they always had coins in their pockets and they made a noise when they walked and you could always go to sleep when you knew they were home. And they were funny and had hair on their arms because they were always outside in the cold weather working. And if they ever shouted it was only because they were worried you might hurt yourself. And they always told you that you were pretty. And you always believed them.

And you always, always believed them.

(But Penny Hammond would just like to say at this point that children should not be held responsible for the illusions forced upon them by traditional male culture.)

Mrs Hammond doesn't like men very much these days. She also doesn't like hot summer afternoons, the sensation of dampness under her arms or the bloody daft clogs that are crippling her feet.

She also doesn't like the fact people keep staring at her and what the hell was so outrageous and unusual about a woman carrying two suitcases? Are women not supposed to carry suitcases or something? Is that the problem? You would have thought that seeing people with suitcases at a holiday resort was not all that out of the bloody ordinary. *(But Penny Hammond would just like to say at this point that she is not on holiday.)*

Maybe people think that she is running away somewhere, escaping to a better life, some fabulous new beginning. *(But Penny Hammond would just like to say at this point no such luck.)*

When you escape what is the most important thing, she wonders, what you are escaping from or what you are escaping to? Or was it the actual act of escape itself? You could probably tell a great deal about a person by how they answer a question like that. Somebody said that they ask you questions like that if you apply to join the police.

Maybe that is what it is like everywhere these days. It is accepted that no one is honest and people only ever reveal themselves accidentally. Or are tricked into doing so. Oh yes, she had no trouble believing that.

She smiles in a way that reveals nothing.

The cases are heavy and seem to be getting heavier; in fact they actually feel a great deal heavier than the last time. This, of course, is simply not possible and she puts it down to the heat. She is beginning to feel that familiar ache in her arms again and her palms are red and hot from the handles but she does not want to stop until she reaches the station. Her back will hurt in the morning like it has done the last couple of times. *(But Penny Hammond would just like to say at this point that it will be worth it.)*

The bus will be along in ten minutes or so and she should be back at the house ages before Darling Malcolm returns. Darling Malcolm is out most free afternoons with his 'friends', the two remaining people on the planet who haven't grown tired of his lies and deceptions – the tall fat stupid one and the bald stupid one. *(But Penny Hammond would just like to say at this point that she knows very well what he really gets up to on his free afternoons.)* For whatever reason, Darling Malcolm is rarely back at home much before late evening.

Whenever her resolve weakens and the muscles in her arms grow tired, she concentrates her thoughts on his silly self-satisfied expression, the pewter tankard with his name on, his unswerving devotion to the works of Sven Hassel, Benny Hill and Clint Eastwood. Or she might think about him doing his press-ups and the way he looked at himself in their hall mirror before he went to see *her.* That horrible little smile of self-congratulation. If all that failed she thinks about his penis – she does this as though it was some hopelessly ill-trained and unreliable family pet. Oh and make no mistake, just for the record, Darling Malcolm definitely had a penis nowadays. He didn't have a 'dick', a 'prick', or a 'cock' anymore – they sounded aggressive and sexual. Too personal. And she couldn't invest that wretched organ with the endearing cuddly sweetness of a 'willy'.

Therefore Darling Malcolm always had a penis nowadays. Objective and medical and anatomical and nothing to do with her, like his liver or his nervous system.

This is the fifth occasion that Penny Hammond has walked this precise path along the Promenade towards the bus stop outside the station. She finds it laborious in the extreme and can think of a dozen things she would rather be doing. Yet she can now see the virtue in completing the task gradually. It would cause far greater anxiety and much longer bouts of worried reflection.

In this respect Sue and Fiona had been absolutely right and yeah, if he is that bloody vain and conceited then let's use it against him! Nothing erodes the mind and lurks so dark within the soul like doubt! Spot on again, girls! And they were giving up their days off as well to help her. Even a Bank Holiday Monday! What a pair of real stars! And with the twins and Fiona's mum being so ill recently . . .

They had been such good friends, really the best friends she could have wished for and she should have listened to them years ago when they tried to warn her about Darling Malcolm.

(But Penny Hammond would just like to say at this point that one day she will return the favour and they can consider that A Promise and she would just love it if they could both be there tomorrow morning to see the results of their labours!)

Of course the plan was a very simple one – but all great

plans were simple. It was just that its execution had required a level of careful planning. But Sue had always been a gifted seamstress even when they were all in school – she was always by far the best in the class. For a while she had actually toyed with the idea of working in the theatre but in the end The Margate Effect got to her and she wound up working in Drapes 'n' Drops making curtains for £34.70 take home every week.

The shop was closed on weekends but Sue had the key and letting themselves into the workshop at the rear of the shop outside opening hours had been for Penny a deeply thrilling experience. It was secret and forbidden. Casting herself as the Hecate of the proceedings, she discovered that conspiracy gave her such a great sense of *belonging*, it was unlike anything she had ever experienced.

The owners of Drapes 'n' Drops had, during the past six months, modernised and upgraded the workshop and it now boasted a couple of impressive high-end electric sewing machines and it was around these that one lunch-time, their daring idea had originally taken form.

Penny Hammond would take Darling Malcolm's clothes every alternate Friday to the dry cleaners (as she always did) and collect them during the following week.

Two work suits, (Darling Malcolm sold Volvos at a showroom in Ramsgate) three jackets, four shirts, and three pairs of trousers made up the bulk of the contents of the two suitcases she now carried. In addition she had recently managed to convince him, without alerting his suspicions, to send his two favourite pairs of Wrangler's as well. This was something she considered a major achievement.

Nowadays, after picking up the clothes, she would make her way to the shop and meet the girls. Then for an hour or so during her lunchtime or after hours, under Sue's expert eye, they worked flat out on the new machines. They took in waistbands and seams and added tucks and darts to shirts and jackets. It was a magnificent job, a most professional piece of work, and no one, aside from possibly another seamstress, would ever detect the alterations.

When the task was complete Penny returned home and hung the clothes in the wardrobe before Darling Malcolm returned.

Everything was normal and did you have a nice time and what's for tea and absolutely nothing was out of the ordinary apart from . . . Well, aside from the fact that nowadays when he dressed for work, his trousers felt a little tighter and recently his jackets had started to be restrictive and uncomfortable for some reason.

It was a bit odd, but at first he wasn't worried, it was those poxy cleaners, that's what it was but there had never been a problem in the past. Maybe it was the beer, no, it wouldn't be that, he cut right down last week and it didn't seem to make a difference. Maybe it was the increased muscle tone but he had to ask, he didn't want to, he hated the idea but he had to . . . do you . . . do you . . . well, do you think I've put on any weight, Pen . . . ?

(But Penny Hammond would just like to say at this point that she couldn't really say, could she?)

Two days ago she had been delighted to inform her co-conspirators that she'd observed that the self-satisfied smile in the hall mirror was now accompanied by a close and careful examination of the flesh around his chin and jaw.

The suitcases now seem to weigh very little as she prepares to board her bus.

(But Penny Hammond would just like to say at this point that next week will be even better . . .)

Never in a million years.

He didn't know quite what he had been expecting in

answer to his question. In fact, he wasn't even aware that he'd formed any particular opinions on the matter.

But an *entertainer*?

Never in a million years.

Not that there was anything wrong with being an *entertainer* of course. (Apart from the fact that announcing yourself as such did tend to raise a number of suspicions over the precise nature of the entertainment involved.) It was just that somehow it didn't sit with the man, not in the way that civil servant, soon-to-retire claims clerk, or local government officer would have.

Barney Langton is not happy about this.

He is thirty-one and three-quarters, a father, a husband, a teacher, a socialist, a motorist, a fantasist, a cyclist, a psychosomatic, a dog lover, a dogsbody and a worrier. He has recently been bought an ice cream by an *entertainer* and has this very afternoon started to judge people by appearances.

'When you say "entertainer",' he offers after a considerable pause, 'what *sort* of entertainer exactly?'

Having invested this enquiry with the suggestion of a suspicion that, to his ears, bordered on direct accusation, Barney smiles in true hopelessness at the gentleman.

Moe returns the smile and confesses in a quiet yet clear voice 'a comedian'.

'Really?'

At this point in their exchange Barney wonders if he might have felt happier if he'd stuck with entertainer. 'That's interesting . . .'

He steals a brief glance at the man and wonders if this explains his odd familiarity, this irritating vague recollection he'd started to experience a few minutes earlier.

Was he famous at all?

He steals another sly glance.

Had he seen him on TV, maybe a long time ago? Maybe on a kids' programme? His name, when he'd introduced himself, didn't sound familiar at all. *Moe Seyton,* he'd said, an odd name really, he was very precise about it too ('Say and not sea – to rhyme with Dayton'). In all probability it was a name he might have remembered but so far nothing . . .

The gentleman demolishes the last of his cornet and speaks through a mouthful of dust and wafer. 'I'm not a very well known or wealthy one, and in all probability, I fear, not a very good one. But it's a job and in some respects, I suppose, I should simply be grateful to still have a . . .'

'What's a comedian?'

'Don't interrupt, Andrew, I've told you about that. And you do know what a comedian is.'

'No I don't.'

'Yes you do, stop being silly.'

'I'm not being silly.'

Transferring a fairly generous helping of ice cream onto his eyebrows as he shields his eyes from the sun, Andrew then looks up at Moe. 'What is a comedian?'

The older man shrugs affably. 'Well, to be honest sometimes I don't think I can actually answer that question. But . . . I tell jokes.'

'Will you tell me one?'

Moe shudders. 'Er . . . I don't think you'd find my jokes funny. They're jokes for old people . . . like me'

'I know a joke, I know a joke . . .'

'Do you?'

'Not now, Andrew.'

'But Daddy I want to say my joke. Let me say my joke, please let me . . .'

'Oh go on then . . .'

'It's a bit of a rude joke . . '

'In that case I don't think we want to hear it . . .'

'What smells and rings?' The boy's face is glowing with a pleasure that he will only know for a few more years. 'Do you know, do you know? What smells? *And* rings. BONG!!!!!!! BONG. Do you get it?'

Moe and Andrew look at each other in a moment of wordless accord.

'Bong . . . BONG!!!!'

'Oh that's a very good joke,' says Moe.

'BONG!!!'

'OK, Andrew.'

'BONG BONG!!'

'Andrew! I said that's enough!!'

In the prickly silence that follows this rebuke Moe glances at his watch for the first time in a while.

Six hours and fifty minutes.

The slightest hint of a frown passes over his face. He doesn't feel particularly tired this afternoon, not like some days, but he needed his nap if only for the neat way it divided his day. It gave things a middle, he thought, a central point around which he could order and arrange his important minutes and hours . . .

'Have you got any?' comes the sudden enquiry that ends this particular reverie.

'I beg your pardon.'

'Kids, I mean have you got any kids?'

'No,' says Moe without the slightest trace of emotion. 'I fear not.'

'Right.' Barney nods at this and overshooting sincerity by some distance finds himself wallowing about in a kind of graveside solemnity.

Moe takes a single, shy, tentative step. 'Well, I really should be making tracks back about now.'

'You heading back to the Seaview, then?'

'Yes, I am.'

Barney's face ceases offering the world its condolences and breaks into semi-smile. 'We have to get back as well. Would you mind if we walked with you?'

'Can we, can we, can we?' trilled an enthusiastic voice – the property of one who has already discovered that enthusiasm is very very very difficult to refuse.

'You might find I walk at a much slower pace but please by all means.'

Moe, Barney and Andrew amble away from the Promenade and cross the road opposite the shop where a boy was once beaten for his refusal to share. The boy is now a man, albeit one who slouches slightly as he walks.

The afternoon sun has mellowed but the pavement is still hot and bright and busy with its warm unwelcome lava of sexless flesh. Commiserating and complaining and punishing and promising and hysterical and miserable and nobody is happy in the whole universe.

He waits a second or two while Moe catches up. 'So you're working down here then?'

'Yes, I'm doing three nights at a club, just Saturday, Sunday and tonight.'

'I see.' Pulling up short of sincere this time, Barney's face crumbles into an expression of apologetic disgust.

'It's not the world's most auspicious venue, in fact it's fairly horrible but . . . what can I say? It pays a few bills . . .'

'True enough.' Barney nods unhappily, like a man who is all too familiar with the ways of commerce.

A young woman with long dark hair brushes past them. She offers them a moment's eye contact and the briefest of smiles. In that instant, one man sees the essential and brutal purity of his basic low desire. He recalls Magritte's words about seeing a woman 'accompanied by her own body'. He struggles for a word and finds an obscure one. One that he has forever linked with seaside and sailors for some reason

– for the spontaneous displays of carnality that occur near salt water. SAUCY. Then once again he surrenders himself to the dismal desperate beauty of it all, the awful crude poetry of her bikini top. Her wet hair. The tiny flecks of sand clinging to her arms. Everything in his life for a moment is frozen somewhere in its own icy irrelevance, lost and distant, its purpose and meaning evaporate.

However, the other man can only see Yul Brynner and Telly Savalas arguing over a deckchair.

. . . and blimey, we've been torpedoed – you'll have to let me share your life jacket! . . .

Both men respond by not responding.

'Er . . . what's the name of this club, then? Maybe I could drop by later and catch your act.'

Moe frowns and chuckles through his nose, producing a vague suggestion of either condescension or anxiety. (At a forensic level it would reveal itself to be the latter.)

'That would be delightful,' he says through a broad smile 'although I don't imagine for one minute that an educated man like yourself would find my act all that amusing. It is, I'm afraid, fairly crude.'

For a moment Barney wonders if the gentleman has just openly confessed to a certain lack of professionalism before the truth dawns on him.

Moe continues. 'Well, I'm at the Grosvenor Place Oddfellows Club and Lodge and they're having their annual Stag Weekend. I rather hope that I needn't be any more specific . . . in front of the young lad.'

'I see. So you're like a . . . what are they called? A blue comic?' asks Barney in a whisper, recalling the phrase from somewhere or other.

'I've been called a great deal worse, believe me. But I'm not over fond of that term I must be honest. Stag act, adult humourist, bachelor comic . . . I think they're all fairly terrible. But I suppose it will have to do until someone thinks of a better one. I always thought that what we did was possibly a little near the knuckle myself but essentially harmless. But others will always insist on branding anything they are unable to hear on radio or television as blue or . . .'

Moe glances for a moment at the boy and then silently mouths the word 'obscene'.

Barney nods and recalls with affection how much happier he was with 'entertainer'.

'But, ultimately . . .' says Moe, in the brave important tones of a man who can begin a sentence with the words *but ultimately* 'if I can get more bookings as a blue comic, then I suppose, reluctantly, I'm a blue comic.'

They walk past the entrance to D
R
E
A
M
L
A
N
D

Whereupon they are instantly interrupted as Andrew launches himself into a series of desperate if not entirely persuasive appeals.

He is silenced finally by a fierce single 'NO!' from his father.

He lets the grown-ups walk on a little way and stares down at his sandals as he draws great big long lines on the pavement, left to right, up and down. A sudden gulping of air and that horrible feeling of warmth around his eyelids. He sniffs and it hurts the back of his mouth. He looks up and gazing unblinkingly straight ahead makes a the sort of solemn vow that only children can make.

'I won't, I won't, I won't . . . ever, ever, ever, again . . .

BONG.

Bong.
bo . . '

Sandra Langton wakes up tasting lemons and metal.

For the cruellest fraction of a second she has forgotten.

It is as though her brain is desperately trying to evolve a process by which it can overcome its own pain.

It manages it only for a split second before the mechanism fails.

Memory takes its hostage once more.

'Guy goes up to a policeman . . .'

A glance to the left . . .

. . . and to the right

'mmmmmmmmmmmm . . . *take it, Satch . . .*'

Sam Taylor leans to one side and raising his left knee slightly, he lifts his buttock fractionally off the chair. Frozen for a few moments in this oddly sculptural posture, his brow furrowed in Rodinesque concentration, he narrows his eyes as he releases a fart of a deeply satisfying character.

A short neat trombone blast of pure tone, a well-rounded FRRRRRRRPPP!

In the stillness of the late afternoon, the dimensions and resulting acoustics of the narrow basement corridor enhance the sound, investing it with a splendid significance. No swell or decay or variation in tone, but a tidy single continuous burst, a stark announcement. He alerts all shipping, deters burglars and wakes campers.

He awaits the rising aroma with something that might have been regarded as anticipation, for isn't this truly the most basic and simple of all man's pleasures? A moment to cherish, the moment when we connect with the child we have so long forgotten, the same child who is now all but dead to us.

A child that found fun and wonder in making smells.

An act that is not modified or improved with experience but remains as pure as infancy itself. Was that why he always smiled? Even now? He couldn't help himself. He didn't smile when he sneezed or coughed, did he?

Apparently all the air we breathe is recycled, it just goes on forever. Somewhere out there or in here (probably not in here actually but somewhere definitely) is the stuff exhaled by Shakespeare or Hitler. It all becomes part of the atmosphere. So, presumably by the same scientific principles, a fart would do the same. That would make sense. So, when you gaze into a distant horizon or the limitless sky, remember that. *Somewhere*, according to Taylor's Law, there must be a few dropped by Julius Caesar and Queen Elizabeth. (That's the first Queen Elizabeth obviously and not the current one. For everyone knows . . .)

Taylor's Law further states that every time you fart, therefore, you produce something eternal, immortal something that will endure for ever. There exists all around us some great vast endless invisible history, one that we all absorb unknowingly and contribute to inadvertently! Certainly not something to feel in any way ashamed about!

Long after all our bones are dust and our good deeds are forgotten somewhere in the atmosphere will be all our farts!

Hanging there like stars!

Now that seems like a very good reason to smile. And so he does.

A second later his nostrils flare slightly in this most private of all delights as he considers the result. A dark beery odour engulfs him for a brief speck of time and he thinks, as he has done for many years, *natural, normal and healthy*. Then he makes small subtle fanning movements with the crumpled manila envelope he has been holding in his hand. This signifies that the moment has passed.

He hates the hot weather for he feels let down and betrayed by his own body. Its processes seemed to stall and malfunction and everything seemed to slow down. Prickly, sticky, thirsty, and he tires too quickly and it was all such an effort. He should be thankful for the chance to take the weight off his feet for a few minutes. It shouldn't be long now. Ten minutes he said . . .

He holds his right hand underneath his nose. His fingers have the distinct odour of a man who has recently been handling frankfurters. Then he tries the left hand. Frankfurters again but also something else this time, something underlying and vague. He holds his hand closer and inhales again. A rubbery smell like the inner tube of a bicycle tyre . . .

This prompts another initial surge of memory, one that is instantly curtailed by the sound of a door opening at the end of the corridor. Sam Taylor is returned to a world of whitewashed walls, service elevators and laundry chutes. He stands up and surveys the figure that walks now towards him. He smiles and discreetly fanning the air behind him with his envelope, he takes a few steps away from his chair.

'I hate fucking hospitals . . .'

From some dark murky recess Sam conjures up that renowned chumminess. 'Ah, good afternoon, Sergeant.'

'Always make me feel ill . . . Seriously, I'm in there no more than five minutes and I'm nauseous, my heart is beating like the clappers and I get this throbbing in my head. I'm supposed to be doing my lawn this afternoon. Actually, I *was* doing my lawn this afternoon.'

'Can't be helped, eh?'

Detective Sergeant ******* would prefer not to be named but is around thirty, lives in Deal and is married with rabbits. A pair of purebred white Chinchillas called Butch and Sundance.

'There's always something on a Bank Holiday. Always. You can guarantee it. I don't know why we even bother with that bloody stupid rota, I really don't. We all get dragged back for some reason or another . . .'

Detective Sergeant ******* shakes his head with a commendable gravity.

'So what have you got?'

'Not all that much yet, I'm afraid.'

'Oh, I'm sure you must have something . . .' With little ceremony or sentiment, Sam Taylor hands the policeman the manila envelope. It contains three ten-pound notes.

'Well . . . her name is Jessica Louise Warne. Seventeen. Lived in Cliftonville. At . . . it's here somewhere . . . ah here we go . . . 36 Prices Avenue, Cliftonville. Very, very dead . . . Probably sometime between eleven and midnight. First reported missing at 2.45 a.m. this morning. She was an only child. Parents are both living and were here a while ago to make a formal identification. I arrived just as they were leaving; one of our boys was driving them home. And Sam, they do not want to be disturbed. Not today! Probably not ever. Is that clear?'

Sam frowns but says nothing.

'Mother is very calm, father swearing vengeance and all the usual stuff . . .'

'Cause of death?'

Detective Sergeant ******* exhales deeply. 'Well . . . so far its been a bit tricky. To be honest, this one is a bit of a . . . well, you know? She was pretty messed up. Extensive bruising to the face and neck, significant damage to the back of the skull. Someone really went to work on her . . .'

'You mean . . . ?'

'Yeah, I think you can rule out any possibility of her wounds being self-inflicted. Or the result of an accident. She was lying near the base of a forty-foot cliff but she has the wrong injuries and the wrong patterns of bruising for someone who had simply fallen. Also, I'm a little troubled by the lack of blood at the scene. If you want my opinion she was either moved or just dumped there in a hurry by someone. We've still got our people going over the area.

Oh and before you even think about it, the whole place is fenced off and I've got two constables at the site today, getting themselves a nice bit of overtime by working an extended shift. They're very knackered and very pissed off and you wouldn't want to give them the excuse they're looking for, would you?'

'OK, OK, point taken. So what else do you know about the girl?'

'Not much at the moment – she seemed a nice girl by all accounts, quite homely.'

'Boyfriends?'

'Give us a chance, Sam.'

'Anything else?'

'Well, as far as we can tell, there doesn't seem to be any evidence of sexual interference at this stage. Robbery might have been a possibility; there was no sign of her purse, which she should have had with her. But personally, I'm not convinced. She was still wearing her watch, a nice one too. Expensive. Sixteenth birthday present . . .'

Sam Taylor sighs. 'It's all a bit sad isn't it?'

'It's fucking tragic. It will be the weekend after next before I get a chance to finish the lawn.'

Detective Sergeant ******* turns and starts to walk away.

'How are the bunnies . . . ?' asks Sam.

But Detective Sergeant ******* does not reply and within moments he has left the corridor through the door by which he entered.

No more than a minute later Sam Taylor is in the phone booth on the ground floor dialling the home number of Simon Wendlebury, the staff photographer for the *Thanet Gazette.*

But Mr Wendlebury is not at home.

*

Simon Wendlebury is twenty-four and yet he has the regrets and disillusionments of a man at least two decades his senior. On public holidays, for largely unaccountable reasons, he feels his gravest and darkest doubts more acutely.

He really doesn't want to be there, *of course he doesn't*, that was obvious, and yet he has so far been unable to even imagine a favourable alternative.

This now fills him with a renewed wonder and confidence in his own worthlessness.

Public holidays and birthdays, always the same and he'd had six birthday cards this year. Six! Two less than last year and that was bad enough. Not much really, is it? (When he died they could hold his memorial service in his father's Rover. Then at least, when they got bored talking about him, they could all go for a little drive . . .)

That was why he had originally let himself be persuaded to take this stupid assignment; it got him away from his four walls for a few hours. It shouldn't take long, they'd said, the Mayor was just going to say a few words, *smile, smile, grin, grin, snap, snap,* and all over in half an hour. The Mayor's mother is going into that old people's home, the posh one up Eaton Road. They're making a bit of a thing about it, which is why they're doing it on a Bank Holiday, that way it's a private matter and not a civic duty. So he won't be wearing his beads either. Get a few of him and his mum and a couple with the staff there. All smiles. This is a great happy joyous event, remember. A positive story. Get a couple of colour shots as well. The last week in August is a notoriously quiet week for news and it may be running on the front page.

And if nothing else in the world was going to make you feel thoroughly depressed . . .

Simon Wendlebury wipes some more imaginary invisible dust from the lens of his Pentax and looks at his watch again.

Then the Pentax.

The Pentax.

Simon Wendlebury's Pentax.

The twenty-first birthday present that had never got waterlogged in the Pacific, or chipped falling out of a helicopter, or damaged by being carelessly tossed in the back of a speeding Jeep, or left in some model's apartment. It had over the years acquired the status of an Inverse Trophy – his *namsilat.* It served as a physical tangible reminder of all that hadn't been achieved in life, a portable monument to unfulfilment. Forever, it would reinforce the futility of optimism. (In Margate, it seemed quite a few people had husbands and wives that served approximately the same purpose. But Mr Simon Wendlebury wasn't married.)

Jesus, come on
a few words, they'd said . . .

'. . . *and I can say with the greatest*
conviction and confidence . . .

. . . a few words? Bloody hell . . .
the poor old dear
was nearly asleep . . .

. . . *Margate has something of which*
it can be justifiably proud . . .

. . . if only I'd got here
before he started . . .

. . . *and in conclusion* . . .

. . . let's not get excited here – he's
already said that once . . .

. . . *at the dawn of a new era* . . .

. . . and aren't we always?

. . . *place into their care*
the daily well-being
and happiness of our loved ones . . .

. . . or our unloved ones . . .

. . . and for my mother,
from this day forward,
like all the residents here . . .

. . . come on, come on . . .

. . . this enriching time of new goals
and fresh challenges . . .

. . . please . . .

. . . a time to set our gaze upon
distant new horizons

. . . I promise
I'll vote for you
for ever and ever . . .

. . . looking forward to regular visits
and I sincerely hope that in
fer-fer-fer-fer years' time . . .

. . . oh please don't anybody
laugh for God's sake . . .

. . . anyway . . .

. . . or am I going
to have to remind
everyone here that
ten years ago, you were
known as Caravan Hughes . . .

. . . autumn years spent
at Eaton House
Old People's Home.

. . . Margate's leading
mobile home specialist . . .

. . . thank you very much.

. . . no, thank you, Caravan,
it's always a pleasure.

There is a smattering of uncertain applause as Alderman Hughes smiles and places a stout, comradely arm around his mother – a gesture that seemed to be expressing solidarity rather than affection. A point not lost on Mrs Hughes but she smiles graciously. Even though she has been on her feet all afternoon and wants a cup of tea. Nobody has offered her as much as a glass of water thank you very much I mean what sort of care is that? And maybe the offer of a biscuit wouldn't have gone amiss. Sandwiches? Where are the sandwiches? A bit late now – it's getting too near suppertime. I thought they'd said that we were having sandwiches. Not much to ask, is it? And the flowers in her room were plastic, sixty-eight next birthday and they fob you off with plastic flowers. What sort of place fobs you off with plastic flowers? What? Do they think people are too old to notice something like that? Its always the details that matter, especially when you're sixty-eight next birthday, little things, always the little things. And the prices they're charging. You'd expect better than plastic flowers. It's like robbery, that's what it is . . .

Surrounded by directors, staff and residents, Alderman Hughes, his mother and their smiles are standing at the foot of the main staircase in the entrance lobby of the Eaton House Residential Home for the Elderly. Recently refurbished for an undisclosed six figure sum ('less than a Kenny Dalglish transfer to Liverpool'), it will pay host to Mrs Hughes for the first time that evening.

From the rear of the group, the cheerless photographer is waving his index finger. 'Your Worship . . .' he says in a colourless voice, 'if you don't mind, just a moment . . .'

'No *Worship* today, son,' says Alderman Hughes, gently tapping his chest like a duchess. 'I'm *sans regalia.* It's just plain simple Brian today . . .'

There are few polite chuckles at this.

OK, Caravan, don't push your luck.

'Right. So, if I could just have you and Mrs Hughes together, if you don't mind, just the pair of you . . .

. . . that's lovely

. . . these fucking better
not be colour, mate,
this is a mauve tie . . .

. . . right, can I have you
a little closer . . .

. . . might come out
looking pink . . .

. . . good . . .

. . . then I'll look like
a right fucking pansy . .

. . . Can you turn towards
each other? . . .

. . . I should have
gone for blue

. . . that's nice . . .

if I end up looking
like some nancy . . .

. . . now, how about a couple of
really big smiles . . .'

Just like the disgraced gym teacher, he lays there breathing in short pants.

Never worked *inhale* well that *inhale* one . . . too *inhale* subtle maybe . . . or it just *inhale* wasn't funny, of course . . .

Otherwise silence.

The pounding, beating, terrible silence.

A car starting.

A door closing.

He keeps his eyes closed for a few moments, unable to face the pious recriminations of the visible universe. He knows it's there waiting for him, but it can wait a bit longer. He retains his grip on the swiftly detumescing organ and while he finds the contours and warmth comforting there is also, for a fleeting second, the odd sensation of feeling that it no longer has any connection to him.

So, now they must part and go their separate ways.

But not just yet.

There was a satisfying bulk to it and it fitted perfectly in the palm of his hand.

A fishmonger on market day.

He would open his eyes in a moment.

But not yet.

In a moment.

There were things to be done.

Something very, very very important that needed to be attended to.

Very very very soon.

Then . . . *then* . . .

Our Father who art in heaven . . .

Hallowed . . .

Oh bloody hell . . .

Moe Seyton instantly opens his eyes and gazes in pilgrim wonder at the perfect pure-white ceiling.

He savours this moment, he would prolong this moment, he would make it last for ever, the moment between a bloody good toss and rejoining the real world.

Welcome to ONAN'S ANAESTHESIA.

He doesn't feel the slightest revulsion or regret, instead he feels that great surge of NOTHINGNESS. Like some great illuminating comet, or some psychic dart piercing human CONSCIOUSNESS and SUDDENLY a man sees EVERYTHING as it is. A SUBLIME experience. A sudden momentary glimpse of the utter worthlessness of the WORLD, the pointlessness of MANKIND and the ULTIMATE final triumph of its VILE ambition. Drained of all PURPOSE, one has the UNIQUE sensation of pure BEING. It lasts barely a moment, but like that fleeting few seconds between waking and sleeping, that divine portal, when you are BOTH and NEITHER, there is that tiny transition between fantasy and reality when your AWARENESS is at its ultimate. There is the greatest sense of PEACE as you COMPREHEND the FUTILITY of all things.

But this was not in any way sad or depressing.

It was FUNNY.

Hovering in the doorway between fantasy and reality – but he was always happy there.

He wasn't so sure about the Our Father bits, that wasn't so funny . . . No, that really wasn't at all funny. It was just another one of those dismal associations from the past. But he doesn't forgive himself. So remind me, when you're a happy, healthy, average, God-fearing Grammar School boy, what are the last things you do before you go to sleep? And I'm afraid I'll have to hurry you . . .

1. Tickle your trouser trout
2. Say your prayers

Maybe you feel the need for absolution or something. But it was an irritation to him that this connection had become something of a habit. By way of consolation he finds somewhere in all this confirmation and proof of the ultimate truth; that the Past is perfectly useless.

He can now see a slight water stain and a hairline crack in the ceiling.

He turns his head and glances at his watch on the bedside table. He sees the converging arrangement of a circle and two lines.

Five hours and eighteen minutes.

Goodbye again then, Catherine. Until the next time. Did I love you? Did I really care about you? No, I don't think so. Be honest now. Nobody's looking. Did I ever wish that I had once laid my head in your lap and wept rivers of salty tears?

Confessed all my sins? Articulated my every fear and doubt? Begged for your understanding and forgiveness? Probably not. Did I ever think that you were the one? The one that would reveal to me all the mysteries in creation? Was it you? Did I miss something? Were you going to redeem me? Save me from the darkness, from all our desperate, endless cruelties? (The neutralising effects of Onan's Anaesthesia, he is well aware, are powerful but short-lived.) Didn't matter any more, it was too late now anyway. Come on now, you were a few years older than me, you might even be dead now . . .

This is the part he hates . . .

She wouldn't even recognise him. She wouldn't even remember him. She never saw him work, maybe that was a shame maybe it wasn't, he told her he was a composer, which wasn't an outright lie, he even showed her a couple of his songs, he just hadn't elaborated any further. We had a few weeks, a month or two, that was our time . . . that was enough . . .

In a sudden burst of manly-male buff and bluster, bluff and buster, pants, buttons, belt in quick succession, Moe fastens his trousers and sits up.

That *was* enough.

Paper handkerchief, wastepaper bin . . .

He concentrates on . . . tasks, objects . . . up – lampshade, down – mantelpiece, down – fire place . . . Ah, yes . . . now . . . 'The Poker Song'. Now, that was something to think about. Not one of his best, not by a long shot. The tune was a bit dreary. Slow and almost hymn like. However, it was in his favourite key . . .

And then he thinks about . . . that kid . . . whatever his name was.

He was actually quite a sweet little boy. Managed to remind of him of what little boys used to be like. God knows, that was rare enough nowadays! The sort of boys he could understand, the ones that you don't see any-more.

A boy who was enjoying his *boyhood.*

The concept like the word seemed to be disappearing from general use. All the kids he saw these days were just like shrunken adults. With more free time and less money. On the whole, he preferred the old-fashioned less threatening variety. Boys that might climb trees, collect stamps, play French cricket . . .

Moe stands up and rubs the small of his back . . . Kits, model aeroplanes, kites . . .

And when I felt her warm embrace I gazed back at the fireplace

He makes fleeting eye contact with his reflection in the mirror over the sink.

If you were passing by that day the chances are you'd hear me say...

In all affairs of the heart it was wise to keep the heart as far away from the thick of things as possible . . .

Poker, poker, I just wanna poker, Poker, poker, I just wanna poker.

But that's the problem with high standards; if you maintain them for long enough and refuse to compromise you eventually slide into a very particular mindset. One that is customarily viewed as the bitterest kind of cynicism. The disappointment is processed and rationalised so it becomes a sort of policy. But that is never the intention. One day you're dreamer and a romantic, an idealist, a fantasist. The next you're some weather-beaten old cynic. Was it all just down to age?

I am old.

So now I must withdraw and return the night to dreamers.

So why Catherine then? Why her? Why not someone . . . someone like that stripper from up north the year before last? Mary. Mary *Thing*. Mary from the dairy. She was amazing. Twenty-two. (She was probably nearer thirty but she said she was twenty-two.) Fantastic body and a nice laugh too. Beautiful long blonde hair . . . but the face is still Catherine's . . .

. . . go-karts . . . conkers . . .

The embers are dying
and it's not worth trying
Poker, poker,
I just wanna poker

Five hours and three minutes.

*

Clack Clack Clack Clack.

Casual.

He inclines one shoulder and leans very slightly against the door frame. Careful now – not arrogant and Sweaty Brando more hesitant and humble and *Scaredy Barney, Scaredy Barney, too scared to join the Army.*

Casual.

He rubs together the palms of harmless hands, behold – here stands a simple honest man – a toiler not a thinker. A worker, a labourer. Casual. Strange word that if you repeat it. Casual, cash-you-all, car-shoe-ill . . . And now comes the difficult part, he thinks, the bit he's been dreading. So far, it had gone reasonably well but then again he'd not really said much. Casual, care-show-all . . . Nothing rhymes with it either. There was a young man who was casual, der-der der-der der-der . . . Keep it all chatty, conversational; make sure it doesn't become an issue or a point of principle. That was easier said than done nowadays. *Did you manage to have forty winks shall I open the window shall I close the window do you want a drink now and by the way I bought you a Crunchie if you're a bit peckish this evening I'll leave it on the dressing table.* Why did she always look at him like that? Was it absolutely necessary? All the time now – it was as though he was perpetually trapped in the precise moment in time that he finally confirmed every single one of her worst fears. No affection, no longing, no hope, no fear – just judgement and doubt. *Mariage à la mode.* You can't beat it. A woman's face is an accusation/a man's face is a confession. Simple. Is that how we read it? The perfect symbiotic union. Three cheers for nature and a round of applause for God! (Whoops, careful.) Had she always looked at him like that? Or was this some recent subtle evolution? Did this arrive with age or (bitter) experience? *Yes we had a lovely walk thank you I thought you liked Crunchies you always used to yes he behaved himself very well didn't moan much but he's a bit tired now hopefully he'll start winding down when he gets out of the bath do you want to go and dry him or shall I?* The near imperceptible narrowing of the mouth and eyes, as though her senses were too exposed or she did not wish to reveal the slightest trace of a reaction. Maybe he was just noticing it because of . . . well, no one would blame her if it was. It can't be easy for her. Oh God, how he was sick of hearing that. He was sick of saying it and thinking it. But it wasn't easy for either of them. Not that she was all that bothered about him. Where was *his* Crunchie? Still, there it is – The Look and now the lingering slow head turn, superior, imperious, as she breaks eye contact. Yet again. This audience is now concluded, you may take your leave . . . Maybe, she knows him as well as she thinks she does . . . Or maybe she doesn't. One day, when the conversation has come to its inevitable standstill, he will shout at the top of his voice LAMPSHADES and ANTHILLS or CREVICE, PAISLEY and COMSUMPTIVE just so he could prove that she doesn't know what he's thinking . . . or maybe . . .

Clack Clack Clack Clack.

'Comedian,' he says eventually, quietly and casually. Although reasonably pleased with the compromise.

'Pardon?'

In his experience, her 'pardons' were not requests for the speaker to repeat a remark but more a simple admonishment for failing to speak clearly enough.

'He's a comedian.'

Sandra Langton opens a suitcase and removes a towel. 'Who is a comedian?'

'The chap I was telling you about. Just now. The one Andy and I met on the way home, the old fellow who's staying here at the hotel.'

'I see.'

'He's not terribly famous or anything but he's been

around for donkey's years and worked with all the greats, he was telling us . . .'

. . . Louis Pasteur, The Green Hornet, Accrington Stanley, Mahatma Gandhi, Jack the Ripper – you're not listening are you?

She lays the towel on the bed, unfolds and then folds it again.

'Really?' she says eventually. She swallows. This was the towel she had taken with her but she hadn't used it because they had given her one. Theirs was white and starched and awful and made her feel like she was dirty or that she was a prisoner or something – that she was (he was) being punished for something. She wanted her own towel, the old orange and green, worn-out and faded towel, it would remind her of home, (a really) she wanted to cover herself with it, withdraw right into it, hide from everything, curl up and fade away, come out again when it was safe and it was all over. (delightful) She would play peek-a-boo like they used to do when she was a baby, she would cover her face *peek-a-boo* and when the towel was taken away (old) she would be lying on her bed again at home looking up at their faces and she would be giggling and they would be smiling and there would be talcum and love and certainty. (bloke) Why couldn't they understand that? She wasn't asking for much, was she? And why wasn't there an all over?

'Sorry?'

'I said he was a really delightful old bloke. It was very interesting talking to him.'

'Who?'

'The chap who is staying at the hotel . . . the comedian . . .'

. . . . Come on, you're doing this on purpose!

'Oh yes.'

'He's doing a . . . what would they call it? Doing a turn?

A spot? Whatever it's called, he's doing one tonight at a club down the road.'

Sandra nods but says nothing.

'Actually I was wondering . . .'

Here we go, he thinks

Here we go, she thinks.

Clack Clack Clack Clack.

'Actually I was wondering if I might take a stroll down later and catch a bit of his act. '

'Uh-huh.'

'Obviously, I'll wait until Andy's settled for the night. Just pop out for an hour or so.

'Right.'

'Like last night.'

'That was nearly three.'

'Eh . . . ?'

'Nearly three hours not *an hour*. You went out for three hours last night.'

Barney chuckles nervously and occupies his hands by fiddling with his watch strap. 'Oh well, it must have been the sea air or something. I must have lost all track of the time. I thought you were asleep.

'I was but you woke me up when you came to bed.'

'Did I? Oh, I'm sorry. You should have . . . no, it doesn't matter.' Barney pauses for a moment and then adds as an afterthought. 'It's great to go for a long walk that time of the day.'

'So you said.'

'When the air just starts to chill in the evening . . .'

She smiles the most illegible of smiles, 'I know,' and Sandra Langton has just revealed as much as she intends to reveal to her husband.

Unable to get back to sleep after Barney's return the previous evening, she had waited for him to fall asleep and for his breathing to become slow and settled. Then, shortly after midnight, she'd slipped on her raincoat and espadrilles and crept carefully out of the room and then out of the Seaview.

Taking her worries for a walk (something she did not infrequently), she searched for the line which followed

Alone I walk through dark nights of betrayal.

She walked for about three-quarters of an hour and smoked three Silk Cut.

Something fail? Love has failed?

She spoke to no one.

However, that is not to say that no-one spoke to her.

HERE BEGINS THE CONFESSION OF SANDRA LANGTON

I left the establishment known as the Seaview Guest House for the purpose of getting some fresh air. It was a warm evening and I was having trouble sleeping. I had been staying at the hotel with my family for a couple of nights. I estimate the time of my departure to be around quarter past midnight, certainly no later than twenty past midnight. It was reasonably quiet and although there was traffic on the road, there were very few people, by which I mean pedestrians, about. It was as I was walking along Marine Parade in an eastwards direction towards the seafront, that a young woman, a girl I would place in her late teens, approached me. She came from behind me suddenly and so I couldn't say from what direction she had come. I was preoccupied that evening about this and that and she really took me by surprise; I nearly jumped out of my skin. She was in a very agitated state and my first thought was that she might have been homeless or sleeping rough. She seemed very excited and out of breath as though she had been running. A thought crossed my mind that she might have escaped from somewhere. She was glancing behind her as though she was expecting to see someone. Or was trying to avoid someone. She walked alongside me for a few yards before she spoke and I thought at first that she might be limping a bit, but then I realised that she was simply trying to walk in stilettos and they were obviously hurting her or she'd not had much practice. One of them, I noticed, had a broken strap. Actually, they looked a bit cheap and poorly made to be honest. That's what happens with cheap shoes – you get what you pay for, unfortunately. The girl had shortish light-coloured hair worn in a cropped spiky style and a pleasant almost pretty face, which she seemed determined to spoil by wearing far too much eye make-up. It had smudged and run down her face and I assumed that she must have been crying at some point. Anyway, it looked frightful. As I said, it wasn't cold that evening and she wasn't wearing a coat or a jacket, just a short skirt and a T-shirt. I didn't pay much attention to the skirt other than the fact that it was far too short. I mean even if you've got a half-decent pair of pins you've still got to draw the line somewhere. But I do recall the T-shirt, which was brightly coloured, pink and white with some writing on it, although I couldn't quite make out what it said. It was definitely a punky-type look I thought and what was that look about – was it supposed to be attractive? I do remember vividly thinking what sort of boy would go for a girl looking like that? Were they going out of their way to be ugly or something? Was that the idea? I mean to be honest, you're going to get stared at and attract attention, aren't you? Dressed like that. Anyway, this girl asked me if she could borrow a couple of pounds. She definitely gave me the impression that she was drunk or intoxicated or worse. She kept placing her hand on my arm as if she didn't want me to walk away from her. She had lost her purse, she said. Oh please, come on! That old one, I thought. She said she had to get back to Cliftonville. Actually, I couldn't have helped her anyway even if I'd wanted to. You see, I didn't have my purse on me – I wasn't intending on walking far and didn't think that I would need it. Besides I wouldn't go giving my money away to strangers just like that just so she can go and spend it on drugs or whatever. That would be a stupid thing to do. And anyway, my father always says you should never give money to beggars as it only prolongs their problems – the solution isn't charity, he says. It's retraining and basic skills. And another thing, you know, they always pick on me, I'm always getting stopped and asked for money, they never pick on Barney, not once, maybe it's something in my face they can see. Maybe they think women are more understanding and sympathetic. Anyway, she was desperate she said. Her parents would be having kittens – well, if they'd let her leave the house looking like that I couldn't imagine them being that bothered if she got home late and all she wanted was a couple of pounds so she could get a minicab. I tried to walk a little quicker and deliberately didn't look at her. She started to sound more intense and anxious. She started to cry. Please, she said, just a couple of pounds, that would be enough to get her home, she'd be there in ten minutes, she said I could write down my address and she'd promise to have the money back to me first thing in the morning. Or I could get in the cab with her and we could go together to her house and she would give me the money then and enough to get back wherever I wanted. I was little worried by this and began to feel uncomfortable. I think it was at this point that I really felt threatened for the first time. We had walked about as far as the Lifeboatsman Memorial and I just felt that I didn't want to be near her, or part of her and her problems. Then she said something about there being a bit of trouble earlier on, that's how she lost her purse, there were some funny people around that evening and she'd been kicked out of a club and please, it wasn't her fault, but they weren't very nice and they were picking on her and they were trying to get her drunk and one of them was touching her and she thought some bloke was following her, please, please, it was really important that she got home as quickly as possible . . .

I didn't speak to her.

I just crossed the road and walked away as quickly as I could.

HERE ENDS THE CONFESSION OF SANDRA LANGTON

'A fellow knocks on the door of a house . . .'

'Daddy, look, there, look, sand in the bubbles, lots and lots, see, why is there sand in the bubbles, if the sand goes down the plug and goes into the sea does it stay in the sea or does it go back to the beach, Daddy, can we go to the beach tomorrow and stay there all day and not come back?

why?

why can't we have a picnic, why do we have to have lunch, why is it for the best, I hate lunch

I'm not

I am not tired, look where I hurt my arm, look, see, it's better

it is

I'm not playing with it, I'm just showing you, bubbles make it better, see, this is how you make it better, look, Daddy, why don't grown-ups ever fall over, why don't they, is it because they're big, you don't fall down do you Daddy, can we see the funny man, tomorrow, our friend, can he come to the beach with us

why not?

why does he have to work, why does he work at the seaside, why isn't he on holiday, he's staying at a hotel so he must be on holiday, you said when people go on holiday they stay in hotels, you did say that

you did

what is sand made of, what would happen if you ate sand,

would you be very ill, do animals eat sand, do fish eat the sand that's in the sea

why not?

why can't the funny man be your friend, Daddy, you could be friends and then you'd be happy if you had a friend, Michael is my friend, friends are good, Michael doesn't like Paul because he pinches and once he threw mud he told on him and Miss was really cross, look Daddy, look at this word here, it says shampoo doesn't it? It's silly

shampoo, sham-poo, hee hee, is that poo, is that made from poo

I don't

I don't always say that, not all the time

I do not I do not

who is THIS here, look Daddy, this man on the shampoo, he looks very silly, is that his nose, why does he look like that, Daddy

I do not

do I?

Punch?

Mister Punch?

hee hee . . . oh . . . Punch and Judy, yes, yes I know, oh Daddy, can we go and see the Punch and Judy tomorrow, please can we, please, Daddy . . .

why can't we?

why isn't there?

why don't they have Punch and Judy anymore?

Daddy?

why . . . ?

why . . . ?

Barney Langton shrugs his shoulders and arranges, with a meticulous precision that borders on ceremony, a towel on the floor.

'One more minute, then out, all right?'

That was enough information. More than enough. There

is no longer a Punch and Judy show in Margate – fact, and that's all an inquisitive six year old needs to know. Any additional information would be entirely superfluous and unnecessary. There is no longer a Punch and Judy show in Margate. The end.

In fact, as he is well aware, there hasn't been a Punch and Judy show in Margate for a very long time. Not since the early twenties, in fact. (Although even that date is debatable.) The usual reasons given for the sudden disappearance of Punch and Judy shows from Margate seafront involved some lofty bureaucratic intervention from an official source. Performing licences, town planners, fire officers and highway regulations often feature. The version that Barney vaguely recalls had something to do with the obstruction of a public right of way.

But you know what they say?

History abhors the random act.

History favours the organisation of past events into easily accessible algebraic formulas. A did B to C which resulted in D. The truth in this case was wildly different from all the stories circulated in the previous sixty years.

One August morning in 1919, a considerable commotion occurred in a small terraced house in Ethelbert Road, Margate. Neighbours reported the sounds of breaking glass and shouting and objects being thrown against the wall. A constable was duly summoned but left shortly afterwards following a short conversation with the gentleman who resided in the house. The constable had, before leaving, assured himself there was no other person on the premises.

The gentleman he had spoken to was known professionally as Tom E. Nosey and was familiar to a great many residents of Margate as he had the Punch and Judy stand on the seafront. Mr Nosey was at the time of the incident in his mid forties and had over the past decade become a popular feature amongst the summer attractions at the beach. But it was later discovered that things hadn't been going all that well for Mr Nosey that past year; he'd had a few health worries, he was drinking against his doctor's advice and his debts were piling up. Furthermore, his wife of six years had moved out and was now planning to start a new life in Italy with a man she had been having a relationship with for the previous year.

He had been to see her the previous evening and pleaded with her to reconsider. He'd made promises and bought flowers and tried to remind her of the old days and explained that their money worries were only temporary but she was adamant and she'd made her decision and she didn't want to discuss it and she was sorry and she thought it would be better if he went now.

Mr Nosey then had a few drinks, walked a bit, slept on the beach for a couple of hours, walked some more and then returned home. In the sort of state he was in, the constable later concluded, you couldn't really blame a bloke for chucking a few plates . . .

He regained his composure sufficiently and he was when all was said and done a professional after all and what would you expect from a chap who'd been nearly thirty years in the business? You wouldn't last thirty years if you were unreliable and you have to keep your personal life as one thing and your work as something totally separate you never let the one affect the other. Besides a man is only as good as his last show and no better. The young 'uns put him where he was today and he had never forgotten that and the morning shows were performed punctually, although a keen observer of the genre may have sensed a certain lack of focus in his work. He left a number of long pauses and the various voices were a little confused at times but that was hardly surprising given the circumstances.

As was his custom, he took a break for lunch between half past twelve and one o'clock. As was also his custom he spent this time in the saloon bar of the Kent Hotel, where, amid convivial company, he ordered his usual lunch of a meat pie, mashed potatoes, peas and gravy, to be accompanied by a brown ale. The regular greetings and pleasantries were observed but it was later noted that he didn't seem as talkative or as cheerful as was his habit. He drank his ale alone at a table and toyed with his food for five minutes. He then returned glass and plate to the bar, empty and largely untouched respectively, and alluding to 'a touch of the old flu' he ordered himself a double brandy. No one was able to recall precisely how many double brandies he subsequently drank in that twenty minutes but a central point between the extremes of estimates, rounded up to the nearest whole number, would be approximately three.

It is possible that it was simply a combination of drinking on an empty stomach, his lack of sleep and the alcohol that was already in his system from the previous evening that resulted in Mr Nosey's random act. But when he returned to his tent just after one o clock he did so on unsteady legs while he was overheard by one passer-by mumbling to himself a series of 'most improper curses'.

At 1.15 p.m. precisely (and if you can't be bloody well punctual you have no reason to be in this business) the pink-and-white striped curtains of the Punch and Judy stand parted and the eponymous Mr Punch greeted his audience. His evident ebullience having not the slightest effect on Judy, who lay indifferent and abandoned at one corner of the tiny stage.

'HELLO boys AND girls, MUMMIES and daddies, how ARE you all THIS afternoon? Are you all READY for our special special show . . . show me the way to go home, hah, this afternoon? Now then, do you know WHO I am? Do YOU? Do you? SHOUT out if you THINK you KNOW THE ANSWER. YES. Yes, that's a very good guess. But you're ALL wrong, I'm afraid. MY name is Mr NOSEY and I LIVE here in sunny Margate in a little HOUSE not very far away. It's a very NICE house, or rather it WAS. It's got a NICE little garden, a kitchen, a nice fireplace and two bedrooms. And OH LOOK, there's MRS NOSEY in one of the bedrooms. LOOK, boys and girls, THERE she is. Can you SEE her? She's ON the bed that HER HUSBAND worked so HARD to pay for. IN a ROOM, that he DECORATED from TOP to BOTTOM only last EASTER. CAN you see her NOW? Of COURSE you can, there she is. Shall we say hello to Mrs NOSEY? HELLO, Mrs NOSEY. Look. She's LYING down, oh YES, she's fucking good at LYING, well she had me fucking fooled I can tell you. But don't worry, BOYS and girls, she's not hurt herself, she's not poorly, she's not GONE TO BED with a pain in her tummy. Oh no, DON'T WORRY. But do you know why she's lying down? Perhaps all you mummies and daddies can answer this one. Lets ask ALL the DADDIES, shall we? What do they say? Nothing? Or maybe THEY CAN'T answer, which means that THEY are either STUPID, blind or very very fucking LUCKY. Mrs NOSEY is lying in BED in HER brand-NEW thirty-bob silky NIGHTIE waiting for SOMEONE to SCREW the FUCKING ARSE off her. Is it Mr NOSEY that she's waiting for? OH no, boys and girls, its NOT him, is it? He's out EARNING a DECENT crust EVERY bloody hour and every day God sends, knackering himself in the process, JUST SO Mrs Nosey can LIE in BED in her brand-fucking NEW thirty-bob silky NIGHTIE . . .

SHUT UP. I haven't FINISHED yet!!!

COME back, where are you GOING? You're GOING TO MISS the best part. Aw, come on now, MADAM . . . Oh well, go on then, PISS off, who NEEDS you ANYWAY?

WHERE were we? OH YES. Here WE are then with MRS Nosey lying on her bed . . . Well not HER bed ACTUALLY, THEIR bed to be strictly fucking ACCURATE in THIS matter. LET'S all go OVER there and see what she's

DOING, shall we? Come with ME, boys and GIRLS. HERE she is. DON'T you THINK she's PRETTY? I USED to think she was pretty TOO! YEAH look at HER, lying there WAITING. And I don't THINK we have AGREED who SHE'S waiting for. STILL no ideas? WELL, I'll FUCKING tell you. She's waiting for her BOYFRIEND! Yes, THAT'S RIGHT, her boyfriend!!! Her CISSYFIED Mary Anne DANCING teacher BOYFRIEND!! NO word of A LIE. As true AS I'm STANDING HERE. That fucking ITALIAN pooftah, MARIO di . . . POOFTAH, Pooftiana POOFTABELLI – fucking ROTTEN POOF FAIRY bastard. WHO do these PEOPLE THINK they are? COMING over here and . . . AND . . . and deliberately STEALING . . . stealing OTHER PEOPLE'S wives? IT'S a fucking LIBERTY, that's what it is! DO YOU KNOW what we do with cheating WHORING wives here IN MARGATE? Do you know WHAT happens to them? COME ON now . . . some of you FUCKING mummies and daddies must know! PUT your minds to it, FOLKS, come on . . . Just SHOUT it out when you KNOW the ANSWER! Don't be SHY, we're all on HOLIDAY. COME ON let yourselves GO!

AM I wasting MY TIME here?

AM I going to have to FUCKING tell you what we do to our nasty SHITTY cheating lying SLUTTY WIVES?

We SMACK 'em in the gob, JUST LIKE THIS. And then we do it AGAIN. WE . . . SMACK . . . THEM . . . on . . . their LYING . . . cheating SLAGGY GOBS. Are you all following this? We do it AGAIN and AGAIN until THEY stop their FUCKING lying. ARE you LISTENING now? DO I now HAVE your ATTENTION? Again and again in the gob JUST LIKE THIS!!

Mr Punch continued his vicious attack on Judy for another few moments in silence before both puppets were hurled from the stall over the heads of the bemused spectators. A little girl at the rear of the crowd, unobserved and cautious, makes her way to where the Judy puppet is lying.

She glances left and right and only when she is absolutely certain does she pick up the puppet and secrete it inside her cardigan. She quickly wanders off to find her mother.

Meanwhile, the act was nearing its finale.

Mr Nosey emerged from the rear of the stall and seized a bucket from a young unaccompanied boy who sat at the front of the remaining dozen or so on-lookers. He then casually unbuttoned his flies and proceeded to urinate into the bucket in full view of his dwindling audience.

This might have been regarded as a fitting climax to such a spectacle, but in his receptacle of choice, Mr Nosey had made perhaps his greatest error of judgement. The unaccompanied boy (who wasn't unaccompanied for very much longer) wasn't your average unaccompanied boy; his grandfather, who will return moments later with a suitably enraged constable, was Fletcher Nicholson, owner of the Kent Hotel, councillor, Rotarian and rumoured high-ranking Freemason.

Poor Mr Nosey.

A bad choice.

Tragically, a year or so after the incident, the boy will die from complications arising from a bout of pneumonia. For many years thereafter, Fletcher Nicholson would always furiously maintain that it all started that afternoon and his grandson had never been right after that terrible disgusting thing was done to him; he was always a sensitive boy, not weak or girly, mind you, he could take care of himself if he had to, but sensitive and it was just such a shock for the lad.

So perhaps it was local embarrassment, a sign of respect or simply an indication of the extraordinary influence Mr Nicholson held for a great number of years as a Freemason. But a Punch and Judy tent was not seen on Margate front after that afternoon.

Mr Nosey was taken away by the constable, who had been

overheard to utter *sotto voce* the immortal phrase 'you've pissed in the wrong bucket this afternoon, sunshine.'

He was put in a cell for the rest of the afternoon to sober up and later, under his real name (Tom E. Nosey was actually an anagram of his true name), he was cautioned and charged. When they were cleaning his cell the following morning they found a small piece of screwed-up paper under the bed. On it was written:

When I loved her
I loved all things

I loved a language that gave me her name
I worshipped a sun that gave me the light that I may
see her
I loved my own hands for they had felt her beauty
I loved the wall where once she had cast a shadow
I loved the shape in the pillow where she lay her head
There I traced the letters of her name across the
hearts of all men

When I loved her
I loved all things

Now I have turned to hate her
And I shall hate all things

'Piss off!'

'Look . . .'

'*Piss!* Off!'

'Now, I know this must be a terrible time . . .'

'Good, so take the hint and piss off! I have asked you nicely but I am not telling you again, Mister Newspaper Man! If you're not off my bloody property in two minutes . . .'

'If you could just listen to me for one minute . . .'

'You lot . . . you really are the scum of the earth! The police have only just gone, it would only take a minute to get them back! Do you want to hang around and see if I'm bloody serious?'

'I know you are . . . and I understand, honestly I do, I'd probably be the same if I was in your shoes'

'Our shoes? Our shoes? Have you the slightest idea what we're both going through at the moment?'

Sam Taylor reverses himself into a thoughtful pause and gazes down at his feet. They are currently occupying space on the neat narrow tarmac path that leads to the front door of 36 Prices Avenue, Cliftonville. The residence of Mr and Mrs Eric Warne. But the Kent and Medway Regional Sales Rep of the Month three months running in 1972 has not withdrawn in defeat. *Persistence. Sincerity.*

Maybe leaning towards sincerity.

'Please, Mr Warne,' *always use the name, be formal, respectful, make eye contact* . . . 'now I don't blame you for acting like this. I would do the same, if some fat sweaty stranger came knocking on my door at a time like this . . .' *a hint, a very slight hint of levity and never shy away from the old self-deprecation.*

Mr Warne, a bemused man in his shirtsleeves and his fifties, a man who has been swept up and dropped back in a version of his life he can no longer recognise, a man who has no experience or resources or answers, a man to whom nothing extraordinary or unusual or noteworthy ever happened, purses his lips as the colour rises in his cheeks again. 'Look, I'm going back indoors and I'm calling the police. It's your choice. But I want you off my property right now.'

'Look, if you could just listen to me for a second?' *always try to sound reasonable, plausible* . . . 'I'm just asking for a moment of your time. I think I might be able to help, maybe only in a small way but I . . .'

'Help? Help? . . .' Mr Warne gazes heavenwards in desperation. 'You've got a bloody nerve, you newspaper people! Do you have any idea of what's going on? What's going on here? We've just got back from the hospital. We've just seen our . . .' He gestures over his shoulder with an accusing thumb towards the hallway visible through the open door. 'Look, I've got a wife in there . . . her life . . . My life will never be the same . . . Help? Help, you say? God, this is almost worth hearing . . .'

Sam quickly reconsiders his next move *to prolong a conversation ask the subject for a drink of water* and seizes his chance. 'I think I can help. Look I realise what has happened to your daughter is a terrible, terrible thing but one of the most important things now is to catch whoever did this. The police will be working hard I'm sure but my paper might be able to do something too.'

'Oh yeah, like what?'

'Well, I was thinking of maybe a £1,000 reward offered for information leading to an arrest.'

There is a second of utter stillness, frozen, as Sam's words drift and circle the two gentleman on the warm late-afternoon breeze but Mr Warne says nothing.

'Look, somebody knows this person, he might be sitting right next to them, right at this moment. Maybe they don't want to talk to the police, or get involved, a lot of people don't trust the police for any number of reasons, but think what they could do with a thousand quid, you'd be tempted, right . . . ?'

'Well . . .'

'It might be just enough to get you to pick up the phone, it may be just enough to make a difference. All we need is a recent picture and a little chat with you. And obviously we'd rather you didn't chat to any of the other papers. But we could run the whole thing on the front page on Thursday's edition. We'll catch this person whoever he is.' *Sincerity. Sincerity.* 'We can all make sure that he will be made to pay for his crimes . . .'

'They should just fucking hang him. Do it down on the front by the clock tower! Or better still let me have a go at him. I'll show you some real justice . . .'

'Er-ic!' The word has a pleasing musical quality, a two-note phrase, the first little more than an accent the second long and drawn out. The instrument is a single female voice, forceful but not entirely lacking compassion. Familiar, indulgent even, it calls rather than admonishes and comes from somewhere behind them, beyond the hallway.

Less than a minute later, Sam Taylor is sitting in the neat unremarkable front room of 36 Prices Avenue, listening to Mr Warne further expound his theories on global justice and his apparent deeply rooted conviction that criminals should be punished, as far as Sam could ascertain, roughly in accordance with medieval woodcuts.

Mrs Delilah Warne, the owner of the voice, sits on the sofa with an unopened photo album resting on her lap. She seems posed and unnatural, the scene hastily arranged by a minor Victorian painter. She glances periodically at her husband, who has remained standing throughout his discourse. Every minute or so he reaches over and touches her hand, a tiny gesture but one that makes Sam shift awkwardly in his seat. Husband and wife together once again in their terrible shared agonies, as they once were a long time ago and as they never will be again. She manages to smile weakly at Sam who smiles back

Something now starts to stir in the dark recesses of the Deputy Editor's memory.

Delilah. *Delilah?* Delilah Warne . . .

'. . . Might seem harsh but the crime rate would drop like a stone overnight . . .'

Delilah Warne . . . *Delilah? Delilah?*

'. . . It's worked in other countries . . .'

With relatively uncharacteristic subtlety, Sam glances at Mrs Warne and just manages to avoid catching her eye. He gazes quickly and innocently at the pictures on the wall behind the sofa. There is a fairly random selection of pictures almost filling the entire wall. They have been oddly thrown together or grouped according to some unapparent system, pictures of things beginning with S, pictures we bought when we'd gone into the shop to buy something else, the overall effect is of the wall of a waiting room. No photos or personal mementos, it is an odd display, which on this particular day seems strangely disconnected, superfluous and irrelevant. A picture of a shire horse, a cottage in the snow, a swan flying, three pictures in a quasi-surrealist style that looked at first glance to be zodiac symbols . . . zodiac symbols? . . . *zodiac symbols?*

At last! Thank you.

'So, this reward you'll be offering' Mr Warne concludes his lecture, sits down next to his wife and looks directly at Sam. 'It will just be for information, right?'

'Information leading to an arrest, it's just a standard expression but it also weeds out a lot of people who might be tempted to just waste the police's time. You know . . . hoax callers and the like . . .'

'Oh Jesus . . .'

'It happens.'

'Bloody bastards, doesn't it just make you want to . . .'

'Eric . . .'

From his inside jacket pocket, Sam removes a pen and a folded piece of paper on which he begins writing. The latter item is actually a bank statement but Sam makes the fairly reasonable assumption that this is unlikely to be noticed. 'We just need a few background details, her hobbies, interests, any clubs she belonged to, did she like any particular TV show or pop star, just stuff like that. If she had a thing about John Travolta or *Coronation Street,* people may feel a connection or an affinity with her, it will make her seem more . . . er . . . er . . . *recognisable as a person.*' Sam mentally wipes his brow with an imaginary forearm and flatters himself that he's managed to get away with it. 'We just need the very briefest outline, that's all. And if you've got a fairly recent photo, one that you think is a reasonably good likeness . . .'

'We already gave one to the police . . .'

'There's a couple of nice ones in here' says Delilah Warne, tapping the photo album with her index finger. 'They were taken a couple of months ago, at her . . . her . . .' and suddenly she has found by awful chance another word she must now forever avoid, another linguistic bear pit she must endeavour to circumnavigate in future. Words that are now (and will always be) preceded by a single tiny inhalation. *Birthday* now joins *bedroom, Christmas, handbag* and dozen or so others. This list will continue to grow on a fairly frequent basis. For Mrs Warne, the greatest pain, will remain forever in the simple and ordinary.

'Thanks,' says Sam, 'that would be great.'

Mr Warne jabs the air with his forefinger at same vague undetermined point somewhere to Sam's left. 'We want it back.'

'Of course. I'll make sure . . .'

Mrs Warne hands Sam a photo of Jessica, happy, pretty and smiling in jeans and a T-shirt, and takes a deep breath. 'Will you have to write about . . . I mean . . . all the . . . all the *details,* all the . . . .'

'Nothing like that, I assure you.' *Once you sense the sale is complete, emphasise the personal relationship that has now developed with the client – affinity, rapport.* 'I'll let you see the piece before it goes to press. I'll make sure personally that it doesn't offend you in any way . . .'

'Is that a promise?' asks Mr Warne with evident hostility.

'It is,' says Sam, in a precise, serious tone. 'The picture is fine by the way, we'll probably crop it down to a head and shoulders but it's perfect.'

'She was interested in astrology,' says Mrs Warne in a sudden flurry of breath and language.

Sam dutifully writes the word down on his bank statement. 'Really?'

'Oh yes, she absolutely loved all that, she always did, didn't she, Ricky?'

Eric Warne grunts through a stiff smile, either in agreement or in awkward acknowledgement of the unanticipated and possibly ill-timed endearment.

'Tarot, palmistry, numerology and we're not just talking about horoscopes now. She had quite a gift. I know I shouldn't say this myself but it was obviously something she got from me.'

Sam's smile, which teeters on the self-satisfied and may therefore have been considered inappropriate under the circumstances, is thankfully brief. 'Yes, I thought I recognised you, you're Madame Delilah, right? Yeah, you used to have that little kiosk thing in the summer didn't you?'

'That's right, dear.'

'I thought so.'

Through narrow eyes, Madame Delilah, Genuine Gypsy Fortune Teller (clairvoyant to the stars – foretells the future – individuals or parties) scrutinises the Newspaper Man. 'I don't recall. Did you ever pay me a visit?'

'No, I . . . but I must have walked past your place hundreds of times over the years. Are you still working?'

'Not as much. I do visits mainly. Sometimes people come here . . .'

'She didn't like him . . . hated him actually,' says Eric Warne abruptly.

'Who?

'Eh?'

'You know, that John Travolta bloke. Jess. She couldn't stand him.'

Madame Delilah frowns her disapproval at this untimely interruption.

It may have been something of a cathartic interlude but Sam could see that she was obviously far happier and infinitely more comfortable talking about herself.

And so she continues. 'We're all connected you know, Mr Taylor. Jess believes that too. We were so similar you know, we were like astral twins – that was what someone told us once. It's quite rare but it's an accepted phenomena. But of course, for each and every one of us there's a great cosmic force that links us and unites us. All of us. Everything is predetermined; it's all in the stars. Past, present, future, it's just part of the same process and we're all part of this great plan, this *continuity* . . .'

'Really?' says Sam politely, writing a most unflattering single syllable word on his bank statement.

'Actually, we're not much more than just pure vibrations, a sort of pulsating energy. But we're all part of an endless cycle of change and rebirth and we are all . . . not like, you know, related in the traditional sense but related by these great invisible connections that bind us together for eternity. In some way on some level we are all of us connected. Even if it's not entirely visible to us. Every tiny thing we do in our lives, every minute that we are alive, even our most insignificant gesture can have repercussions for all eternity. You see, Mr Taylor, we must all acknowledge and then master these connections in order to live out our lives naturally. Actually, I was an African prince in a past life. I had a palace and servants and all that sort of stuff.'

'Really?' says Sam, fearing that he might have just repeated himself.

'You have a friend in trouble, don't you?' she announces suddenly.

'I do?'

'Yes, he has darkness and the clouds of a great torment are about him. I keep getting this picture in my mind of the tarot card called The Devil. But at this moment in time this person feels troubled, he feels alone and helpless, I sense a great peril.'

'Does he?'

'He can only be saved by love ... no, wait ... or by someone he loves ... or loved ...'

'Well, that's very ... interesting. I'm sure I'll bear all that in mind.' Metaphysical or paranormal speculation had played little or no part in the Deputy Editor's life up until this afternoon and this state of affairs is considered unlikely to modify itself to any discernable extent in the future. 'Now, to just get back to Jessica for a moment.' Sam starts to shift uncomfortably in his chair. 'Any particular friends, maybe someone we could talk to, who might like to say a few words about her?'

Oh God ... why now?

No, no! OK, so it happened once during the Queen's speech on the radio one Christmas, once watching racing from Haydock Park, once listening to *Round the Horne* ... No, no ...

But beneath dark mysterious folds of 75% Terylene, 25% cotton, machine wash cold, do not tumble, warm iron, waist 40/regular leg, something is definitely stirring. A set of nerves called the parasympathetic system is activated, the vessels are expanding and the blood flow is now increasing dramatically. The muscle wall in the Sam's corpora cavernosa relaxes allowing the blood to flow more freely. Then veins compress and the blood is trapped inside the corpora cavernosa.

In short, Sam Taylor experiences, for reasons he can hardly begin to fathom, a completely spontaneous erection.

He crosses his legs.

The member in question measures exactly six and a half inches when fully engorged (although he was in the habit of rounding it up to the nearest inch), rising slightly at an angle of roughly twenty degrees from the horizontal and bending very slightly to the left. It had been seen in its unaroused state by a total of 107 people, 23 of whom are now dead and in its aroused state by 16 people all of whom are currently living, yet only 7 of these have any tangible memory of the organ in question, of these 7, 2 would be classed as unskilled, 3 as semi-skilled, 1 as skilled and 1 as N/A. Six currently reside in the United Kingdom, while one now lives in New Zealand.

He uncrosses his legs.

'Special friends you mean?' asks Mrs Warne. 'Jess had so many friends. She was such an extremely popular girl. Always was. You can ask anyone.'

'I'm sure.'

'But there's a couple of girls that she used to see a lot. Claire was one and Loretta. They sometimes went around as a three but recently she's been seeing more of Loretta.'

'Oh yes and she's another one who doesn't want to show her bloody face around here either, not if she knows what's good for her . . .'

'Oh Eric, come on, stop it now . . .'

'Say, what you like, the fact remains . . .'

'Sorry, Mr Taylor,' says Mrs Warne. She then goes on to explain that her husband is still a bit upset about Loretta. Jessica had planned to meet her the previous evening as they were intending to go to Folkestone together.

'To see a film or something, they said. Then just as she's getting ready to leave, about seven o clock, wasn't it? Yeah, about then, this Loretta rings to say she has got to do something really important and she won't be able to make it. Jess was really upset by this, she felt really let down. She was so looking forward to going out. We suggested as it was a nice evening that maybe she should walk into Margate and see if she could find any of her other friends . . .'

'You see, you see! There you are! You see what I'm saying! If that Loretta hadn't let her down she would have been in bloody Folkestone all evening!'

Sam nods and looking up from his bank statement a moment later he sees that Mr Warne is crying. 'Er, right . . . OK . . . so where can I find these girls then? Addresses, surnames?'

Mrs Warne gives Sam the requested information and notices that for some reason the Deputy Editor suddenly seems in a great hurry to leave.

Four hours and forty-seven minutes

Here goes . . .

Clack . . . Clack

Again.

Clack . . .

Jesus.

Clack . . . Clack.

Tracing the arc of some far-off bliss-oblivious perilous seabird, Moe Seyton takes careful mock aim through the window once again.

Clack.

God, it was a heavy pull on the trigger with the hammer uncocked; he'd completely forgotten about that, maybe it was something to do with its age or the general deterioration of the mechanism. It wouldn't be rust, would it? But it must be getting on for seventy years old, more probably, certainly older than him. He takes aim once more.

Clack . . .

Always more difficult than you imagine . . . Supposedly the great advantage of a Mark IV Webley service revolver . . .

Clack . . . Clack

was this double action mechanism, which allowed you to fire with the hammer cocked in the usual firing position . . .

Clack . . .

and also with it uncocked like this, if you needed to get a shot off quickly . . .

. . . Clack

but bloody hell it was stiff. Let's try it with the hammer off then. OK, chimney pot on the far right . . . do you have any last requests . . . take aim

Click . . . Clack

Yes, that was much more like it, a much lighter trigger action. Click . . . Clack

Made in Birmingham originally, if I remember rightly. God they must have made thousands and thousands of these during the Great War. Although, interestingly enough, revolvers

Click . . . Clack

have actually been around a lot longer than you would think . . . they used them

Click . . . Clack

in the Crimean War, I believe.

Click . . . Clack

Here we go then. Question one, part one . . .

Click . . . Clack

Oh God, there he goes again!

Click . . . Clack

What is that bloody noise?

What in God's name can he be doing in there? It sounds like he's got a belt going around in a washing machine or maybe he's learning to skip.

I don't know. How on earth can I be expected to concentrate with all that going on?

Barney Langton, in reasonably contended spirits, is currently sitting on the toilet in the bathroom on the second floor of the Seaview. The bathroom is located next to the room occupied by Moe. In fact, separated only by a wall of fairly recent construction, he is less than ten feet away from where the comedian is still testing his revolver.

Barney is not attending to any particular ablution or bodily function, he is simply enjoying ten minutes to himself following Andy's bath. He is answering a questionnaire in this month's copy of *Rogue*, a gentlemen's magazine, which announces itself on its front cover as 'Top Quality Entertainment for Men for Under a Quid'. Unashamedly lowbrow in content and format, *Rogue* eschewed all aspirations to sophistication in favour of page after page of fairly basic titillation. The questionnaire currently under review is one of very few pages of text this month. Barney had purchased the magazine thc previous morning and had secreted it within the pages of the *Observer* business section, where it had, to his knowledge, not been discovered.

In fairness, this was an occasional rather than frequent indulgence but it served as a welcome enough diversion at times like these.

Where were we? Oh yes.

Question one part one. Er . . . No. Never.

From the shampoo bottle on the side of the bath, Mr Punch eyes Barney with deep linear suspicion. He is in no mood for self-deception this evening. His voice is a squeaky soprano but firm and drained of all emotion.

They all say that.

Moving on then, Question one part two. Er . . . what did I say before? 17 or 18?

I think you said 18.

OK. Question two. Never.

Come on, I'll bet you have . . . you're just too embarrassed to admit it.

Question three. Once a week. Once a week, that is, if we're lucky. Once a fortnight is probably more accurate.

Mr Punch shrugs with exaggerated cartoon objectivity. *If you're in any doubt maybe you should just try to be honest.*

Question four. Six. 'Up until current partner' it says – but does that mean we include them in the total then or leave them out? And is 'current' strictly defined as regular or most recent?

I suppose that's largely up to you.

Go for six then, I suppose. Right then, here we go, the next question . . .

Click . . . Clack

Question five. Favourite position. Er . . . doggy probably . . . why am I tempted to say roaming midfielder?

Try and take it a bit more seriously, will you, there's a good chap . . .

Barney now starts to grow bored and he scans the next couple of questions half-heartedly. Question eleven addresses the subject of methods employed by which ejaculation can be delayed.

That's easy.

So what's the answer then?

I'm not absolutely sure I want to tell you.

Mr Punch dances and sings in mocking tones. *Scaredy Barney, Scaredy Barney, too scared to leave his mummy. Come on now, you started this.*

I know but it sounds silly.

Mr Punch smiles. *Listen, son, I don't really think you're in a position to judge what is or what is not silly.*

That's true enough.

Click . . . Clack

But we're all men here

OK. I . . . what was the question again?

What methods have you employed to delay ejaculation or prolong lovemaking?

Oh yes, of course.

Come on, spit it out.

OK. David Coleman. There. I said it.

You what?

David Coleman.

That's what I thought you said.

I think about David Coleman. To delay . . . you know . . .

The sports commentator?

Yes that's him. I never do it on purpose or anything he just sort of pops into my head.

I see. So, what does he actually do?

He commentates. Obviously.

A look of fear suddenly distorts Mr Punch's features. *Oh Christ, not on you, I hope.*

Oh God, no! It's just like a rerun of his commentary on some notable athletics events of the past.

Of course, you mean like his legendary lachrymose outbursts during Ann Packer's famous 800 metres victory at the Tokyo Olympics?

No, no, much more recent than that.

Like what then?

Um . . .

Go on.

And Bedford KICKS for home . . .

I see.

Jenkins has got a FLYER!

Does it work?

Usually works for me.

Well, there you are then

Click . . . Clack

Like I say, it just pops into my head, I have no idea why. He is just suddenly there and I can't do anything about it. So, what do other chaps think about?

You'd be surprised.

Would I? Oh good. That's a relief.

I think we should move on to question twelve now.

I don't want to answer that. Well, I don't actually know to be honest with you. Besides, I'm not that bothered about it and I have never been interested enough to find out.

Why don't you do it now, no one can see you.

No, I don't want to.

Mr Punch lets out a long sigh. *OK, so I'll just put you down as Below Average, that should cover it. Now, question thirteen.*

Click . . . Clack

The most unusual place I have ever had sex?

That's the one.

Why don't we skip that one?

Why?

Well, because there isn't one really. An unusual place, that is. Nowhere that springs to mind.

Oh dear, you're quite a sheltered little soul, aren't you?

Am I?

You seem to be.

I don't think that's entirely fair.

In fact, to be honest with you, you strike me as being, on the whole, a little on the inhibited side. Maybe this is why you're so frustrated most of the time.

Who said I was frustrated?

Warming to the subject, Mr Punch becomes suddenly animated. *For one thing, this whole conversation, which as you are no doubt aware is entirely delusional, is probably born more or less entirely out of deeply rooted sexual frustrations.*

Now wait a minute.

Click . . . Clack

Or are you going to indulge yourself yet again by pretending that all this has got something to do with what you loftily perceive to be moral anxiety or guilt?

Well . . .

Or that I am simply your conscience manifest?

I . . . er

Pull the other one!

But I'm not frustrated.

That's easy to say. Scaredy Barney, Scaredy Barney, too scared to join the Army.

I'm not just saying it. You should have seen me a few years ago! I wasn't at all inhibited!

Yes, but that was responsive not instigative!

Click . . . Clack

But being inhibited isn't the same as lacking imagination. I might own up to that, maybe. I'm not particularly inventive or creative in that respect but that doesn't mean I'm inhibited. It's a completely separate issue.

But surely you can't claim to be truly uninhibited if you fail to be instigative. That notion is utterly absurd.

Look, I'm not getting into a debate about this with you.

Click . . . Clack

So what was her name then?

Who?

Mr Punch taps the end of his nose and looks pleased with himself. *You know, this girl you've been making references and allusions to all day.*

Oh, I'm definitely not telling you that.

Click . . . Clack

Was it the lure of the forbidden? Was she young?

Why are you asking me this?

Click . . . Clack

Come on, you are just so desperate to confess and repent, to be absolved and forgiven. It's written all over you! People like you are all the same!

No, that's not true at all! I resent that!

She's just like me, isn't she? Go on, admit it, confess, confess! She's just another one of your harmless delusional fantasies, isn't she? You know, it wouldn't do you any harm to knock around with some real, non-fictional people once in a while.

That's not fair!

Juke-er box, juke-er box
No . . . not like this
Juke-er box, juke-er box
Please . . .
Clack Clack Clack Clack.
Click . . . Clack
Click . . . Clack
Clack Clack Clack Clack.

'Geezer is sitting on his own in the pub one day . . .'

Absorbed in the moment, Alderman Hughes trims his prodigious nasal hair with a small manicure scissors.

'Be careful with those, they're new.'

'Yes I know, I bought them for you.'

'That's hardly the point is it, really? You just be careful with them.'

'OK, Mum.'

'And be careful with that mirror too, I don't need you breathing all over it and steaming it up. It's a nice mirror that . . . or rather it was a nice mirror . . .'

Exhaling sibilantly through his teeth, his worship makes fleeting eye contact with his reflection and gently shakes his head.

Nearly done, nearly done, how come they grow so quickly, just . . . *thatonethere* . . . I never used to do it this often, I'm certain I didn't . . . didn't need to, very unattractive, lends the face an almost thuggish, Neanderthal aspect . . . *andthenthisone* . . . I did it last week, I'm sure I did . . . mostly grey too nowadays, maybe its all to do with age . . . *onemoreand* . . . ouch!

Yes.

Finished.

Cupping and shielding the results of the aforesaid act in his hand as though transporting a wounded bird, he makes his way to the wastepaper basket where discreetly and without undue ceremony he concludes his grooming procedure (for is he not his mother's son?) He then places the scissors and the mirror on the corner of the bed next to his mother. 'Thanks,' he says through the smile that he keeps solely for these occasions.

Mrs Hughes shakes her head in vigorous dismay. 'Oh, for goodness' sake! Not there! Put them in the bathroom. That's where they belong!'

Alderman Hughes reflects on duty, virtue and the Ten Commandments and removes the items as requested.

'If I have to stay here,' she says, slightly louder than absolutely necessary, 'I might as well try and keep the place neat and tidy.'

'What was that?'

'Nothing. And on your way back, Brian, can you open the window? There's a good fellow. I don't know why they have to have it so hot in here, I really don't. You would have thought, wouldn't you? It's boiling. I said to the chap downstairs I did, I said we're old people not tropical flipping plants. I'll be coming out in a rash soon if it carries on. Besides, it's not good for anyone to be cooped up like this on a hot day without any fresh air.'

Alderman Hughes opens the window and looks at his watch, it's just coming up to six thirty and he wonders how soon he can get away and do so with his conscience unblemished.

'There you go, why don't we move this armchair back a bit then you can come and sit at the window?'

'Why do you imagine I would want to do that?'

'Er . . . enjoy the view, maybe?'

'Don't be silly, Brian, why would I want to look at that? Until I get some proper nets, not these flimsy cheap ones, I'll probably keep the curtains closed most of the time.'

'What do you mean, Ma?'

'Well, correct me if I'm wrong but I thought you told me I'd be having a view of the sea.'

'I know, but we did go through this before, didn't we? Some of the rooms at the front of the house have got sort of indirect sea views, I believe, but then you're right on a fairly busy main road and I thought you'd prefer the peace and quiet. I've told you I was very lucky and this is one of the best suites in the whole building.'

'So you keep telling me.'

'Come on, Ma. It's a great place, I just can't see how anyone could fail to love it here.'

'It's quite simple, I just don't want to look out at the backs of people's houses, that's all. It was certainly not my intention to spend my so-called autumn years sitting here on my b.t.m. contemplating the rear of someone's garage!'

Alderman Hughes suppresses a tiny smile. 'Oh come on, it's not that bad.'

'Of course it is, it's even worse than that! Look straight ahead of you! You see that? You see that building right opposite? That horrible unsightly edifice, that thing with the concrete wall is, I am reliably informed, a Workingman's Club or some such. Well, I don't recall them being in any great and desperate hurry to point that out to us when we signed the papers, do you? Yes, somehow that managed to slip their minds that day, didn't it? You would have thought, wouldn't you? So, I would rather not sit at the window if you don't mind!'

They make momentary eye contact.

And for a moment, it rushes back.

Just a boy and his mother.

A boy growing up without a father, growing up without brothers or sisters.

Just a boy and his mother.

They laughed together and they were always brave. They

laughed together and nothing could hurt them. It was their protection against anything and everything. It was a special thing that nobody else knew about.

In his dreams and memories they still always seem to be laughing.

Together, they had once marvelled at the absurdity of the world and of all things – ladies who had to draw big red circles around their mouths in case they forgot where to put their cakes, the little dogs that would float away like balloons if you didn't hold on very tightly to their strings. Only they knew that milkmen were made of milk (which was why they always left puddles on the doorstep) and that if you went too long without wearing your jumper it went back to being a sheep.

They could always laugh.

Not any more.

Gone again.

'Whatever you say, Ma . . .'

Together, they had once marvelled at the absurdity of the world and of all things – nowadays they have settled into simply marvelling at the absurdity of each other.

Alderman Hughes gingerly lifts the lid on the cardboard box that is currently resting on the dressing table. 'Have you got much more unpacking to do?'

'No, there's not much, I'll do it later.'

'I thought you were going to throw some of this stuff out.'

'I never said that. You told me that I should throw some stuff out. That is the actual truth of the matter as I recall it.'

'I didn't think you'd want to keep this stuff.'

'I wasn't aware that we'd discussed the matter.'

Alderman Hughes removes from the cardboard box a moth-eaten ancient teddy bear and a singularly odd-looking doll, a curious article with an ugly garishly painted face, one that upon closer inspection reveals a deeply disturbing countenance. The slight sense of vague unease it evokes has not dimmed in forty years and without thinking he turns away. Yes, to be fair, one could possibly imagine the former being an object of a child's affection but never the latter.

'I don't know, Ma. For the life of me, I never knew why you hung onto these for so long. You never really kept anything much, you never used to keep souvenirs or things like that and you never seemed particularly attached to anything in the old house. Even when you lost that photo album that time, you never seemed all that bothered to be honest. But you always held onto these horrible things for some reason. I never understood that.' He holds up for inspection the items under discussion. 'I remember for years they lived in the bottom of your wardrobe, didn't they? And I wasn't allowed to play with them. This manky old teddy and this hideous doll here, say hello, chaps . . . *Hello.* God, they can't be very hygienic. I dread to think what germs are lurking here. They're probably a major health risk.'

'It's not a doll, it's a puppet and it's very special, please just leave them alone, Brian. Just leave them there . . .'

They lapse into an uneasy silence and within a matter of minutes Alderman Hughes has said his farewells, kissed her on the cheek, written phone numbers at which he can be contacted all evening, opened the paper at the TV page and promised to return in the morning.

Emotionless, Mrs Hughes stands at the window for a few moments surveying the scene. She then takes her two ancient companions and arranges them on her bed. As she does so she says softly to the less worn and threadbare of the two items,

'I did try to give you back, didn't I? I didn't mean to keep you. I went looking for a policeman and when I found one he told me he was busy and to look after you. He didn't say how long for, did he? I mean I was only nine, I wasn't to know, was I?'

Somewhere else, somewhere good, somewhere nice, someone nice sings 'Summer Nights' . . .

There is that *moment* in the life of every man (a truly unfortunate man may of course experience any number of *moments*). The *moment* when despite all his best attempts at obstruction, duplicity and denial and all his skill at manoeuvring and manipulating his way out of responsibility and accountability, a *moment* of true fate when suddenly it all just falls away and finally he is revealed to himself not as he wishes to be, not as he believes himself to be, but as he actually is.

When all illusion is cast aside.

When there are no more half-truths.

No more excuses.

When his every vile obscure intention is made manifest, every ghastly deception, every clouded motive, every dubious instinct is suddenly and irrevocably exposed. In this place, he now stands publicly, for all to see! A flawed-raw terrified all-too-human being, naked, without hope, obscene, weak, utterly and unspeakably ALONE and useless . . . useless . . . useless.

In Sam Taylor's life, his *moment* occurs at 6.42 p.m. August 28th, 1978.

Sick with memory, he sits alone at a table in the Cliftonville Arms, a public house of stern, fairly foreboding countenance, located roughly opposite the junction of Prices Avenue and Northdown Road.

Somewhere else, somewhere good, somewhere nice, someone nice sings 'Summer Nights' . . .

He lifts his Guinness carefully to his mouth, it is cold and heavy and he doesn't even know if he wants it anymore and his hand is shaking and he was right not to drive, very sensible, not in his condition, just wait a while, go back later, maybe wait until tomorrow, the Capri should be safe where it is, outside the Warnes' house . . .

Sam Taylor coughs and manages to spill a mouthful of Guinness onto his trousers.

The three young men at the bar, who with Mr Taylor constitute the entire clientele of the Cliftonville Arms at this time, turn and look at him. They stare without the slightest amusement or pity.

Fuck. Fuck. Fuck. Fuck.

Sam wipes his trousers with his handkerchief.

Fuck. Fuck. Fuck . . .

He reaches into his pocket and produces a cigarette packet and a creased and folded bank statement. From another pocket he produces a box of Swan Vestas and a photograph. His body tenses slightly.

Fuck. Fuck. Fuck . . .

She knew didn't she – of course she did – she knows everything – you could tell – the first moment she saw me – the second I set foot in the place – she knew exactly what was going on – they always said she was really good – not like most of them – none of that old talldarkstranger and crossmypalmwithsilver nonsense – they used to say she had a real gift – so why did she say that thing about the devil – she must have had a reason – what was she trying to say – that was why she kept staring at me the whole time – like she could see right through me – God, it was like she was just playing with me – like she was enjoying it or something – why didn't she say something – just come right out and say it – did she want me to feel like this – did she want me to suffer – so I could feel just a tiny minute fraction of her suffering – she knows all right – I know she does.

Meanwhile, one of the young men at the bar, the tallest of the three, returns from putting more money into the jukebox and says something to his friends after which they all turn and look at Sam. One of them laughs coldly.

2,4,6,7 . . . Fuck. Fuck. Fuck. Sam lights a John Player Special while counting the remaining cigarettes in the packet. Fuck. Fuck. There were two unopened packets in the car. Fuck. Fuck.

Hot now. Sweating too.

His mouth is dry and he can feel his tongue. He takes a slow careful communion sip of the Guinness.

Blood of Christ – what did she say – I'm sure I didn't write it down – no it's not here – didn't think it was important at the time – something about all our lives being connected in some way – its obvious what she was trying to imply – she was so calm about it all when I think about it – like she'd almost been expecting me or something – I should never have gone – I should have cleared it first – not that it was a problem – I made the right decision – no doubt about it – five o'clock on a Bank Holiday afternoon – there is no one around to clear it with – I'll go and have a chat with him first thing in the morning – he'll be fine – you can't risk missing a story like this one – but I should have sent someone else – I could have spent the rest of the day with Moe – gone and had a nice early supper somewhere – my shout – but instead – this – why did it happen today – why couldn't the car have broken down today and not last week – she knew – she knew – she knows everything – but I didn't know – I swear I didn't know – you have got to believe me – I had absolutely no idea – I knew she had a friend – someone that she saw a lot of – but she only mentioned it in passing – I never knew anything about her – I never even knew her name – I swear.

Somewhere else, somewhere good, somewhere nice, someone nice sings 'Summer Nights' . . .

HERE BEGINS THE CONFESSION OF SAMUEL PETER TAYLOR

Just over a year ago, in common with many other local firms, the *Thanet Gazette* joined the East Kent Business Incentive programme. As part of this plan, we were encouraged to find jobs for local school leavers. Usually they would be eighteen and upwards, certainly no younger and they would usually be employed in fairly junior, fairly menial positions. Doing mainly administrative work and running errands. The money isn't great obviously but it's better than the dole and it gives them valuable experience of working in an office environment. That's the reasoning behind it anyway. To be honest, half the time we were hard pressed to find things for them to do. We've had about half a dozen of them come and go during the past year. A young girl started after Easter but she left us after a few months when she got a full-time job in Boots. Her place was subsequently taken by Colin Featherhead, who is still working at the paper. The young girl's name was Loretta Bowden. She had left school after a fairly poor showing at her A levels and was looking to work rather than go onto to any higher education. I have to say I liked her the moment I set eyes on her. She was always happy and I know it's a terrible cliché but every time she entered a room it was like someone had opened a long-forgotten window, the place instantly seemed so full of air and light. I should perhaps pause before progressing any further and clarify the current Taylor Marital State. Put simply – there isn't one. My wife and I were divorced in 1974 and I have lived alone ever since.

I don't recall saying very much to Loretta beyond a hello for the first couple of days but then she came on a couple of assignments with me and we used to talk in the car. She was a smart girl, funny too, and she's got a wicked sense of humour. Flirtatious maybe, but in a very subtle, knowing way. Not overt or tarty. It was my birthday in May and she made me a card, it was really sweet, she'd drawn a picture of a tortoise because I'd mentioned to her that I liked tortoises. She's like that. I took her out with me a couple of times, we went to the last few football games of the season together, stuff like that. We talked about all sorts of things, films, politics, religion, and the more she talked the more comfortable she felt with me. She started telling me about her home life. Her father had left them a few years ago and she didn't get on with her mum's boyfriend. They were always arguing, she said, fighting almost constantly. One day she came to work with a bruise over her eye. By this point I was starting to dread her days off, I would be in a foul mood if I thought I wouldn't be seeing her. She was eighteen and I was fifty-one. We have the lifespan of Jesus between us, I used to tell her. She thought that was very funny. We shouldn't worry, Jesus often comes between people she says. I was all too aware I was making a fool of myself but I didn't care and that's when I *knew*. I started to give her lifts home. One night we popped into the pub and then we popped into the pub every night. I would always enquire if she had a date that evening or if she was seeing a boyfriend and she would always say something like why can't you be my boyfriend tonight? Or why do I need a boyfriend if I'm with you? One evening after she'd come to work with another bruise, a really bad one, we stopped off for a drink and she just asked pretty much out of the blue if she could stay with me as she couldn't face going home. What could I say? That was when it started. Now the thing is whenever you see a man in this situation, an older, a much older man like me, it is always easy to rush to conclusions and judgements and to be honest I have made such judgements myself in the past but it's not as straightforward as it may seem. It's not actually about sex, I promise you, that's the simple truth, yes I have had sex with Loretta, I'm not denying it. Not all that often actually, a few times, it's been great, fantastic, but that's not what is important. Loretta makes me feel like it's not all behind me, it's not all gone, wasted, pissed away, forgotten, finished. She has reminded me that there is still so much to be done. Listen, old man, wake up! Possibility is now a possibility! She has shown me that even in some wretched overweight broken-down old fool like me that there is still a heart in there beating somewhere. I can still fall victim to my passions. There is still enthusiasm there – I can feel it! It's like this sudden great energy burning inside me – and you can't know what that is like after all this time! It is THAT I promise you and not the sex! I'm *only* fifty-one, I keep telling myself. I'm not old yet. One hundred and one is old! Understand this! Loretta is precisely that which obscures my death from me! Anyone that possesses that gift is worth making an idiot of yourself over! She masks my decay and my decline. Tell me I'm wrong! Look, just try to understand. It wasn't just about her, it was about how I felt, what it felt like to be Samuel stupid bloody Taylor, when I was with her. It wasn't about her young supple body, it was about how it felt to be inside this old ugly one as we touched and made contact. She'd managed to connect me with my own life. Plugged me back in! Simple as that and of course I was grateful. Of course I bought her presents, it was the very least I could do. I still do. As planned, she went to work in Boots at, I believe, the end of June but we've carried on seeing each other. We've managed to keep our relationship secret until now. Obviously, we have both been extremely careful and there are certain places where we can't be seen together. But we've managed to find a handful of places out on the roads around Sandwich and Deal where we can go and have a drink or a meal and just be together without any great risk of being spotted. I've just bought her a moped so she can get to places under her own steam. She's taking her driving test next month; if she passes I'll get her a little car, a little mini or something. She said she fancies a Capri like mine for herself but I told there's absolutely no way! Yes, I know how this all appears and I'm well aware what people will think. Truly, I have no illusions, whatsoever. It isn't easy to understand, I know, but I feel I'm the most fortunate person on the planet. I don't actually feel that I'm doing anything wrong. Maybe in five years' time it will be easier for both of us. I know she feels the same and I'm sure she often has the same insecurities and worries as me. We see each other fairly regularly, a couple of times a week. She tells her mum every now and again that she's staying with a friend or something and she comes over and spends the night with me. I ring her every day at work and we talk then but sometimes I have days when that's not enough and I just have to be with her, I just have to find a way to see her. I get myself into this highly anxious state. I was in this real panic on Sunday around teatime, shaking and sweating. I was in a right old mess. She rang me from a call box as she often did on her way to somewhere else; there's one at the end of her road. I was so upset on the phone to her, I was pleading with her to come over. She said she couldn't make it, she'd arranged to go to the cinema with a friend of hers. You see, she recently befriended a girl a year or so younger than herself, she's taken her under her wing a bit and I think she feels very responsible for her. This was the girl she was going out with on Sunday night. But cross my heart, I had no idea who this girl was and Loretta never referred to her by name. However, she did talk about her a lot, how they'd recently been chatting about getting a flat together and I admit I was starting to get sick of it. I was just jealous, I suppose, pathetic really but I just didn't want her confiding in this friend and this friend advising her to get rid of me. I could just imagine them talking about me and laughing the way girls do. It just started to gnaw at me over the last couple of weeks, I know it was probably silly but I was certain she was keeping our phone calls to a minimum and she always seemed in a hurry to hang up or somebody seemed to be waiting to use the phone. I am now fully aware of the situation but I was becoming increasingly terrified that I was losing her and that this new friend of hers was partially or rather more than partially responsible. So, on Sunday night when she told me she was seeing this friend, I have to confess I just lost it. Completely. I broke down and started sobbing, I begged her and begged her to come round. I was going on and on like I was a thing possessed. She said she couldn't let a friend down, particularly as she was a bit younger and she didn't want to leave her on her own, very sorry and all that. She was quite firm about this and I didn't like it. I don't remember exactly what I said to her but I couldn't let it happen, I couldn't let her walk away, so I told her in so many words that if she didn't come round I would end the relationship once and for all and that would be that. I can see now that it was an incredibly stupid childish thing to do, just because I was feeling so jealous. Pathetic isn't it? So, Loretta arrived at my front door about half an hour or so after our phone call and I made a point of not mentioning her friend for the rest of the evening. I thought that was the mature thing to do.

HERE ENDS THE CONFESSION OF SAMUEL PETER TAYLOR

*

Fig. 1

Fig. 2

'I would like to start by drawing your attention to these two images on the screen behind me . . .'

Two minutes, three minutes and now five minutes and the auditorium is still only three-quarters full. He feels a twinge of slight disappointment as he lines up the acetates on the overhead projector. It is only vanity, he tells himself, and he should ignore it. In fairness, you might have been forgiven for thinking that a little bit of controversy would have been good for business. Strange. Maybe things were just different over here. Let's not forget the word blasé is not English!

'These two pictures were taken roughly at the same time just a little over a century ago. Figure 1 being taken a little before figure 2. I imagine that given the nature of my talk this evening you shouldn't have too much trouble identifying the subject of these pictures. Yes, it is a bit of a giveaway, I fear.'

No polite laugh, no response, they are still openly hostile to him.

Barney Langton leaves the Seaview and turns left; he walks slowly and purposefully in the opposite direction to the seafront in a roughly south-westwardly direction.

'I imagine that you may be very familiar with these pictures but I ask you to look very closely at them. Indulge me. Come on, guys, I'm a visitor here!'

No response again. They were really going to make him work, make him sweat. Just like last time.

'OK, I would ask you to play very close attention to the shape of the eyebrows in both figure 1 and figure 2, even though we are viewing from two slightly different angles, they both share a very particular arc, here and here at the corner of the eye. Concentrate on this area here, where the eyebrow meets the nose in figure 1 and again on this area in figure 2. Also observe in both pictures the actual overall shape of the eyes, we can easily make out almost identical oval shapes. Consider then the width of the bridge of the nose. What we are looking at here is I believe . . .'

Here we go, no turning back now.

At the junction with Garfield Road, Barney Langton crosses Marine Terrace and walks on the opposite side of the road.

'. . . two photographs of the same man, taken a short while apart. If you approach the data dispassionately then that is the only possible conclusion you can draw. Figure 1 and figure 2 depict the same man. However, figure 1 is, we are told, Paul Verlaine and figure 2 is allegedly Arthur Rimbaud . . .'

Now the noise, at last the noise, it comes at him from all sides, some angry, some with questions. Requesting silence, he holds up his hands in an unconscious gesture of surrender. This makes little difference and he busies himself for a moment removing the first two pictures from the projector and replacing them with two more.

'Figure 2 is actually a detail from a slightly less well-known photograph of Rimbaud. It was taken by Étienne Crajat in 1871, the photographer responsible for the more famous and universally recognisable portrait of Rimbaud taken in the same year. This more obscure portrait was, however, generally considered at the time to be the most accurate and faithful portrayal of the poet.'

A less contentious point, obviously. They quieten again and now he notices her for the first time.

'So now, let's examine in greater detail these two portraits of *supposedly* Verlaine and Rimbaud, from which the two previous enlargements were taken. Let's take a good look at the original pictures. Figure 3, Verlaine, on the left and figure 4 is Rimbaud on the right. As we study these pictures another very interesting detail emerges. If we concentrate our attention for a moment on the lower half of the portraits we immediately discover that both subjects are wearing identical clothes. Not a similar style or type of garment but literally identical. Observe the shape and this particular edging on the lapel of the jacket, the buttons on the waistcoat, even this rather raggedy old necktie. These are the same clothes. Identical. Please judge for yourself, look at the evidence, this is not my interpretation, it's not some wild unsubstantiated guess but a matter of very obvious, very self-evident fact.'

The girl looks at the screen, then at him for a moment and then back at the screen. In that moment, however, he thinks he detects the slightest smile. It suggests encouragement rather than solidarity but he continues in noticeably more confident tones.

'Now something strange seems to be happening here and it was this that first began to gnaw away at me a couple of years ago. What was it telling me, what was the bigger picture? Had I stumbled upon something . . .'

It was a fairly traditional rhetorical device but in this case it was definitely an ill-advised one. The noise starts again. He looks at the girl who smiles again and shakes her head

Barney makes a right turn into Hatfeild Road.

God, why did he do that? He was talking about himself, fatal, *fatal* mistake; he just sounded vain and pompous. He'd shifted away from his subject and into some irrelevant inflating self-promotion.

Once again, he feels as though he just pinned a brightly coloured paper target over his heart.

Think quickly. The noise increases. A polystyrene cup missile hits the podium. Think, man . . .

'So what WE must do in this case is train OUR minds to explore alternatives. If WE can move our fixed points of view just fractionally then an interesting possibility presents itself. Is there an order to this? Is this a conscious, if you will, *deception* being played on US? Is the word, in point of fact, *hoax*?'

They settle slightly and the noise shrinks to an ambient drone.

'OK. Let's start with a few fairly indisputable facts. Arthur Rimbaud was one of the greatest French poets of the last century and possibly, many would claim, of all time. He was born in Charleville in 1854 and showed himself to be intellectually precocious and gifted with a great healthy loathing of convention and authority. Following his own visionary credo he wrote a series of extraordinary poems, largely unpublished during his lifetime, before abandoning literature completely in his late teens and embarking on a series of business ventures in Africa. Whilst a schoolboy in Charleville, he had sent some examples of his work to the poet Paul Verlaine in Paris. Verlaine was one of the very few contemporary poets Rimbaud admired and Verlaine was sufficiently impressed by the boy's work to invite him to Paris. This was September 1871, Verlaine was twenty-eight and Rimbaud sixteen. For two years thereafter the poets had an intense, violent, brutal affair that was only brought to an end by Verlaine's imprisonment for shooting Rimbaud in the wrist at the climax of one of their quarrels. They met one final time after this, which again ended in violence, and they never set eyes on each other again.'

The girl is nodding and writing something. Something related to a smile is playing on her lips. She turns fractionally and as she does he reads the word L'ANARCHIE on her T-shirt.

'These are the simple substantiated facts and few would

dispute them. In the past there were attempts to impose a purely *platonic* basis for their relationship but nowadays, in our more enlightened times, very few people would waste their time on such an absurdity.

'So, historically, there are three distinct Rimbauds. There is the Charleville Rimbaud, the Paris Rimbaud and the Africa Rimbaud. This evening I am only interested in the Paris Rimbaud or as I prefer to call him the Verlaine Rimbaud . . .'

Barney reaches the end of Hatfeild Road and raising his eyes above and far beyond the sights and sounds of the seaside early evening, he gazes out at the horizon. He smiles to himself. He sees the sun mixed with the sea . . .

Together.

Yeah but . . .

Even their language had begun to erode, not just communication nowadays, even definition! True. In the past couple of days they both seemed to have concluded independently that they have been mistaking *Together* with *Proximity*. How long for? He did things and she did things *nearby*. Their only connection nowadays was geographic – never once social or emotional. They were simply proximate to each other. Local. God, how long can they go on like this?

'The Verlaine Rimbaud or the Hoax Rimbaud . . .'

Noise again, polystyrene cups, a few people seem to be leaving but this time he feels in control, he knows that by using that very term he will incite them. He is well aware of the controversy he is in the process of creating.

'Please understand I'm not trying to claim that Rimbaud didn't exist or that in his youth he didn't write some fine verse but that the writings of the Charleville Rimbaud are, to quote Henri Lafitte in one of the first critical biographies of the poet, "merely the tantalising appetiser of the feast to follow". I only ask that you open your minds and consider with me an alternative to the accepted wisdom. Let's remind ourselves of certain truths. That Rimbaud's greatest work, the work upon which his reputation is built, was written during his relationship with Verlaine, at a time when they actually lived together for long periods. That Verlaine wrote virtually no poetry for the first year they were together. That when he did start writing he did so in a style that showed a remarkable similarity to Rimbaud's at the time. That the majority of Rimbaud's original manuscripts from this period are in Verlaine's handwriting. That Rimbaud would allegedly dictate his poems to Verlaine. That as they are parting after their final acrimonious meeting (which according to some sources has Rimbaud beating Verlaine unconscious and abandoning him at the roadside) Rimbaud simply hands over to Verlaine a pile of papers. These papers contain arguably the greatest sequence of poems ever written in the French language, namely *Les Illuminations.* So, they argue, they fight and then as they are separating, never to see each other ever again, Rimbaud just hands over the only copy of his finest work! Just ask yourself for a moment, how likely, how plausible is such a scenario? Yet these facts can be checked in any account of the lives of the poets. Furthermore, there is no doubt whatsoever that Rimbaud wrote no further poems of any consequence after this fateful meeting.'

The girl looks at him and grips the end of her pen tightly between her teeth.

'It is frankly absurd to suggest that they never collaborated in any way and I don't think it can simply be dismissed as a fantasy or some idle academic distraction to wonder if Verlaine had a hand in Rimbaud's work. The question that we need to address is how much. To answer this we must concentrate our attention on Verlaine. If there has been any deception, or, shall we allow ourselves to say, a hoax, then he is certainly the perpetrator. Verlaine's reputation has suffered over the past century, largely resulting from his being cast by history as Rimbaud's straight man but of course he was also a major poetic talent in his own right. He had survived a childhood during which he was endlessly indulged and mollycoddled by an overprotective mother and he grew to maturity ancient before his time. A dull, unattractive civil servant, he was bald, bisexual and alcoholic by his mid twenties. In matters of the heart, his taste in men had always been for the younger and, if one may be permitted to generalise, rougher types and all his life he was attracted to what he regarded as the rebel and the outsider (remember that he wrote that very heartfelt poem about Kasper Hauser) – obviously because they represented an aspect of his own childhood he would dearly love to recapture or live again vicariously. All that his own dear sweet old *maman* had never allowed for her delicate, precious boy during his youth. But these young boys, with whom he consorted, were everything the old-before-his-time poet yearned to have been. One need only read Verlaine's more graphic or scatological works to sense in the poet's contrived voice an attempt to grasp the nuance or the reckless abandonment of an adolescent's writing.

'There were homosexual encounters in Verlaine's life, both before and after, but Rimbaud, it could be argued, was perhaps the greatest love of his life. But beyond simply being a partner, Rimbaud was his intellectual equal, his alter ego and the means by which he would for all eternity reinvent, perhaps even reclaim his own adolescence. In pursuit of this goal, it is my belief that the Rimbaud poems written between 1871 and 1873 are the work of Verlaine.'

Noise again, too much to be heard over, can't quite make out what they're shouting, probably a good thing. He checks but the girl isn't looking at him anymore.

'There are a vast number of clues dotted around the place that confirm this hypothesis. Fellow poet Léon Valade, who may have been taken into Verlaine's confidence, or heard a rumour, wrote in a letter of 1871 of a meeting with Verlaine during which he is introduced to Rimbaud. He refers to the young poet as being '*sous les auspices de Verlaine,* ***son inventeur***'.There is no alternative translation other than 'under the auspices of Verlaine, **his inventor**'. Inventor indeed? A curious choice of word when one might expect to read 'friend', 'acquaintance', even 'partner' perhaps or possibly 'mentor'. Interestingly, both Monsieur Valade and the recipient of the letter, Émile Blémont, feature in Fantin-Latour's legendary group portrait *Un coin de table* alongside Verlaine and Rimbaud. As a matter of interest, I do believe that there are certain sexual ambiguities in the representations of Rimbaud and Verlaine in that particular painting. For example, studied closely and in isolation, one might easily conclude that Verlaine resembles uncannily a woman disguised as a man, whilst Rimbaud looks like a man disguised as a woman. Another trick, another deception? Who knows?'

But the sea is never as blue as you think it will be.

OK, point taken . . .

An incredibly poor metaphor but a reasonably fair observation.

It's greener . . . brown even.

So how do you manage to hate, well . . . *nothing*?

To effectively despise space or to live in utter dread of emptiness? How does that which is missing so unsettle a person? (Is this where religion starts from?) But there was no escape from it, was there? That endless, cavernous wretched space between them. Barely recognisable or even visible to each other. Only echoes now, traces, suggestions. Something implied or half recognised, or momentarily caught out of the corner of one eye. Regrets gathered in shadow, took physical form and now walked and wailed like ghosts stalking the perimeters of their days and nights.

But the girl is looking at him again, now her expression is bordering on the vaguely maternal.

'So Monsieur Valade has given us a tantalising clue, perhaps no more than a hint, but what of Verlaine? Did he leave us with anything to back up my hypothesis? Did he leave us any hints? Were the two pictures we looked at earlier a bold attempt at the most obvious visual confession? A wig, a shave and the assistance of any theatrical make-up artist and such a Jekyll and Hyde duplicity is a simple task. Étienne Crajat, the photographer, who took both pictures, had of course been attacked by Rimbaud wielding a sword stick. Perhaps he was happy to indulge in a joke at his assailant's expense, or take a sort of mild revenge. It is true that the images of Rimbaud from this period differ wildly from each other. One need only look at the most famous portrait and contrasting this with the Verlaine fake, we can see that the jaw lines are entirely different.

'But what about written evidence? We must remember that Verlaine, like many writers of this period, enjoyed playfully advertising his verbal prowess by indulging in puns and word games. Of course one need only think of his *Poétes Maudits* of 1888, his famous critical study of Rimbaud amongst others. In this piece he refers to himself as '*Pauvre Lélian*', a perfect anagram of his name.'

A handful of people noisily leave the auditorium, one pauses to throw an empty Cola can towards the podium. It falls short of its intended target by a considerable margin.

'Perhaps we need to go right back to the very beginning. Perhaps to the earliest poem of Rimbaud's Paris period, the poem he allegedly brought to Paris in his pocket the first time he met Verlaine. Still considered by some to be his finest poem in verse, '*Le Bateau ivre*'. 'The Drunken Boat', is certainly one of his most important works. Without doubt, this would be the first poem that Verlaine wrote under

Rimbaud's name, and it certainly shows a staggering improvement on the poems that the Charleville Rimbaud had written. This is truly the first work of a major poet. There are, I believe, a number of clues dotted around the text, the most significant is the great word game that Verlaine plays in the opening line. Remember that this is the very first line of the first poem written by the hoax Rimbaud. This only becomes apparent when the poem is read out loud. The poem opens with the great declaration:

Comme je descendais . . .

As I went down or was going down. Written down the meaning is clear but read aloud this line effortlessly transforms itself into:

Comme jeux de santé . . .

Like games of health, literally 'LIKE HEALTHY GAMES'. This is how he announces himself. It's like an opening fanfare. *Comme jeux de santé.* His intention is crystal clear. There is no harm intended in the deception. These are only games, entertainments, merely a series of exercises. Something that will be good for him, *comme jeux de santé,* one that might bring about a literal and indeed literary rejuvenation.'

They're booing now, well, he could have expected that. Being greeted with a respectful silence was the last thing he wanted. Critics adore controversy. Given the choice between reputation and controversy

or respect and controversy

or prestige and controversy

he would *always* choose controversy. It was no contest. But they are shouting now and throwing things, plastic cups and cans. The girl glances behind her and starts to look a little worried. She gathers up her papers. People are standing up and some are now starting to walk towards him.

He is talking about the hugely dubious printing history of the first edition of Rimbaud's *Une saison en enfer* and suggesting that the character of La Vierge Folle bears ONLY the hallmarks of Verlaine's dreary and notorious self-loathing, but by then he's running. Not, as so many critics have claimed, a mocking, incisive portrait of an ex-lover but an exercise in the most profound narcissistic self-pity by a mawkish windbag. Suddenly, he's running down red carpeted staircases with the girl just behind him and the roar of the crowd in his ears.

Marble maybe and columns flash past him and he is laughing and shouting at the top of his voice. 'Exiled and banished for heresy and blasphemy and crimes against French literature! You just don't get it, do you? I have got something important to say! Why can't you just listen for once? You idiots! You absolute fucking morons! Don't you see? YOUR Rimbaud would have been proud of me!'

The girl takes his arm as they run down the steps and into the street. He glances back and takes a final look at the Sorbonne or was it L'Académie française? Shouldn't we be standing near a landmark of some description? The Eiffel Tower? Notre-Dame? The Sacré Cœur? It was difficult to know if you'd never been to Paris. It wasn't supposed to be a huge place but how small can it be? He'd always wanted to go but you know how it is. She reckons we wouldn't like the food. And everything is really expensive there. God, what a joke! The French teacher who had never been to France! That was another thing he'd just thought about. How come he was delivering his lecture in English? He'd not actually considered that. That was very stupid. Maybe they have translators working at the Sorbonne like they do at the UN. It was possible. Big important place like that, people from all over the world go there. Why shouldn't his lecture be in English?

And the more he thought about it he concluded that it definitely had to be the Sorbonne, no question about it. It just had to be there. Really. Perhaps it was just the name but it has such a perfect ring to it. Sor-*bonne*. A word so effortlessly and utterly French. Sor-*bonne*. Vin du Pays de Sorbonne . . . Bœuf Sorbonne . . . Renault Sorbonne.

Exhausted, they finally push open the doors to her apartment whereupon he takes Sorbonne in his arms and kisses her gently on her eyelids.

She smiles and lets out a barely audible sigh. '*Un peu de musique, chérie? Est-ce que tu veux entendre encore ta chanson?*'

There follows a quick survey of the collection of LPs carelessly strewn about the floor in one corner of the tiny room. She claps her pretty little hands together in delight as she makes her selection and hands him the sleeve.

It has the sort of picture on the cover that makes you want to weep. To cry with the vague, unspecific longing no person can possibly understand before thirty. It is an image that instantly disconnects you from terrible and painful Nowadays and takes you back somewhere you know to be better and nicer and safer.

His song. That was nice.

She carefully places the needle on the disc. '*Et voilà – seulement pour toi!*'

Crrru crkkk cuurrrkkk crruuuu . . .

He taps his foot to a descending bass line. 'You know, I hate goodbyes, Sorbonne . . .'

Juke-er box, juke-er box . . .

Diagrammatically, the orbit of one man's life might be represented as a circle. Two men's would therefore be drawn as two circles (A, B) When the circumferences of these two circles, regardless of their individual dimensions, intersect they must, by the laws of geometry, do so at two separate points (*x*, *y*). Thus;

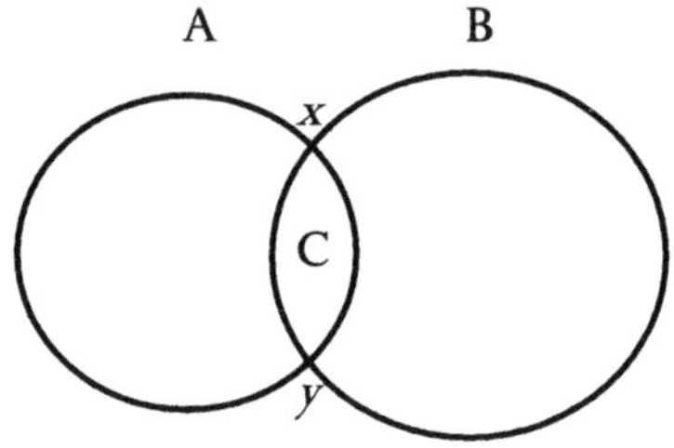

This in turns creates a third figure (C). We could call this third figure an ellipse or an imperfect circle.

A formula which takes into consideration variations in circumference and the points of dissection would thus be able to calculate the precise level or extent of this imperfection.

After waking up slightly disorientated after his doze, Moe Seyton finds the fresh air quite invigorating. Strange dream he had just then – the underlying narrative of which he fails to recall, just a feeling of vague elation and a series of disconnected details. A pyramid . . . music . . . animals, confined but wild, like circus animals, and the odd sensation that he was somehow invisible, like a phantom, observing but unobserved.

No trace of what had been on his mind, no sign of a Mark IV Webley Service Revolver, not the slightest hint of Catherine, nothing of the sort. Very odd.

He performs a quick calculation, takes a few more steps and stops abruptly.

Three hours and thirty-nine min . . . thirty-eight minutes

Not long now.

The time has come.

And he knows exactly what he is going to say.

He approaches slowly so as not to startle him.

'Hello there.'

'Pard . . . ? Oh hi, sorry, I do apologise I was miles away.' Barney Langton smiles and realises what his problem is.

His problem is the same as what it has always been.

His problem is that he is nothing of the sort.

'That's quite all right.'

'I just came out to get some air and I wandered down here to have a look at the sea.'

The line drawn from *x* to *y* is therefore the diameter of the figure C. Its Axis of Imperfection.

'I saw you from up the road there; I was just taking my evening constitutional. I call it my evening constitutional, of course, just to make me sound important but really I find that it's good for the old voice to get some air before a show.'

Barney nods. 'Of course.'

'Also,' says Moe, lighting a cigarette, 'if I'm going to smell of fags I'd like them to be my own. I'm sorry, would you care for one yourself?'

Barney is about to decline, about to declare himself a non-smoker, about to advertise his virtue . . .

But this evening he is starting to wonder about the virtue of virtue.

'Yes please, go on then, why not? Thank you. As long as you're sure you don't mind?'

They lean against the low whitewashed wall that runs parallel to Hatfeild Road and stare in silence at the sea together for a few moments. The pair of heads in the postcard peeping over the fence of the nudist colony. *Blimey, they never said anything about a* ***BARBEQUE!!!***

Idly, they watch a wet over-excited dog chasing after a football. Barney glances at his cigarette and wonders by what polite conversational means he might raise the subject of the noise coming from Moe's room earlier. He ruminates on various possible lines of enquiry but each seems as though he is making some sort of complaint. Or worse, was embarking upon some disingenuous preamble to a complaint.

Moe finally turns to Barney and smiles. 'So where's the young fellow now then? That young Andy.'

'He's in bed. Worn out by it all, I expect.'

'He's a good lad.'

'Yeah, I suppose he is. He wears me out and he can be a pain sometimes, especially when he's on holiday! Six is a very difficult age! They don't warn you about that. But he's got a good heart in there.'

'I thought he was a charming little chap.'

'Thank you and you made quite an impression him too. Yeah, he was talking about you non-stop earlier. I think it's difficult for him. He can't seem to understand that grown-ups might laugh at different things to children.'

Moe takes a long considerate drag on his Gold Leaf.

History will always require a witness.

He begins.

'Well, to be fair to him, in some respects, you could say that he's actually quite correct in that. It's quite true. Oh, the situations change, of course, the context is different but what we find humorous is actually fairly universal. Whether it's clowns or smutty jokes, there is always that same sense of subversion. That what we recognise and understand is being distorted in some way. How much we recognise and understand obviously changes with age but the underlying *method,* if you will, remains the same.'

Barney considers this whilst successfully managing to suppress a cough. 'I've never really thought that much about it,' he says in all truthfulness. 'But I imagine that there must be as much theory to it as there is to, say . . . music.'

Moe smiles at this. 'Yes, I think that's a very fair comparison. Very fair. So much is about nuance and timing and those aspects that are felt rather than learned. And I should know. Great comedy is, according to some, very much like a great musical performance. It's very hard to pin down, very hard to accurately describe. We can't explain why this particular Chaplin gag works so well or why this phrase from Mozart or whoever is so moving. It remains just that little bit beyond our comprehension, at the very limits of our understanding. And it's this, I suppose, that leads the uninitiated into the realms of metaphysics, investing a great performance with a mysterious or even a *magical* quality.'

'I've never thought of it like that,' says Barney as he turns away to surreptitiously dispose of his Gold Leaf.

'I've never been able to judge what people will laugh at. Forty years in the trade and I still don't know. Sometimes I have got it right and other times I have been so far off the mark.' Moe shrugs. 'Maybe if I'd had it all figured out I wouldn't be here now talking to you.'

'But do you watch TV regularly? I have to monitor what Andy sits in front of. It's terrible. People laugh at the most unbelievable rubbish.'

'I'm sure.'

'And their taste in music is not much better.'

'I've no doubt you're right. But to get back to your earlier point, I actually got into comedy through music. So I have always appreciated the connection. That's what I wanted to do originally. It just didn't happen that way. Instead I became a Purveyor of Madcap Merriment, as it used to say on the bills . . . NOBBY NEWTON – "the Naughtiest Mouth in the South, Mister Laughs Galore . . ."

Moe's voice trails off into a brief moment of reflection and Barney glimpses in the older man's eyes only a fleeting hint of sadness for Moe Seyton is not a man who ever fell victim to frustration, anger or bitterness.

'Mister Laughs Galore! That was me. What a terrible title

to be saddled with! But I was still doing music even if Nobby Newton did shortly after become known as a Composer and Performer of Risqué and Ribald Songs.'

'There's no disgrace in that, is there? I mean, Shakespeare composed a few himself.'

'True enough, my young friend. But, as far as I'm aware, the great Bard managed to have a fairly illustrious career without feeling the necessity to compose "I Can't Quite Put My Finger on It".'

'Oh dear, well, it's his loss I'm sure.'

'I must have written well over a hundred in my time, I've thankfully forgotten most of them. I recorded a dozen or so sides back in the forties and a couple of them did rather well. But you know what they say. Second only to its treatment of women, time is *most* unkind to comedy. As far as comic songs are concerned, it shows no mercy whatsoever.'

Moe Seyton looks at his watch.

Three hours and thirty-one minutes.

'And now I'm The Last of the Great Front-Cloth Comics. Or I'm supposed to be, at least until eleven o'clock tonight.'

'Are you?'

'Frankly, I haven't the faintest idea. But I will tell you a true story. You know, it wasn't just the idea of money or fame back then, it wasn't like I was yearning after the promise of travel or popularity particularly. If I'm honest, that never really interested me all that much. It was nothing like that. It might sound crass but I just loved the idea of being able to make people laugh. Simple as that! Don't get me wrong – not for their benefit, don't be ridiculous, just for mine! You see, for me, comedy always seemed like some fabulous great *power*. You used to hear people saying that it was a gift to be able to make people laugh. That might be true but I couldn't see it like that. It was just this magnificent *power* some people had. To make someone laugh, just like that, a stranger, to make them convulse with laughter, make them weak from laughing – that's a terribly powerful sensation, I'm telling you. I wasn't as good as some, I'm well aware of that, but I had a few good years and there's nothing like it, I promise you. You go out there in front of hundreds of people, sometimes they're rude, sometimes they can be downright hostile but as soon as they laugh you feel absolutely in control of the situation. Through their laughter they are exposed and vulnerable, it is like you have been able to find their weaknesses whilst not revealing your own. They are helpless before you. Suddenly they need you. Then you feel that rush of power and you have to keep it at the same level, so you're like a prizefighter bouncing on your toes, jabbing away, again and again, bam, bam . . . you've found a spot – you keep on it. No respite. That, for me, has always been the thrill of comedy. It's being able to do that, night after night after night. To see a pretty young girl, to see her with tears in her eyes and helpless with laughter, well, it's the nearest thing to an unwitting consent that I could ever imagine. When you're a comedian, you have the power to do this. It is an amazing feeling. I don't expect you can imagine what it's like. But it's fantastic. It didn't matter about the money. If I could have got up there every night I would have done it for nothing if I had been able to. Just to stand up there. Well, that's what it used to be like, of course it's all changed now. They don't laugh like that anymore. Not at what I do anyway. You see radio was our medium, we could adapt to it, it was a logical extension but when television arrived it changed everything. We were comics not actors, I couldn't act, none of us could! So the stage was all we had left. Not that we've got that anymore either! I know it might make me sound old and silly but that's why I've been coming back year after year. It's not the money, it never was, it's just that thrill I very occasionally experienced, just a moment maybe once in an evening, just a fleeting spark that just somehow reminded me of what that *power* had once been like. That's what used to keep me going. You know, there has never been anything like it . . . it was better than booze, fags . . . and even sex.'

Silence.

Broken only by the rhythmic sound he makes by clicking his tongue against the roof of his mouth, Barney digests what he has just heard and considers a reply.

Clack Clack Clack Clack.

'So, do you still miss the old days?' he asks after due consideration.

'Sometimes I do. I suppose I must do. I miss the bigger crowds, the bigger venues certainly. But I went my own way, I may have made some very poor decisions along the way, I would be the first to admit it but I don't regret anything. What would be the point now? I did what I felt I had to do. It is as simple as that. I was true to my craft and I do apologise if that sounds terribly pretentious but it meant something in those days. A long, long time ago it meant something. I was doing what I felt I had to do and nobody, agents, managers, bookers, nobody was going to tell me any different. I wouldn't take the easy path and for better or worse I stuck to my guns. Of course there's a downside to that. As your audiences dwindle, you naturally doubt your ability and you start to wonder about this famous craft of yours. But I know one thing for sure, my friend, when I was good I was bloody good.'

'The power?'

'Definitely. Sometimes it's a gamble, you might be trying something completely new, not just relying on all the old safe tried and tested material, all the old songs, then it's a bit of a risk, if that comes off then it's even more of a thrill. Of course sometimes it doesn't come off, then it's agony. The dark pit opens up in front of you! And there is no tragedy so great, no man so impotent as the unfunny clown. And by taking risks with your material you always come up against that possibility. Mind you, when I played the Alhambra in '47 I was playing it terribly safe, or so I thought, and that was my greatest disaster *ever*, my personal Wall Street Crash. Of course, one may take the moral from that as being that there is great virtue in staying true to your craft.'

'What sort of risks exactly?'

'My friend Sam, with whom I spent the afternoon, seems convinced I was some ancient punk rocker, some impossibly dangerous rebel comedian, just trying to shock people, pushing at the boundaries of acceptable taste, years ahead of my time, but really that's just him being dramatic I think. Nowadays all I hear is Max this, Max that and the chap's been dead for fifteen years! It is amazing that you can still buy all his stuff on LPs! One of these days they'll put a statue up in the middle of Brighton in his honour! I didn't even mind him pinching bits of my act because I really believed that I was better. Or that he was just tame by comparison. Perhaps I should be flattered but I was just trying to make the people laugh. I really thought that my sort of material was funny, I found it funny, but like I said I wasn't always the best judge of what people laugh at. Some people found it funny but a lot of people would complain that I was, in the lingo of the time, *too near the knuckle*. Chuck in the odd word, which is, after all, the common argot of your audience and you are suddenly the devil himself! Public enemy number one. They wanted risqué – I was just plain risky. You might have imagined it would have endeared one to one's audience, speaking in their vernacular and about the central preoccupations of their lives! Sex and what have you. But no, it defies common sense but people just wanted innuendo, suggestion, implication. I was always just far too obvious! I never understood that but if you want rational in your life, steer well clear of comedy! But I was good once, even if I say so myself. So, the choice was clean up the act, go a bit cheeky and a bit spicy or shuffle back and forth between private clubs, with no management, too poor to afford a band, unable to do any songs, just slotted in between strippers. Well, the money got less and less and the strippers got older and older. It was getting harder and harder to get work and so Nobby "retired" in the sixties and I started working under different names but the momentum had gone and it was never the same.'

'That's really sad.'

'In a way, but I had brought it on myself. Nobby was Nobby and he was never going to make it as some terrible third-rate Max Miller. I just couldn't do that to myself. I probably thought I was just being noble – thinking like an artist and not a businessman! Fatal in this game! But times have changed, the business is totally different now – God, it's beyond unrecognisable! Adult comedians, blue comedians are everywhere and I'm just another old fart with a microphone. They all have their histories and their tragedies and I have mine.'

'It doesn't sound very glamorous.'

'It's the least glamorous thing on the planet and then finally one morning you wake up and you realise the power has long gone, the thrill is no more and that basically the love of it has gone utterly and completely. A Bank Holiday turn in Margate once a year just for old time's sake, or so I tell myself, but it's shallow compensation. Listen carefully, can you hear that? The melody transposes itself over the bridge, there's a tricky passage in double time and suddenly you find yourself stuck forever in some mournful minor key.'

Barney looks at Moe but says nothing.

They turn and begin to make their way back towards the Seaview.

'B♭ minor, F minor, back to B♭ minor, on and on like

that. You see, is it actually better for a man to produce or create something that is mediocre or worthless or just second rate, or would it be better for him to just produce a nice round nothing at all? Personally, I have no idea but I intend to find out very soon! Oh, I've been through similar periods in the past but this time I know I am serious, I'm finished with it. Completely. I have been thinking about it for a long, long time but my mind is made up. It's over. I've finally had enough. When I finish here tonight, that will be it for me. I'm not coming back next year. Not here not anywhere. I just can't face it any more. It's time to put it all away. When I get off stage later I will be officially retired! An ex-comedian.'

Barney can think of nothing to say in response to this.

'Sadly, I don't have the sort of profile anymore where one can make announcements about this sort of thing. There's no agent, manager or press office anymore. It's just me. But I've told you now and that dog over there so it's like making a public announcement, isn't it? I hope you don't mind. I have been rather rambling I realise. But I've been planning this for months and I knew when I came down here that this was going to be the last time. I've thought about it for so long.'

'How does it feel?'

Moe grins. 'Actually it feels OK.' This being a fairly accurate, if a little over-simplified, summary of his resulting emotions.

Barney smiles back. 'Well, as long as you're happy with your decision.'

'It just feels right, I know I'm doing the right thing. Anyway, thank you for listening to me but I just need to ask you one small further favour.'

Barney looks surprised. 'Yeah, sure. Please ask away.'

'If you can get away for an hour or so later, I'd be very grateful if you could come to the Oddfellows Club and

Lodge tonight and catch my show. Well, my final show. Do you think that might be at all possible? It starts at ten o'clock. Er . . . gentlemen only, I'm afraid.'

Barney shrugs his shoulders. 'Yeah, I don't imagine that will be a problem.'

'Oh good. You see, my young friend, it's important that you're there. As they always used to say HISTORY REQUIRES A WITNESS.'

'It does?'

'Yes, I think I'm going to make tonight's show a bit special, as it's my last one. I've been mulling it over for a while and I think I'd like to end on a high note, maybe do something a little bit, shall we say, *different.* I'd like you there to see it. Don't look so worried. Just think Camelot.'

'Think what?'

'Camelot.'

Barney frowns. 'The place or the film?'

'The film.'

'OK?'

'That bit right at the end when King Arthur is about to go into battle knowing that he will be killed and the whole thing is hopeless. He is tormented by the thought that all they ever tried to do, all their great work will be completely forgotten. It was all therefore for nothing. Then right at the very end, he meets a boy who promises that he will record and retell all their great victories and then King Arthur goes off happily to get slaughtered.'

'Sir Thomas Malory.'

'I'm sorry?'

'The boy is Sir Thomas Malory. He's an allegory. He wasn't even born for five hundred years.'

'Well, I'm sure the principle still probably applies!'

'OK, well I'll aim to be there just as the slaughter starts then.'

'Good man. Ten o'clock sharp then.'

They stand on the kerb on the opposite side of the road from the Seaview for a few moments and wait for a break in the traffic. After a few moments a carmine-red 1972 Triumph Stag with saddle tan interior slows to a halt and the driver gestures for Moe and Barney to cross the road.

Three hours and thirteen minutes.

Meanwhile, the *x–y* axis of imperfection in this case has now been established.

'Now, there's this husband and wife . . .'

The driver of the 1972 carmine-red Triumph Stag with the saddle tan interior is a man named Malcolm Hammond. Mr Hammond is not a happy man, in fact by general consensus of his friends and relatives, he is judged to be having a Few Problems at the Minute. These problems to which they allude are diverse and varied and need not concern us at present. He is, however, at this precise moment concentrating exclusively on his weight problem. As he stops his car at the traffic lights in front of the clock tower, he glances again in the rear-view mirror, and again and again, he can't stop himself, he moves his chin to the left, then fractionally to the right, the left, he pouts, tilts his head, nothing looked all that different, his face didn't seem any fatter but really he wasn't the person to judge, was he? I mean it's difficult when it's your own face and you have to see it every day. It's just too familiar. Besides his increasing waistline was beyond all doubt. A man's trousers don't lie!

Malcolm Hammond has not eaten anything all day and a vague suggestion of a headache now hovers at his temples. He should be walking more too, taking more exercise every day not just when he felt like it. He should be walking now. He shouldn't really be driving, not for short trips like this.

But be fair, who's going to look at a bloke if he's walking? Come on, you need a set of wheels for the ladies, that's obvious. And you never know, do you? Never know when the opportunity will present itself.

Then again who is going to look at a fat bloke wearing jogging trousers? The pair that he had to buy on Saturday because he couldn't get his gut into his Wrangler's anymore!

He'd been on a fairly strict diet for a couple of weeks but it didn't seem to be making an awful lot of difference. None at all in fact. Actually, it was starting to make him feel really frustrated and annoyed, he couldn't help it. He's been tense and agitated and it was all just getting on top of him. It made him, yeah, angry. Jumpy. It was like that business with that stupid girl last night. He knew he was in the right, he'd heard exactly what she said, oh yeah, she said he was *making a mistake* or that he'd *misheard* her, all the bloody excuses, it was under her breath but he'd heard well enough, always had good hearing, you shouldn't go around making personal comments like that, after all, he was only trying to be friendly and she had no right to make personal comments. It was bloody rude and who did the little tart think she was anyway making personal comments? Whatever you say, she needed to be taught a few manners . . .

Maybe you could still get those diet pills from the doctor like his mum had all those years ago. Or are they banned nowadays? They were very good she said. They might help, just give him a bit of a head start. That's all it would need. It had never been a problem before, maybe it was his age, but thirty-one didn't strike him somehow as being a medically significant age. It was hardly middle-aged, was it? He used to be so bloody skinny too. Years ago, that was. In school they used to call him Petit Mal because of his size and the fact that there was another much taller boy in his class who was also called Malcolm.

Penny wasn't exactly being a great help was she? Vanity, she says, it's all vanity, like it's all just so amusing to her.

Like she found him simply comical and ridiculous. He'd tried to talk to her about changing his diet and buying different foods but she hadn't shown even the slightest interest. Vanity, it's all vanity.

That was the funny thing. Maybe he was noticing her a little more than usual because of his own current problem but she was really looking good at the moment. If anything she actually seemed to have lost a few pounds recently and how sickening was that.

Vanity, it's all vanity.

. . . yeah, she did, she looked great the other day, really fantastic, she'd been sunbathing out the back, those couple of hot days we had last week, and she was in the kitchen just wearing her bikini (it was a new white or light-coloured one) she must have bought it recently, and it made her skin look really brown and God, the things that go through your mind, they know as well, that's why they do it, they drive us to think such thoughts, I don't think we can be held entirely responsible, can we? (not entirely) we couldn't do it on our own, we always get the blame but they're the predators, not us, they always look so unaware, so innocent but they're very aware, they're always aware, like that bloody girl last night, she knew exactly what she was doing, acting all innocent and scared but she knew what was going on (oh yeah, she knew all right) but that day she was in her bikini, she was just making a cup of tea or something when I walked in but she knew exactly what she was doing, she knew what I was thinking, and I was just looking at her, I couldn't help it, I was just taking it all in, and it was like ten years ago and I'd just seen her for the first time, she had hair up and I kept looking at her neck (I remembered things from way back), stuff I didn't actually want to think about, I was totally overwhelmed and that stuff can make you think funny things . . .

The traffic lights change to green at the precise moment Barney Langton pushes open the door of room 203. He is greeted by a pair of near simultaneous hand gestures. With exaggerated solicitude, a single finger-to-mouth motion craves his silence while somewhat gracelessly the other hand draws to his attention the figure currently sleeping on the single divan.

Their wordless pantomime at a conclusion, Barney sits himself gingerly on the edge of the chair by the dressing table and looks at his hands. In here it was different. No beginnings anymore, no endings either, no overtures, no finales, just the hollow echoing eternity of the moment.

He glances at his reflection for a second and then hastily turns away. Nowadays, he looked older in the evenings, there was no reason for this of course but there was a distinct life-scarred weariness to his features that he fancied he only noticed at this time of the day. Beyond attributing it vaguely to tiredness, he had little or no wish to delve any further into this anomaly. He checks again. Look, there he is! Mister Ancient and Defeated. Christ! What *happened*?

In the musty musky semi-darkness, he now looks back towards her.

She is turning the pages of her magazine and he can see the outline of her breasts rising and falling fractionally under her lightweight dressing gown as she does so.

He should look away.

Rising and falling.

. . . there too for a moment in the folds of the gown is the raised suggestion of a nipple, oh, this is not good, and again, oh, how I have come to dread this desire, I loathe the way it occupies and overwhelms a person, it gives you such a complete advantage over me, I feel so helpless and subservient, and by the way, it's hard to be happy about the fact that nowadays whatever pornographic image inspires a fantasy it has all too frequently reverted back to a recollection of you by its conclusion, that was deeply depressing (like announcing one's paucity of imagination, declining an offer of one of the last remaining liberties) and again, oh God, I could at least feel on an equal footing if I thought you were doing all this deliberately, that would allow us at the very least a sense of common

purpose, actually, that might be quite erotic, but no, you have always been an inadvertent temptress, haven't you? (the accidental seductress) . . .

Beyond the old bathing pool, at the eastern tip of the esplanade, a Triumph Stag pulls to a halt in Palm Bay Avenue at what is imagined to be a discreet distance from three police vehicles that are already parked there. Malcolm Hammond leaves the engine running and observes the activity. Three . . . four . . . uniform, maybe one plainclothes unless he's press of course. Whatever the count it was hardly the frenzied activity he was expecting and he actually found it all a little depressing. It made it all seem insignificant somehow, like it wasn't worth the effort. Not on a Bank Holiday when everyone had better things to do.

Maybe she's been sunbathing again.

. . . sometimes I ask you to repeat yourself, you hate that, don't you? you ask me if I need a hearing test, but I hear perfectly well, I just like watching your mouth move when you're talking, I can't help it, I still find it really exciting (it doesn't matter what you're saying) you can be nagging or complaining or accusing, its just that mouth, it gets me every time, all I can think about is how soon can I connect with it, pardon, could you repeat that, I'm sorry . . .

He adjusts his sitting position and straightens his back.

. . . some women just seem to have this gift, this incredible talent that's not put-on or phoney (or enhanced by things bought from magazines or mail-order catalogues), it's just a pure, natural gift I suppose, they just exude this promise, this suggestion all the time and it's in everything they do (although they don't have to actually do anything) it's something they are and it's just there all the time, almost as though they couldn't prevent it even if they wanted to, it will always be revealed somehow and in time everything else just becomes secondary (it's biology probably), but to live with it day in and day out over the years it just becomes overpowering, you get a little intimidated by it, what makes you feel most like a man can also in some ways make you feel the complete opposite in your own

eyes, you're weak and totally helpless (vulnerable I suppose) and you just can't compete with stuff like that . . .

Suddenly he starts to feel a slight constriction in his chest. The atmosphere in there feels airless and confined and he wants to open the window.

. . . this is not a good time to be a man, not any more, there's so much we have to think about nowadays, so much has changed in the past decade or so, we are probably unrecognisable to our grandfathers, did they ever worry about their proficiency as a lover? (worry if they gave a woman satisfaction every time?) which if we're all honest has nothing to do with the woman in question and everything to do with good old-fashioned masculine pride, actually that's one thing that's remained fairly constant (it's just modified itself a little), it now hides itself quite successfully behind our new identity with all our awareness and sensitivity, did you have an orgasm? – good and was I great? (of course I was, I'm a sexual bloody miracle), but then again it's just something else for us to worry about, isn't it? more doubt, more anxiety, are you sure? because I know that sometimes women just pretend, how do I know that, because I read it in one of your stupid magazines and nowadays I want to ask you every single time we do it just to make sure but I don't say anything (I'm too scared to) then I want to ask you if you thought you were with another bloke while we were doing it, but I don't know how I could ask a question like that (out of the blue) and so I keep quiet and sometimes I wonder if it is the same now for you as it was in the beginning (but let's be fair here that's not an easy one to ask either), and then there's the boys you say you can't remember any more, is that true or were they all fantastic and handsome and all had huge cocks and you just don't want to tell me? (do you still think about them?), were you thinking about them the last time and you can't imagine, no, you really could never imagine, how much I want to know the answer (but you know I would never be able to just ask you a question like that) and have you ever wondered what it would be like to be with another woman? sometimes it tears me up inside but I just can't

say anything to you, not about things like that, to voice an anxiety honestly and candidly, you must understand, is so difficult, it's the exposure I couldn't stand (that vulnerability) also I would just sound like a whining child, which brings us back to this man thing again, sometimes it all gets difficult for me . . .

He puts a hand to his temple and feels the throb-BING pul-SING vein with the tips of his fingers.

. . . that's another thing, you must realise that when I mentioned all those things that day, it wasn't because I'm deranged or perverted, (don't be silly, you mustn't think like that) the honest truth is that I just thought it might be fun for both of us to try something different, I mean it's been a few years now and things get into a kind of routine and I thought it might liven things up a bit, OK on reflection I can see that it was a huge mistake but you didn't have to make me feel so low and so dirty, did you? you might laugh at this but I had thought it was something we could do together (it could be like an adventure for us), give us something else to talk about so that we wouldn't ALWAYS have to talk about that other stuff (that's all it was), it was probably not the best time and I probably phrased it the wrong way but there was no need to react the way you did, anyway, it's not all that disgusting nowadays and you often read about it (I think you'd actually be surprised just how many couples do it), besides, it doesn't hurt to try these things once in a while, you don't know what you're missing, I don't know why but I thought it would give us a sort of connection again (we could share secrets together), have an aspect to our life that was exclusively ours and completely private, maybe it would open the door onto something new and exciting for us, I can't bear to think that it's all behind me now (that the only excitement I will ever know in my life has already passed), but no, no, I had a filthy mind and I wasn't to go near you or touch you, I was to keep away from you, me and my disgusting desires and you lock the bedroom door (and I have felt so locked out of your life for such a long time) so I sleep on the sofa again and again and on and on it went until it all becomes blurred and confusing (and

while we're on the subject, are you the victim here or am I?) do we at some point share the responsibility for what happens afterwards, at what point do action and reaction separate? I mean, what did you think I was going to do? come on, you can't just ignore that sort of stuff, it gets to you, yes, part of this is about you (and you must surely know that), you have to see that everything is connected (yes, everything), you just can't avoid that or step outside that, even the tiniest things we do have implications somewhere, it all affects someone or something (sooner or later), so did you really think I could just take something like that and just go on with my life as if nothing had happened . . .

Barney feels uncomfortable now, his hands are shaking and he knows that he will have to move in a moment, in a moment, in a moment.

. . . I don't think anyone would say I was a bad person, not out and out bad, all my life I have always tried to do something approaching the right thing (or the right thing as I see it) but I have failings (I know I do), I have weaknesses, I can try and be honest about them but it's not easy, I have a conscience but conscience can be an indulgence at times (a confession in certain cases benefits only the confessor) and besides conscience thrives far better in a vacuum, under laboratory conditions, and it's not always easy for it to find its place out here in the great scheme of things, besides, if you think about it, it's a social and moral issue and is therefore flexible (and consequently individual and I am therefore exercising my prerogative), but all of this is just my way of fighting back, my way of trying to make sense of things, that's all, you made your response to it and I made mine, they're not the same but the principle remains common, we're just trying to get through it all and that's all we can do, but nothing is solely responsible, nothing is ever solely responsible for anything, it doesn't work like that, our lives are just this seemingly infinite sequence of chaotic unrelated tiny sub-atomic events, instant and fleeting (like the beating of a bird's wing, a bee sting or a heartbeat), after which the who we are and the what we are changes for ever, whether we

acknowledge this or recognise this at the time, everything turns on that moment, you can't avoid this, everything is partially responsible for everything else, all that is the case, trace a line back and back and so much is based on an initial random spark of chance and nothing else, OK, I am partially to blame, I am partially responsible but I'm only part of long vast infinite chain that shares responsibility and I'm sorry to point it out, my darling, but you're part of that chain too . . .

The figure lost in thought sitting in the driving seat of the stationary Triumph is finally noticed by one of the uniformed officers standing on the opposite side of the road.

. . . sometimes you misunderstand me, you see me only as what it suits you to see, only as what you imagine me to be, but sometimes you get me all wrong, it's like you just don't know me at all any more, it's not just about the sex, it's about that contact we have and that closeness that comes with it, that's all I really want sometimes (it's not just about tits and cocks), it's just the only time I feel that we're completely together, when I really feel like I am yours and you want me, nowadays it's all we have and now I'm denied even that, you don't want me anywhere near you, so if I am to be refused all contact with you, what happens to me? what am I supposed to do? all I wanted was to feel like a man again (to feel some connection somewhere) I wanted to talk but it just came out wrong, but you wouldn't listen, you kept walking away, I was just trying to explain things to you and I needed you to listen to me, you kept turning your back to me, yeah I lost my temper but I was just trying to take control of the situation (any situation) and of course I regret it, sometimes I think I regret everything I have ever done in my entire stupid life . . .

The young uniformed constable now approaches the car with careful big-booted-movealongnowsir footsteps and tries to attract the attention of the driver. Malcolm Hammond glances at him and instinctively revs the engine a few times. The Triumph takes off and within seconds it has accelerated over the brow of the hill and is heading towards Cliftonville.

The car's progress is vigilantly observed by young Constable Steven Parkwood, who also takes a moment to make a careful note of the registration number.

Two hours and forty minutes.

Not long now.

Not long at all.

Moe Seyton sits on the corner of his bed and counts out six five-pound notes. He then places these in a neat pile on the bedside cabinet. He feels particularly calm at this moment. After finally securing his witness a little while ago, he began to feel, as they used to say, a little more at ease with himself. It had all gone terribly well, far better than he would have dared to dream, and now there was to be no turning back. Mr Langton seemed quite happy to go along with the idea and had required nothing in the way of even the slightest persuasion; perhaps he is just grateful for the chance to get out for the evening.

Moe allows himself the slightest smile and wordlessly congratulates himself on his good fortune.

It was a blessing, wasn't it? Although uncomfortable with the term, he can think of no other expression that better captured the sensation. On reflection it was probably for the best that Sam was unavailable and had to cancel, which forced Moe to seek out his contingency witness. Sam's approach would have been obviously journalistic, too immediate, too superficial. Instant. Sensational. He was perhaps a little under-qualified to do justice to the complexities of the situation. And there had been far too many distortions, too many half-truths in the past. In all honesty, his whole career was once based on rumour and supposition. And very little else. Now the truth might be its final absolution.

An article would be fleeting, transitory, IT WOULD NEVER GROW IN THE TELLING, it would simply fade and be forgotten.

And what would it take to have the story buried somewhere on page 16, where it would never be seen by anyone other than the select minority of readers who entertained themselves by browsing planning applications? That was always a risk. Another bad storm? It wouldn't take much.

In fact it wouldn't take much more than a local murder, would it?

Mr Langton will appreciate the grand sweep and significance of this evening, far more than Sam. The younger man was certainly a smart enough chap, a teacher, a bit of a thinker, God, maybe he's even a bit of an academic on the quiet. Yes, it all makes sense now, even the very nature of their first fated meeting in Marine Gardens!

He would be sure to fully grasp the situation and all its complexities. After all, he had already given him plenty of background information.

Furthermore, it stands to reason that a witness must record what he witnesses, otherwise he has no business being a witness. It's obvious if you think about it. He must observe and record – simple, that is what is expected of a witness. Mr Langton will understand that. Therefore he must have the means and the method to record that which he has observed.

And of this task he will be, without any doubt or question, infinitely capable.

Like Thomas Malory?

Well, a bit like Thomas Malory.

Something far grander and lasting than an article!

Not a biography, no, that would be too dreary for words and there are far too many already. Besides a Has Been is infinitely more bankable than a Never Was. Something else? He could perhaps use it all as a basis for a play for the radio or maybe even a story, a novel based on just the events of today. That would certainly be a job for him, if he was up to it.

'What thou seest – write in a book.'

Revelations, Mr Langton. Good old Revelations!

Moe sighs and stares into endless infinite magnolia.

Morte de Moe?

I don't think so.

Eeny Meeny Miney Moe?

He winces and experiences something that might have been distantly related to indigestion.

Oh dear! That was too terrible to even contemplate, although he recalls with a certain shame that this was in fact the title of a tiny article about him that appeared in *Variety Pages* in 1969. Interestingly, the article made no mention whatsoever of Nobby, yet it remained (had he troubled himself to consider) his most recent press notice. Certainly on a national level.

Or Dreamland, he could call it Dreamland. Add a bit of local colour?

Maybe not.

Then suddenly Moe grins and nods emphatically to himself.

Aaaaaah yes indeed, now you're talking! That's the one!

EVERY OTHER INCH A GENTLEMAN.

That would do him!

Walpole said that once years ago allegedly in reference to the novelist Michael Arlen and the term had always had a particular resonance. In fact, he has always longed for the opportunity that he might claim it as his own! Indeed, for as long as he could remember, he has been rather hoping that the term would even serve as his obituary. A simple four-line announcement in the local paper or in reasonably modest inch-high letters on a once-polished marble tombstone.

Somewhere.

Forgotten.

Overgrown.

But that could be the title, couldn't it? He can picture it in his mind now.

Perfect.

There was even a time, a long time ago, when he'd actually pestered Kaiser Sullivan to bill him as 'Nobby Newton – Every Other Inch A Gentleman'. Sadly to no avail. Kaiser was absolutely convinced that they would drag the Lord Chancellor back from his holidays if he tried anything like that! It was too obvious, too direct, Kaiser said and he absolutely insisted they stayed with 'The Naughtiest Mouth in the South'.

Maybe he was right then but times change.

EVERY OTHER INCH A GENTLEMAN.

Yes, he liked that.

He could live with that.

Smiling to himself, devious, diabolic and eternal, he picks up the thirty pounds from the bedside cabinet and skips lightly out of his room and down the stairs.

Two hours and thirty-one minutes.

On the ground floor he makes his way into the dining room and finds her sitting alone in the corner smoking and reading the *TV Times*. The room is otherwise completely deserted.

'Evening, Mrs B.' he says cheerfully.

Startled, Dorothy Burton looks up. 'Oh Mr Seyton, I am sorry, I am SO sorry but we're not serving an evening meal tonight what with it being a Bank Holiday and everything. Did you not see it on the board? Someone should have told you.' She stubs out her cigarette and narrows her mouth pensively. Then she manoeuvres herself into the moment that she senses is passing between them. 'I could make you a little sandwich or something if you like, there's some cold ham and cheese left over, I'm sure I could manage something . . .'

Moe shakes his head. 'No, honestly, it's fine, really, don't put yourself to any trouble, I had a big lunch and I expect I'll pick something up at the Oddfellows later.'

'But it wouldn't be the slightest trouble, I was going to make myself a little something actually, besides you look as though you could do with feeding up a bit nowadays.' She waves her finger in the direction of his abdomen with self-conscious familiarity rather than strict anatomical accuracy. 'You've been looking a little on the thin side lately, I fancy.'

Moe instinctively takes a slight cautious step backwards. 'I don't think so but maybe you're right. I'll tell you what, I'll buy some chips on the way to the club.'

Dorothy Burton manages a brave smile as another petal falls from another flower and floats downwards and downward into the darkness and then disappears for ever.

'Well, just as long as you know that the offer is there, Mr Seyton.'

Moe now places the pile of five-pound notes on the table in front of her. 'Actually, the reason I came by was that I wanted to drop this off with you.'

'Oh did you want it putting in the safe, did you, Mr Seyton?'

'No, no. I just thought I'd settle up with you now.'

'You don't have to do that now . . .'

'Well, I'm not sure, well, that is to say, I actually have no idea. I'm just . . . Put it this way I don't know when I'll be err . . . checking out.' He winces. 'Er . . . I may be leaving very early in the morning tomorrow so I thought I'd pop in now and settle up with you. If that's OK with you?'

'That's fine, I'll make you up a bill and get your change for you.'

She gets up and without looking at him she makes her way back towards the front desk.

Moe calls after her. 'Oh please keep the change, what little there is. You know you've always been a great help to me over the years, haven't you?'

She doesn't hear him.

Two hours and twenty-two minutes.

Still kneeling, Mrs Hughes opens her eyes.

Amen.

She has just prayed for her son (not that he deserves it) and her grandchildren (selfish little monsters). She has prayed for her sister (far too busy with her own family now), her friends who are still living (when they can be bothered of course), and she has remembered those whose lives touched hers and who have since passed on (God rest them).

Uncharacteristically humble in her prayers, Mrs Hughes has developed the slightly curious habit over many years of referring to herself in the third person throughout. As though the act of asking for things directly might be considered inappropriate. Stiff in the language of an official invitation, her devotions have a distinctly formal tone, *Mrs Catherine Elizabeth Hughes would like . . . Your servant Catherine Hughes humbly asks.*

As is her long-established custom, she has thought about her parents and then for a moment as she concludes her prayers she recalls the long-gone husband, the father of her son. The image has been distorted over the years, his face now, in her memory, a cartoon facsimile of the original, no more than shapes and shadows, lacking detail, better that way maybe. She can no longer recall the warmth or the desire it once inspired. She has learnt to forget the sensation of breathlessness it once aroused and she can no longer remember ever saying that her heart was beating like a wild thing. Like something glimpsed in a hearth fire, it glows for a second and then fades.

He is best forgotten.

She reaches up for the small item resting in the saucer on top of the dressing table. Perhaps not worthy of her prayers exactly but possibly deserving of a little gratitude is a gentleman named Leo H. Sternbach. If it wasn't for his timely invention, it is doubtful Mrs Hughes would ever have a good night's sleep.

Tonight, like every night, Mrs Hughes salutes his endeavours and achievements with a 5mg Mogadon capsule.

Now, steadying herself on the dressing table chair, she slowly rises to her feet. Alternating Ows and Ahs she counts her thoracic vertebrae in strict rhythmic succession.

Ow Ah Ow Ah

Ow Ah Ow Ah

Ow Ah

Ow

Ah

Vertical.

She exhales deeply and pushes open her window another couple of inches.

Then him again, never for more than a split second but always at that precise moment. This was another face and this one she could recall with absolute clarity for some reason, like he was sitting in the next room and she'd just left him. The face smiles a lopsided and ironic all-too-knowing smile. She never gave him a second thought at any other time of the day, never, not even for a moment but for some reason always for that fleeting second or two there he was! It was daft, stupid really but many years ago, she had been fairly intimate with a young man of a fairly atheistic turn of mind. He always used to ask her if she said a prayer to the person who invented prayers. Shouldn't they at least get some credit, he used to say.

Ha ha ha, Mister Cleverclogs! You're such a comedian, aren't you?

She has not seen this man for four decades but later this evening their paths will cross one final time.

It is already dark when Barney Langton leaves the Seaview. There is a chill now in the air that saddens him – bringing with it as it does the clear implication that their summer is now almost over. Just above the sound of his own footsteps, the soft swirling distant sea and the last late homesick homeward holiday makers in their sandy and sulking cars, he hears.

'Good evening, Sir . . .'

Unaccustomed to being addressed in this manner, Barney Langton simply ignores the request. The 'Sir' with which he is more familiar is generally speaking a two-syllable word. It was approximately Sir-*er* and spoken exclusively by young adults in the fourteen to sixteen age group. No adult in his experience had ever called him 'Sir,' and Barney, standing at the bottom of the steps outside the Seaview, turns right and begins to walk away in the direction of the clock tower.

'Just a moment, Sir . . .'

According to Moe's instructions, he still had about an hour before the comedian took the stage at the club and he thought he'd prefer to spend it walking rather than hanging around their hotel room for half an hour and taking the car. Having consulted the map in the entrance hall of the Seaview, he had concluded that it wasn't that far and he might get the chance to enjoy a beer or two. Besides, she didn't seem in a particularly good mood either. It was probably better to get away before it all blew up again . . .

'Sir, could you just spare us a moment . . .'

On his third attempt, Detective Sergeant ******* employs the additional tactic of tapping the object of his entreaties on the shoulder. 'If you would be so kind, we'll only take up a minute of your time.'

Barney turns around and finds himself face to face with the Detective Sergeant, who is holding up a badge for his inspection. In the orange glow of the streetlamp, the policeman's face is lined and weary, lending him the aspect of a man a good ten years his senior. Two other uniformed constables are standing a few yards behind him chatting to an elderly woman with a shopping trolley.

'Are you a resident of this guest house?' Detective Sergeant ******* inclines his head in the direction of the Seaview lest there be any confusion whatsoever.

'Yes I am.'

'And were you here last night, Sir?'

Barney nods and shifts his weight from one foot to the other as his lifelong fear of authority manifests itself in the usual over-obsequious solicitude. 'Yes I was, indeed, yes.'

Detective Sergeant ******* sucks air through his teeth and looks suitably grave. 'There's been a serious crime committed, Sir, and we're just trying to put some sort of timeframe around the victim's last known movements. Basically, we're attempting to calculate various times of the possible routes the young lady might have taken, that's why you may see a few officers around the place this evening.'

'Last known movements?'

'Er, yes Sir, obviously I cannot pass on specific details at this stage but the weight of evidence we have so far collected does suggest that we are in pursuit of a murderer.'

'Oh my God . . .'

'Indeed. Anyway, we think the young lady probably walked past here last night, possibly more than once. It is our understanding, Sir, that she was rather intoxicated, so she might have been behaving in a way that drew attention to herself. I just wondered, Sir, if you might have heard anything last night. This would have been sometime around midnight, sounds of a struggle or shouting maybe.'

Barney thinks for a moment and then shrugs his shoulders. 'I'm sorry I can't be of any help but I don't recall hearing anything. Nothing at all.'

'OK, Sir. I don't want to take up another minute of your time but if I could just ask you to have a look at a photo. This will only take a moment.'

'Certainly.'

Detective Sergeant ******* turns and calls to one of the constables. 'Parkwood, just let me have that photo a minute, will you?'

'What photo, Sir?'

'You know, that nice picture of those little kittens we always take out with us. Come on, Parkwood, just give us the picture of the girl, I haven't got all night.'

'Here you are, Guv.'

'Thank you,' says ******* tersely. He hands the picture to Barney. 'If you wouldn't mind just having a quick look at the girl in the picture for me. Just to see if it rings any bells. It's a fairly recent photo so we are given to believe that it's a good likeness.'

Barney looks at the picture.

Barney looks at the picture.

See Barney look at the picture.

Then he plays with his ball.

See Barney play.

See Barney play.

'Ring any bells, Sir?'

Barney looks at the picture.

Barney looks at the picture.

Barney says to the policeman.

'What time did you say she might have been passing here?'

'Working with the information we have, Sir, and within

the absolute limits of our timeframe, we would be looking at some point between 11 p.m. and 1 a.m.'

'Between 11 and 1?'

'That's what I said, Sir.'

Barney shakes his head.

See Barney shake his head.

See Barney give the photo back.

'I'm sorry I really can't help you. I'm sorry.'

'Not a problem, Sir. I'm sorry to have wasted your time. Have a good evening, Sir.'

'Thanks.'

Detective Sergeant ******* and his two constables walk away quickly and Barney watches them as they make their way towards the off-licence.

Barney swallows and forces himself to inhale deeply. Once. Twice. Hold it. And then out slowly. Hands are thrust deep deeply deeper deepest into jacket pockets but he can still feel them shaking. Oh God, oh Christ! It wasn't even the bloody picture, that was the stupid thing, (even though you could just about make out the freckle on the base of her neck). But he didn't need to see it, no point, as soon as he'd heard the word *intoxicated* he bloody knew, he bloody knew. Hold it again. Count to ten. And

Out-oh Jesus, that poor girl.

He had told the truth, *he had told the truth* he repeats the phrase again and again as if hoping to wring every last drop of comfort from it. Had he heard any commotion outside the Seaview? *he had told the truth.* Had he seen the girl between 11 and 1? *he had told the truth.*

Yet at the very epicentre of all uncertainty there is always a certainty – one knowable, indisputable moment of clarity.

But Barney can draw scant consolation from the knowledge that he has not told the story in its entirety. Nothing but the truth, perhaps, but far from the whole truth.

HERE BEGINS THE CONFESSION OF BARNEY LANGTON

On August 27th, 1978, I was staying in Margate at the Seaview Guest House on Royal Terrace. I was in the company of my wife Sandra and our son Andrew. Andrew is six and after our supper, Sandra was reading to him prior to getting him settled in bed for the night. It was around 7.30 p.m, possibly a little later but certainly no later than quarter to eight, and as it was a mild evening I thought I would go for a little stroll for half an hour. I didn't have any particular plans although I did take the book I have been reading with me, a translation of *Rimbaud par lui-même* by Yves Bonnefoy. I had no firm ideas but I thought if I found a pub with a beer garden or something similar I could pass an agreeable twenty minutes or so on a summer evening with a half a pint of shandy and my book. I was walking eastwards from the Seaview in the direction of the town when I passed the Shakespeare, a fairly modest public house but one boasting, I was quite delighted to discover, a couple of tables with benches on the pavement outside. A couple were sitting at one while the other was unoccupied. It seemed ideal; I purchased my shandy and sat down at the vacant pavement table. I must have been there for ten, fifteen minutes and I'd almost finished my shandy when, without any warning or preamble, this young girl sat herself down at my table. She said nothing and I paid little or no attention to her and just continued reading my book. You must understand that I made absolutely no attempt to start a conversation, I didn't even smile at her or say hello. Although I did notice that she didn't bring a drink to the table with her so I just sort of assumed she was waiting for someone. Out of the corner of my eye I could also see that she was rather fidgety, rather animated I suppose, for one who was sitting down, she looked anxious, she looked at her watch a lot, maybe the person she was waiting for was late, I thought. I took another sip of my shandy and returned to Monsieur Bonnefoy. The couple moved away from the other table but the girl remained sitting on the bench opposite me. Then suddenly straight out of blue she says, 'What's that you're reading?' Just like that. I had said absolutely nothing to her by this point, I'd not even made eye contact. It must be understood that she opened the conversation, not me. Anyway, just to be polite, I told her that it was a study of Rimbaud and when she inevitably asked who he was I told her that he was a great French poet. 'I'll bet it's dead boring,' I think, were her exact words on receiving this information and then she confessed to me that she'd always hated French in school. She'd given it up after she'd messed up her O level, she said, choosing, sensibly or otherwise, not to elaborate any further. So, at this point I casually mentioned that I was actually a French teacher, and she sort of laughed and looked a bit embarrassed. Then she told me that she'd had a terrible French teacher called Mr Maitland and she hated his lessons and had quickly lost interest in the subject. I think she added something at that point about Cancerians being poor at learning languages. Something of that nature. Then she said I was probably a much better teacher and I thanked her for the compliment. We then lapsed into silence for a minute or two and I looked at her properly for the first time. Now I don't know why precisely but the funny thing was that, for some reason, I got it into my head that she looked French. Ironic really in the light of what I had just learned but there was just something intangibly Parisian about her look and her manner. I could just picture her sitting at a pavement café on the Left Bank or attending lectures at the Sorbonne. She had quite a pretty face and in her style of dressing she was, well, I believe the term in fairly popular use at the moment, is a *punkette.* But she wasn't overtly radical or confrontational about it, her take was very much a watered-down, provincial, seaside-town version. She was wearing a bright Day-Glo pink and white T-shirt with a screen-printed picture of Gene Vincent and the word L'ANARCHIE with the individual letters assembled so it looked like a blackmail note. Her hair was cropped quite short, a bit like Jean Seberg in *À bout de souffle*, and she wore lots of dark eye make-up. It's a look I really like and I have to confess that I thought she looked great. But at this point, I felt that our brief exchange had reached its conclusion and I was just about to start heading back to the Seaview. I'd closed my book and was preparing to make my farewells when the girl asked me if there was a public pay phone inside the pub and I said that I hadn't seen one. She seemed troubled by this for some reason and then asked me if I knew of another one nearby. I apologised and said that the only one I was aware of was the one in the railway station, although I was certain that there would be one nearer than that. I suggested that we asked the barman but she just started telling me that she wanted to phone her parents. She told me that she'd come out for the evening on her own and was starting to wonder if she'd done the right thing. Maybe they could come and pick her up. But as soon as she'd vocalised this notion it was evident that it was one that had little or no appeal. But she was obviously in rather a quandary about it all. She told me she'd been let down by her friend but was determined to enjoy herself anyway. I said that she had the right idea. She said she was a bit nervous about being out on her own but I told her she was young, it was a lovely warm evening and she should be out there enjoying herself, while she still could. I think I said half-jokingly at this point that she had a duty to live up to her T-shirt, she laughed at that. Maybe it was reading Rimbaud, I don't know, but before I knew it I was Jean-Paul Belmondo, persuading her, urging her to stay out and have a great time on her own. You're young, I told her, do something wild or one day you'll wake up and you'll have kids and a car and there will never be that chance again. Believe me, I told her, that day will come soon enough. I mentioned that there were many things in my life that I regretted doing but there were far more things that I regretted *not* doing. If I could go back in time, I said, I would take advantage of every possibility, of every chance I was offered, I would find every unlocked door and search out any window that had been left fractionally open. Life is in its chances. One day, when it was all too late, she would understand this. She needed to grasp all this experience now while she was young and in tune with her times, while she was connected, while she was certain. Oh yes, she said, she completely agreed with me, but she still seemed a little on the apprehensive side. The world is a dull enough place anyway, I told her, this is a great opportunity to add some colour to it. I suppose with all the stark neon clarity and cruelty of hindsight, I can see that I was probably talking completely selfishly and subjectively about me and my life and not about hers. She kept saying but you're a teacher and I said yes but once, a long long time ago, I used to be a human being. I wish you'd been my teacher, she said, and we laughed. She said she was still feeling a bit nervous about being out so stupidly I suggested that she maybe had a drink to calm her nerves. It was an insane suggestion but it just seemed the right thing at that moment. She admitted that she'd already had a glass or two from the sherry bottle her father kept in their sideboard. Unfortunately, she said, she'd done this on an empty stomach and it made her feel a little queasy but she said she felt fine now. I asked her how old she was and she said eighteen. I must have looked a little dubious because she immediately reiterated that she was really, honestly, ask anyone, eighteen brownies honour. So the next minute, without really pausing to question what

I'm doing I'm back inside the Shakespeare at the bar buying the girl her choice of tipple, namely a Southern Comfort. It did strike me as a ludicrous choice for a girl of her age but I took some solace in the fact that Monsieur Belmondo, under the same circumstances, would have probably complied with the young lady's request. But I know that it was a stupid stupid thing to do and I can find no rationalisation for my actions. I should have just sneaked away at that point but I took her drink back outside and she must have finished it within a minute. She then said she was starting to feel better and a little less nervous about the evening but then she insisted that she bought me a drink. I told her I was only having a half of shandy before I went back to my hotel but before I could protest any further she'd gone into the pub herself and returned with another half of shandy for me and another Southern Comfort for her. She drank the second one as quickly as the first. Cheers, she said and confessed that she would have been bored out of her mind if she'd actually gone home for the evening. Two hours of the telly and her dad going on about her hair all the time. She thanked me for talking her out of it and for buying her a drink. She told me she was going off to have a great night and promised that at the end of it she would remember our little chat and thank me. She gave me a little wave, said goodbye and walked off towards the town. She ambled and swayed a bit and looked very uncertain on her feet. I think I probably wondered if the Southern Comforts had been such a good idea. But as soon as she was out of sight, I abandoned my second shandy, which I'd hardly touched and left the Shakespeare. Maybe it was the heat or the fact that apart from the shandy I had not drunk very much all day, but I felt I was starting to get a headache. So, rather than go back to my hotel, I went for a walk, I just strolled up and down the seafront as far as the Lido and beyond hoping that my head would clear. I really don't know how long I was walking. A couple of hours I suppose. I was so lost in my reveries I suppose that I just lost track of the time. I got back to the Seaview about 10.30, I think. But I didn't see the girl again. I didn't see her until I was shown the photograph. Of course I recognised her, I recognised her in an instant. She looked terribly French, you see. But you know, it's amazing what actually goes through your mind when you are forced to confront something like this, but it's never quite how you imagine, is it? That awful sudden terrible awareness of the utter frailty of all things. That realisation that there are no certainties and there can never be. It all seems so ephemeral, doesn't it? And every day we walk alongside it never daring to glance over the edge. At such times, rare as they may be, I suppose a sort of ancient *Homo sapiens* instinct takes over and, like any other father I imagine, I just find myself worrying what the future holds for my son.

HERE ENDS THE CONFESSION OF BARNEY LANGTON

August 28th, 2005, Margate, England.

In a room on the second floor of the Hayland Rock Hotel, Andrew Langton paces the floor.

One must remain logical and detached at all times.

However, this is easier said than done.

Sometimes the frail hairline boundary between sanity and insanity is to be discovered within our capacity to view coincidence objectively.

One should view coincidence with little more than passing interest as simply a naturally occurring phenomenon and not something to which one should attach great significance.

He wanders back to the window and the dressing table

upon which stands his Apple G4 PowerBook. He reads again the words 'Dear Sir' in 12-point Helvetica. Then nothing, just the cursor endlessly blinking, taunting, mocking, accusing . . .

The purpose and main objective of the letter had never been in the slightest doubt; it was only its general tone that was proving so problematic. He had made the right decision to come away on his own for a couple of days, definitely, yet this final detail had not been made appreciably any easier. But they could manage without him for a day or so. He would switch his phone back on in an hour or so and give them a call. He did promise.

He sighs.

This wasn't about intellect, this was all about inspiration. The former may fail you temporarily but the latter can elude you indefinitely.

Words, he would graciously concede, were not exactly his strong point. The line that he trotted out with fairly tedious regularity (now have I ever told you) was that English was his second language and that he was only fluent in numbers. (Oh ha ha ha Andrew, you are just *so* witty.) It was, he would announce in his defence, a positive virtue for a financial analyst; in fact it was virtually a prerequisite. And let's not forget who it was who put the anal in analyst? (Oh Andrew, that is so *naughty*!)

'Financial anal-yst, MSc (App. Maths) LSE and amateur number cruncher, weekends and Bank Holidays,' he confesses to his invisible companions.

Ten minutes later, he pauses after having written 'the purpose of this letter is to record for posterity' and stares blankly once more out of the window. He watches three forty-something cyclists passing the hotel. One wears a red Brigate Rosse T-shirt with the word 'Brigate' misspelled – a *d* in place of the *t*. All three are riding foreign-made bikes, one French and two Italian. It strikes him that Margate is a rather curious destination for someone on a cycling holiday. But then of course his own reasons for being there are no less obscure.

Originally, it was actually his father's suggestion. The subject had come up in conversation a week or so ago. He'd just mentioned in passing that he needed a couple of days peace and quiet away from Lucy and Josh as he was working on something. Without even enquiring upon the nature of the work, his father had immediately suggested Margate. Margate! Bang, just like that! They had been there once many years ago on a family holiday but Andrew would have to confess to having little or no memory of either the town or the specific holiday. Furthermore, nothing he had seen in the past twenty-four hours had rekindled any dormant memories and, unclouded by sentiment or any great ghastly longing to recapture his childhood, he maintained an icy objectivity towards his surroundings.

'Things happen in Margate.'

That was what his father had said, as though he had felt compelled to justify this apparently hasty choice of destination. But he had said nothing further on the subject. This was a fairly typical remark from a man who had recently developed the habit of speaking as though his every utterance required an exclamation mark. It added a certain dramatic flair to his conversations, although periodically he managed to sound like a particularly bratty teenager, albeit a rather articulate one.

'Things happen in Margate!'

Andrew removes his glasses and cleans the lenses with the end of his T-shirt. He yawns.

Off the subject, off the subject . . .

Come on.

In his mind he returns again to the second paragraph and continues.

Coincidence is simply seeing patterns and systems and connections where there are none. A pattern that occurs in numbers (like primes) is mathematics and not coincidence. That is the accepted wisdom. Mathematics is order, coincidence is chance. On the one hand you have numeracy and on the other numerology, apparently, distinct and unconnected in any way whatsoever. Yet the more you advance into the former the more you stumble upon certain grey areas, points where the two worlds actually touch. Indeed patterns sometimes were hard to avoid. Like perfect numbers. Perfect numbers, numbers equal to the sum of their divisors, are comparatively rare. 6 is a perfect number (1+2+3=6), the next one in the sequence is 28, then 496, after which the numbers get really big. The largest one so far discovered, the 39th in the sequence, has more than four million digits. The other interesting thing about perfect numbers is that they are all even and all end in a 6 or an 8. That is a pattern and patterns are acceptable in mathematics. Indeed patterns represent a sort of order. It's only when we start looking for some underlying metaphysical factor that operates beneath that pattern, or we begin to attach too much significance to any particular pattern, that we leave behind the world of pure mathematics.

He sits at his PowerBook and writes a rough paraphrase of the above.

Yes, that was the right tone, no personal details just theory and background. Now came the tricky bit.

He starts to pace again. He looks at his watch.

Two hours and ten minutes.

Approximately.

Rounded up to the nearest five minutes.

He has drafted this letter twenty, probably a hundred times in his mind but this has not made its final execution any easier. But he knew that he was fortunate to have found Mr P., not many solicitors were prepared to work at five o'clock on a Sunday, if only for ten minutes. He'd called him the previous morning after finding his name in the *Yellow Pages* he'd borrowed from reception. His was only the second number he'd called. Andrew had been deliberately vague about the purpose of the meeting but Mr P. hadn't seemed particularly bothered or surprised by this and his general tone throughout their brief conversation remained polite and accommodating. Even when Andrew requested that he remain anonymous throughout their brief association. But he felt safer that way. Taken out of context, at this stage, some of what he was saying might make him sound absolutely bonkers and he is aware of this.

He will naturally be paying in cash for the service.

But it is going to cost him, he knows this, but he also knows that he will sleep well tonight, for the first time in months, knowing that a copy of his letter is sealed, dated and placed in Mr P.'s safe. Then he will be insured against any possible controversy in the future, against anyone else claiming his ideas as their own. It would be some time before he was ready to go public with any of this, he knows he needs more time, much more time . . .

It wasn't necessary to explain how he'd stumbled upon the figures or that the American-made Modular Professional 800X software which he ran on his desktop at home had set him back thousands of pounds.

It was just about the figures.

And how he loved figures! There was always something to discover, always something new. When he was younger he had been fascinated by the qualities of particular numbers; there were the hidden properties of 17 (the only prime number that is the sum of four consecutive primes) or 64 (the lowest number that is both the square and the cube of other numbers), and he had once derived such a thrill (yes the word was thrill) from discovering that zero qualifies as an even number.

Nowadays, his particular area of interest was repeating

numbers, numbers both sides of the decimal point, and he continued to find within them an almost aesthetic perfection and divinity that touched him far deeper than any poem or painting. In the patterns and order, an order that was so infinite and changeless, he saw the hand of God.

It was just about the figures.

So it will start with a single figure, Langton's Number, as he had come to term it, namely 11472.

The number 11472 has some unique properties; first, the square root of 11472 to the first three decimal places is a repeating number, 107.107.

Furthermore, 11472 divided into 1 results in

0.00008716875871687587168758716875871687587168758716875871687587168758716875871687587168758717 . . .

This is another fascinating number with a seven-digit sequence repeating itself.

There is more. When you take this precise seven-digit sequence 8716875 and multiply it by 11472 we arrive at another curious repeating number – 99999990000.

These numbers are without precedent and Andrew Langton, after citing two further examples, will then quite calmly and rationally conclude his letter by asserting that the cube of 11472 (1509793026048) when taken to its logical conclusion in what he terms its 'ultimate equation', namely

$$1509793026048^{1509793026048^{1509793026048}}$$

will prove to be the numeric equivalent of infinity. Otherwise

$$1509793026048^{1509793026048^{1509793026048}} = \infty$$

Over the past year, he has run countless diagnostics and tests on the Modular software and he is absolutely certain that there are no bugs, viruses or glitches in the system. On many occasions in the past he has worked with vast numbers and performed all manner of calculations using the software yet every time he begins to plot the properties of 1509793026048 the whole system crashes. Every single time! He has tried other systems running different software and always with the same result. Nothing is able to process this particular data. It would seem that 1509793026048 to the power of 1509793026048 to the power of 1509793026048 is a number that is beyond all possible calculation. Yet it should be (however vast) an integer that could feasibly be represented numerically. One could rationally speculate that such a number could therefore only be the numeric equivalent of infinity. Nothing else would make sense.

But there it was.

For all to see.

∞

That symbol.

For as long as he can remember he has been absolutely fascinated by the infinity symbol. Ever since he was a teenager, he has been drawn to its mysterious beauty and a purity of line that is as near perfect as he can imagine. For many years he's been particularly obsessed with its centre, where the figure crossed itself and the lines intersected. Unlike a circle or an ellipse, which might have been used to represent something eternal with no obvious beginning or end, the infinity symbol had at its very centre this point of intersection. To the extent that he had once speculated that at specific points in space and time a similar intersection would naturally and inevitably occur.

A moment at which all events, past, present and future merge.

Infinity.

Beyond this, beyond Langton's Number, he has begun to hypothesise an abstract sequence of numbers commencing with Langton 1 or *L*1 (otherwise ∞ +1).

He would present his absolute formulaic proof in due course as he still needed to explore further the complexities and numeric powers of 11472 and 11472^3.

He returns to his Apple and continues typing. Once again, he restricts himself to the basic points of his theory. It is doubtful that there would be any virtue in revealing that 11/4/72 is Andrew Langton's date of birth.

Over the past few months, he has sought comfort in the fact that it is a birth date he shares with thousands of others (at least ten notables on the Internet Movie Database), but he still feels a distinct chill whenever he sees that particular sequence of numbers. It is the ultimate coincidence, he tells himself, but still no more than a coincidence. There is no significance, no order, no pattern, there is no *purpose* to it, the number is random and he happened upon it completely by chance at one time when he simply needed a five-digit number for a calculation. It just seemed an obvious choice.

He never asks 'why?' anymore, he can't allow himself to.

Don't even think about it.

It is just about the figures.

11472

The numeric portal to infinity.

Also the common numeric representation of the birth date of the man who discovered it.

A coincidence.

Of course it is.

Don't even think about it.

Andrew prints a copy of the letter and then immediately deletes the file from his PowerBook. Once it is stamped and secure in his safe, he will give Mr P. a pass code, which can be used to gain access to his letter in the future. After discounting several possible alternatives he settles on MARGATE1978.

Don't even think about it.

There is now only one final task to complete before he sets out for his meeting. He takes the final page of his letter and with his left hand he scrawls a flamboyant looping signature at the end of the text. It is virtually indecipherable, which is, of course, his intention. However, if it was to be studied very carefully, some of the individual letters would reveal themselves.

Further meticulous scrutiny would eventually divulge the following possible sequence of characters:

'M' (?) 'O' 'E' 'S' (?) 'E' '?' 'T'(?) 'O' 'N'.

'Chap walks into a nightclub . . .'

Brogues have an interesting and not widely known history.

The word itself derives from brogan, a type of simple, primitive footwear worn by poorer Scottish Highlanders. The brogan was made by wrapping a piece of deerskin or cowhide around each foot and holding it in place with a thin piece of leather known as a thong. Despite contending with the adverse terrain and weather conditions, the brogan was not intended to be waterproof and holes were cut in the skin and the hide to let the water out as they tramped across rivers and streams. The pattern of holes punched in the outer leather layer of the modern brogue derives entirely from this historic practice.

Similarly unknown to a great many people is the fact that linoleum was invented in 1860 by an English gentleman named Frederick Walton. Walton worked as a rubber manufacturer and was driven to discover a cheaper alternative to an expensive rubber composition called Kamptulicon. According to the generally accepted version, his inspiration came from observing the skin of oxidised linseed oil that forms on paint.

The industrious Mr Walton also gave the world Anaglypta amongst other things.

The name linoleum comes from the Latin word *linum*, which means 'flax'. Flax, interestingly enough, supplied the fabric for the infant Jesus' swaddling clothes and also for his burial shroud.

We may pause and fleetingly reflect on brogues and linoleum as at approximately 9.35 p.m., an example of the former makes a series of brief contacts with an example of the latter.

The former is a size 10, in a dark tan, and purchased in 1969 for 59/11*d* (plus postage and handling) from an advert in the *Daily Mail* and is the property of M. Seyton Esq.

The latter, in alternating waxed and polished squares of black and mid-charcoal, covers the main entrance lobby to the Grosvenor Place Oddfellows Club and Lodge, Grosvenor Place, Margate, Kent.

The first contact between the two is a crisp single snare drum accent, the second is an axe hitting ancient wood, the third is a gun shot . . .

He stops sharply and looks at his surroundings.

Built in the mid-sixties the Grosvenor Place Oddfellows Club and Lodge is not the world's most attractive building but it has an air of reassuring functionality that perversely appeals to Moe. Given his state of mind it seems a most appropriate venue.

He has very recently disembarked from a minicab, which he took for the half a mile or so trip between the Seaview and the club. Usually, he makes this journey on foot but this evening he felt the added extravagance was justified. It added a significance and grandeur to the evening. Similarly grand was his telling the cabbie to keep the change from a ten-pound note. This was rather generous as the fare was only £1.50.

But he did things like that, they were saying to each other in dark corners, their faces lost in shadow deep in their imagined whispered conversations, *he was like that . . . he was decent enough . . . and funny too . . .*

He had even made a point of having a couple of words with the chap on the door. He'd mentioned that he would have a guest arriving shortly but he'd lingered a while exchanging pleasantries. Something which he had not done on previous evenings . . . *always a very civil gent . . . and one of the funniest, they reckon . . .*

Moe pauses for a moment and reaches behind his back. He traces the reassuring outline of his Webley Mark IV army service revolver, which is firmly and discretely tucked into the belt of his trousers. Undetectable. *But there was nothing that would have suggested . . . good heavens absolutely nothing that might have even implied . . .*

'Sorry about the smell,' says a sudden sharp voice to his immediate left.

Moe turns. 'Ah, good evening, Shuffle.'

Henry 'Shuffle' Montgomery (the nickname attached itself a great many years ago due to his particular manner of walking) is a short, stout amiable man with thick eyebrows that arch perpetually upwards in an attitude of vague astonishment. This lends him a slightly bemused demeanour. Dapper in fawn corduroy and paisley cravat, Mr Montgomery also practises a neat line in self-deprecation and whistles with a vibrato that would shame a canary. As far as Moe can ascertain, Shuffle's role at the club remains essentially ambiguous; he is either the janitor who regularly steps up to the mike as the club's MC and warm-up man. Or he simply *is* the MC and he just chooses to help out in whatever way he can. Moe's view on the subject tends towards the latter but lacks any real conviction.

'Evening, Moe. I think the flipping khazi's blocked again or something. You wouldn't credit what some folk try and flush down the bog. But why does it always happen in hot weather? That's what I would like to know.'

Moe frowns. 'I can't smell anything, I promise you.'

'You mean you didn't catch a whiff of that awful sewer sort of smell when you came in?'

'Not a thing.'

'Oh well. I'd better check anyway.' He takes a few steps towards the gents and then stops and turns around. 'Oh Moe, nearly forgot, the boss says he would like a word.'

Moe inhales lavishly. 'Well, you just tell him that I would like to have TWO words with him. Then ask him if he can guess what those two words might be.'

Shuffle shakes his head and looks intently at Moe. 'Nah, I think maybe that would be best coming from you!'

Moe says nothing but puts his hands up in fake surrender.

'Look, Moe, are you absolutely sure you can't smell anything?' asks Shuffle, wincing accordingly. 'It's bloody revolting!'

'Sorry.'

'Your nose needs glasses, mate.'

'Good crowd tonight?'

'Well, I wouldn't call them that. They'd both probably get offended!'

Moe smiles. 'Tell you what, Shuffle, why don't I clean the latrines tonight and you headline the show?'

'Nah, it's not bad really. Actually it's filling up quite nicely for a Bank Holiday. And it's still fairly early. Have a look for yourself.'

'I will.'

Shuffle Montgomery shuffles off eponymously towards the gents once more and Moe approaches the main double doors to the Geoffrey Chaucer Room. He pushes open the doors a fraction of an inch and peers inside. His first impressions are olfactory – bodies, stale sweat, aftershave, wood polish, tobacco and alcohol battling each other in the oppressive humidity. (Someone has had the sense to open a few windows this evening. Thank God.) Then the quick head count, sixty, possibly seventy, Shuffle was right, not a bad turn-out. At the far end of the room on the tiny stage, Gigi Sinclair performs her first routine of the evening to a recording of a song by Serge Gainsbourg; she will return to the stage later in the evening in a red wig when she will be introduced as Sandy St Moritz. Nice girl, not a bad mover, good tits and always punctual, lives in Herne Bay, well, somebody has to . . . Couple of empty tables near the front there, Mr Langton will get a good view . . . he'll be here soon . . . damn, someone's coming.

Moe quickly reverses away from the door but not before he hears an angry patron complaining about 'that awful bloody stench'. He then hurries down the adjacent corridor. Past the cloakrooms, the toilets and front office, down a couple of steps and now he is standing in front of a door onto which is affixed a page torn from an exercise book. In bold hasty strokes the letters M. S. are scrawled across the paper. He pushes open the door and turns on the light.

A mirror, a sink, a dressing table, a single chair, an ashtray, a clothes rail, a wastepaper bin and a small wardrobe. This is to be the inventory of Moe Seyton's final dressing room.

Mindful of the item in his trouser belt he perches himself gingerly on the edge of the chair and looks at his watch.

One hour and nineteen minutes.

Then he makes an amendment to his inventory, a clean drinking glass by the side of the sink. Forgot that was there. Too good a chance to pass up, he thinks. So he now opens the small wardrobe where, at the rear of its single drawer and shrouded in an old scarf, he has been hiding a quarter bottle of Johnny Walker these past two nights.

Then something catches his eye, something immediately recognisable, something that wasn't there the previous evening, or was it? Maybe he didn't notice it. No, he would have seen it, maybe it's just being stored there, maybe it belongs to someone who works here and they've just parked it here, still it can't do any harm . . .

And with that, Moe carefully unfastens the vinyl case and removes a Spanish guitar.

Then after pouring himself a reasonably modest-sized measure of whisky, he sits himself carefully once more on the chair and cradles the guitar in his lap. It's been years, he thinks, decades maybe since he has played one of these. Piano was the number-one instrument back then, never a greatly accomplished player but competent enough to get by, pick out a tune and hold a beat, certainly all those songs were written on the piano, but you never saw that many guitars in dance bands back in the old days, it was more a classical instrument . . .

He runs his hand over the strings and arranges his fingers into chord shapes he fancies he can still recall.

Is that C or F?

Doesn't sound too out of tune either, can't have been in there all that long or it's a half-decent instrument. Would never have bothered with the guitar at all but it was easy to drag around with you and after the war when things got a bit lean, something was needed that was more portable than a piano and cheaper than a band, the guitar seemed the best available option, it was certainly preferable to the accordion.

He strums a chord as a slow arpeggio.

Hang on, no that must be F and then that's E, is that right?

Took a couple of lessons, just enough to get by, so the songs weren't dropped from the act, which they would have been and that would have been a shame and Kaiser had some pretty strong ideas on the subject too, so that went on for a couple of years. Never really progressed much further beyond the basics.

If that's E then that is the minor third so that must be E

minor, yes that makes sense. He strums the chord. So if we can do that C chord to E minor and that's a tricky change. 1–2, 1–2, then up to the F major chord . . .

Then guided by instinct or memory or something darker he can barely comprehend, he sings very softly, his voice quavering and lost in the moment, for the first time in over a quarter of a century.

Then a gentle tapping on the door and a voice is heard from the other side.

'Moe, Moe, do you mind if I have a word?'

One hour and eleven minutes.

Illuminated by single spotlight, the short man is banging the microphone with the palm of his hand whilst gesturing frantically at a shadowy figure standing at the side of the stage. Eventually the short man speaks.

'Hello, hello, is this working now? Let's try it again. Good evening, gents, I said good evening, gents. Oh fucking hell that's quiet, isn't it? Can anybody hear me? Hello, hello? Is this thing switched on? Jesus fucking Christ, has Marcel what's his face been using our PA again? Turn the volume up, Ken for fuck's sake, good lad, come on don't be shy, this is a stag show not a fucking vicar's tea party! That's better. Yeah, all the fucking way up, there's a good chap, right all the way up, ooooooh, that's nice! Ooooooh, just there, oooooooooh, yes, yes, you naughty man! That's better! Can you hear me at the back now? Excellent. It's good to be loud. Thank you, Sir. Yeah and you too. God bless you. Right then, my name is Shuffle Montgomery and I'm your MC for the rest of the evening. So there'll be no fucking funny business, all right? I'd like to welcome you all to Margate, that is of course if you're not from Margate. So, gents, quick show of hands, how many of us are from Margate? How many of us are local? Come raise them high above your head, nothing to be ashamed of. So, most of us are from Margate. Great, three fucking big cheers for Margate! Great place Margate, isn't it? Best place in the world. Here, you know why Jesus wasn't born in Margate, don't you . . . yes thank you Sir, we all know it's an old one and thanks for that. You're wrong anyway, he wasn't born in Margate because the place was full of loud-mouthed fucking ignorant idiots who like to ruin everyone's fucking evening! Thank you. Somebody throw a bucket of water over him. Hey, it's not the easiest job in the world this, you know, its hard work standing up here. Its not like working in an office or driving a bus, you know, anyone can do that. Actually, my friend has got a great job. My friend has got the easiest and most brilliant fucking job in the world. True, it's fucking fantastic! He performs illegal backstreet abortions for women with phantom pregnancies! I'm telling you, easiest job in the world, raking it in, he is too. Anyway it's great to see so many of you here tonight. I love Margate, it's a great fucking place, right? Bloody fantastic. Well, it's too late to go anywhere else tonight, right? You might as well stay here. We've got some more delectable young ladies coming up here to entertain you a little later on but right now, gents, let's get the comedian on. A very, very funny man who's been coming down to see us on our Bank Holiday stag weekends for a good few years now. He'll make you laugh and if he doesn't then we don't have to pay him! Just kidding. A warm Margate welcome please . . .'

Atop two massive columns, in a semicircular arch of great bold roman letters, the Menagerie of Folly announced itself in the most eye-catching manner. Nowadays, however, it was starting to look a little weather-beaten, seedy even, more like a carnival, she thinks, noting with a slight distaste that the final Y is now dislodging itself. She takes her father's cold hand and walks quickly to keep up with him. She has been visiting as long as she can remember, sometimes with her family, with old friends but often on her own. It is not a place she likes particularly yet it is one that retains a reassuring familiarity.

The music keeps playing but it doesn't bother her. She is determined to enjoy herself today.

The Euclidean Circus would be too hot today, her dad tells her again, it was always packed anyway. It was the Menagerie's main attraction and the queues seemed to stretch as far as every horizon. She tugs her father's hand but he doesn't respond. Please, she silently implores. The Euclidean Circus, upon which the menagerie's international reputation had been built, was where they housed their collection of impossibly complicated geometrical figures, brought together under one roof from all over the world.

Beyond description and imagination, these complex three-dimensional figures (some rare examples existed in four dimensions and included a particular sound frequency as an essential property), were so far beyond the usual laws of classification that they were known simply by their Folly Numbers. Some had such an unbelievable beauty and you caught yourself drawing breath at the very sight of them. Often you saw people weeping, as you imagine they might at the opera, moved beyond endurance. People would stand for hours, days sometimes, in front of these figures, some of which, over the years, had been invested with an almost mystical healing power. Indeed some enjoyed a sort of cultlike reverence and worship. Although there were a number of these, Folly Number 7078 had been one of the first and remained to this day possibly the most famous. The 7078 was special, a figure in Series 7 had a number of sides equal to a prime and the 078 resonated a G natural in harmony with an A sharp, a perfect minor third. Every day a handful of the shaven-headed faithful 7078ers would gather in front of it to sing and chant and scatter rose petals. Harmless really, her dad said.

But there were other figures too, those that were kept in the inner second room. Those were different. They were quite simply the ultimate affirmation of the old adage that the greatest possible evil can only be represented in a linear form. These figures were grotesque and terrifying in their perfectly ascribed malevolence. She knew all about them but she'd never been allowed to see them. When you're a big girl, her dad was always saying. More so than the figures in the first room, these fragile, vulnerable exhibits required an environment of a precise constant temperature. This ensured that the figures' precise angles and relative dimensions remained fixed and 'mathematically constant'. On summer days the second room was too hot for even the most devoted geometratic.

Please, she asks again as they pass a smiling 7078er who offers her a rose petal.

It is then that she notices that the music has stopped playing.

They walk past the Dark Enclosures again, she hates this part of the trip. She hates the way they call to her, hates the way they look at her. It was all too distressing. The Dark Enclosures were a series of dimly lit cages located around the perimeter wall of the menagerie and in these cages were the beasts. Nameless, unrecognisable creatures, unlike anything dreamt of by Noah or Darwin, half-blind, mutant, hybrid, hideous creatures – each and every one the last surviving specimen of its species. They were kept here away from the main part of the menagerie so that their endless wailing did not distress the visitors too unduly. So fearful of their imminent extinction these tragic creatures, all of them psychotic and deeply paranoid, never slept or even stood still for a moment.

She glances at the cage where Folly Number 451 886 is incarcerated. The huge hulking faceless entity turns towards her. Part bear, part walrus, part virus with hair, horns and scales and a gaping foul slit in its abdomen, through which and by which it performed all its functions. It smells absolutely revolting, she thinks, like it was rotting and decaying in front of her, moment by moment. She wants to turn away but something compels her to look at him. Then she sees the doll in the bottom of the cage and wants to cry. It was a well-documented fact that these animals would attempt sexual congress with anything in a last desperate attempt to propagate the species. They would attempt it with their food, the bars of their cage, even their own reflections, this final futile instinct made all the more poignant by the fact that they were all infertile. Sometimes people visiting the Menagerie would entertain themselves by throwing something into one of the cages, like a doll in this case, just to watch the resulting desperate pantomime.

Some people could be so cruel.

451 886 turns away but she hears his voice in her head.

'. . . not a fucking vicar's tea party!'

It is a voice that is not near but it is not far.

What?

What did he say?

She looks for her father but he has gone and she can no longer see him.

'. . . *It's good to be loud . . .'*

Pardon.

She wants her dad, she wants to chase after him but doesn't know in what direction to run.

'. . . *no fucking funny business, all right?*

What?

She is starting to feel scared and tries to shut out the voice.

'. . . *loud-mouthed fucking . . .'*

I don't want to hear this. I want my dad.

'. . . *ignorant idiots . . .'*

And at this precise moment Mrs Catherine Hughes is suddenly and untimely wrenched from her benzodiazepine-fuelled dreams. She opens her eyes and and sits up, shaking her self into full consciousness.

She is confused but hears the voice again.

'. . . *I love Margate, it's a great fucking place, right?'*

Her mouth falls open in horror.

Words. Just words. All over the place, just everywhere. Falling tumbling, stumbling towards meaning and context. Towards definition, towards recognition.

She stands up and it all becomes clear in that moment.

She drinks the glass of water on the bedside cabinet and picks up the telephone receiever. She dials 9 for an outside line and then dials the number on the piece of paper by the phone.

Within a minute the restrained dulcet tones of her initial inquiries had been superceded by a more strident urgent manner of speaking.

'No, now you just listen to me, Brian . . . no, listen, I said. This is not what we are paying hundreds of pounds a month for . . . no, quite right . . . and I'm not about to have my sleep interupted every single night by such foul language. For goodness' sake, we're all pensioners . . . surely we're entitled to a little peace at our age. No, I'm telling you, you will do something and you will do something now! Right now this minute . . . Of course it's not a private club if I can hear every word! How can it be private . . . Don't be stupid, Brian, I pointed it out to you earlier, if you could have been bothered to listen to me and I told you this was going to happen What? . . . Well, I think at my age I should be allowed to sleep with the window open if I so choose, don't you think? Or would you rather I just suffocated? . . . No, I won't calm down . . . It's criminal that's what it is and it shouldn't be allowed . . . On my very first night here as well! You'd think there'd be laws to protect people from that sort of thing. It was revolting. I don't care who you have to call or who you have to get out of bed but I want this sorted out now . . . I can't sleep with this . . . this obscenity, yes and I mean that quite literally. You've never heard such language, it made me feel sick to my stomach . . . I thought Margate was a nice little seaside town, not a place where decent people would have to put up with that sort of language. I mean do these people consider it entertainment or something, is it funny to them? Or clever? Is this what we have desended into? No . . . I know but as I have just explained to you, if I can hear it and hear every word as clear as day, how can anyone say that it's private? It didn't sound very private earlier on, I can tell you . . . yes, I know I had to drag you away from your dinner but this is important, somebody will put it in the oven for you, I'm sure . . . Just make a couple of calls will you? And do it now please, Brian, I would like to get to sleep sometime before tomorrow if it's all the same with you . . . My first night here, my first night and what a way to spend it . . .'

*

The applause that greeted his arrival onto the small stage was sporadic. However, a few whistles and a loud cheer from a group of young men sat around a table near the rear fire doors qualified as some consolation.

Then silence.

He is here. Table on the right.

He smiles but says nothing. Instead he stares at the stage and shifts from one foot to the other as though perhaps deliberating over what might be the ideal point to stand.

Finally, here stands a man selecting both his space and his time.

Fifty-six minutes.

Discreetly he passes his hand beneath his jacket and checks one final time the article tucked into his trouser belt. Just to make sure.

Yes.

He is ready now.

He takes the microphone from its stand.

HERE BEGINS THE CONFESSION OF MOE SEYTON

Good evening, gents, and welcome to Grosvenor Place Oddfellows Club and Lodge, nice to see so many of you out enjoying yourselves this evening. I mean that. Best enjoy it while you can, eh, gents, because you never know, do you? I mean you never *really* know, do you? It's true. In fact I'd like to start with a change from my intended opening this evening and tell you a little story. A true story as it happens. Just now I was in my dressing room and Tony, he's the manager of the club, came to see me and told me a rather sad tale. You see, a young girl, she must have been sixteen or seventeen, came to the door of the club last night and asked to come in. This must have been around nine thirtyish. Oh come on now, do be quiet, gents, settle down.

Tony was chatting to her out there in the lobby by the entrance and seemed to be at the point of letting her in. This was just too much, I thought. I had overheard most of their conversation but at that point I felt that I simply had to intervene. I took him to one side and remonstrated with him in the strongest possible terms and reminded him that it was a stag night and he was supposed to be operating a strict gents-only door policy. Black and white, as simple as that. Besides I thought, quite frankly, that she was a bit dishevelled-looking and was acting a bit . . . well, forward I suppose. I quite reasonably assumed that she was slightly the worse for drink. The girl had quite evidently spun him some yarn or another and I didn't quite catch the gist but she was laughing and sort of leaning on him in a very obvious, very tactile way, and you can probably imagine the scene I'm sure. Tony insisted that he could sneak her in and he would keep an eye on her. Come on, he said, no one would know she was there, she could sit at the side of the stage and be virtually invisible. But I stood firm with him and told him you can't have a door policy and then just change it, it wouldn't be fair on the other customers. It wasn't fair on anybody. Besides if one of the members caught a glimpse of her, goodness knows what sort of fuss could be made over it. No, please don't shout things out, not tonight, I want you all to listen to this, it's important. Besides, you could see the other side too and I think it would be fair to say that the nature of our ENTERTAINMENT this weekend is particularly unsuitable for a young lady. Maybe she should have been protected from witnessing a show of this nature. And I also sensed, I don't know how, that she was going to be trouble. I just felt it. When you have stood in front of an audience for as long as I have you get a nose for where there's going to be trouble. You just know who is going to start shouting and generally giving you a hard time. Yes, thank you very much for that, sir, how very inventive and original of you! Anyway, I just thought she was going to be a problem. I told Tony to get rid of her, actually I told him that either the girl takes a walk or I do. Tragically, I just learned from Tony about ten minutes ago, that a couple of hours or so after we stopped her coming in last night, that girl was dead. Killed, murdered, a young girl with her whole life in front of her, finished, over. Just like that. The police are still looking for the person or persons responsible but it is a fairly safe bet that if I'd kept my mouth shut and we'd let her in last night there is every chance she would be alive now. You know, gents, that's a terrible thing to think about, isn't it? I mean how do you all feel about that? Do you think that was cruel or evil or heartless to turn her away like that or do you think you would have done the same thing? You see all my life I have set myself against authority, against rules and regulations, against RESTRICTION in all its forms. The one time I played the game, the one occasion I did the correct and right thing, it had the most tragic CONSEQUENCE. Isn't that just the most EXTRAORDINARY thing? Think about that for a moment. Settle down please. Thank you. Look at him over there, that's Mister Langton, that is. He is my WITNESS this evening. You getting all this, are you? Good man. To be honest with you, this is not how I'd intended to start this evening as I've actually planned something very special for us all tonight. But I suppose it serves as a good jumping-off point – in fact you might say that this is only the start of my confession to you tonight. You see, one of the THEORIES about comedy is that we laugh at its very SUBVERSION of our reality – how unlike real life it is. Comedy is the displacement of CONTEXT: alligators don't live in the jungle, they walk into pubs and order drinks. This is how we RECOGNISE comedy, it's often how a joke announces itself, with this obvious contextual anomaly. A great painting may be considered great because it represents or interprets perfectly, for example, a landscape or a still life. But COMEDY cannot be a reflection of that reality; it must subvert or distort it in some way. Great comedy is GREAT subversion. That being the case, gentlemen, I fully intend to give you all the FUNNIEST evening of your lives! You see, a great comedian is a TRICKSTER, a falsifier, someone who twists your perspective of the world, hopefully he does this in a way that amuses you, or makes you laugh but for all that he's perpetrating a DECEPTION. You may think this is harmless enough, of course, but the TRICK is wholly dependent upon your BELIEF in this. You are as innocent as CUCKOLDS, all of you! Or is this also a trick? Ha ha, I know the answer to that but you don't! I am the TRICKSTER and I'm not saying. Not that you can trust what I say anyway! Don't make the mistake! A comedian is never a clown, but a deceiver! Conjurer, jester, juggler, DEVIL! You see we present you with a SLANT on your life, whilst momentarily REMOVING you from it. No other ART form does that. COMEDY is not funny, my friends. But it has its FUNCTION. You view it as an amusement, titillation perhaps. Yes, you too, sir, kindly sit down while I'm talking. You might learn something. Titillation, distraction, whatever. But what happens when you are SATURATED with titillation and amusement? Eventually you lose sight of what you are being DISTRACTED from. When you lose sight of MEANING in your life, you have no purpose or any reason for being here, you are lost, FINISHED, over. There are no great causes left anymore, no great CRUSADES, we've lived through two great wars, WITNESSED bloodshed and carnage on a scale UNIMAGINED by previous generations. But now there are precious few beliefs worth FIGHTING for – it's just titillation and distraction and frankly I mourn the fact that this appears to have replaced our need for SUPERSTITION! Nowadays it is simply TITILLATION and DISTRACTION, endlessly locked into some kind of loop. But you must realise that this doesn't reflect your lives any more, or enhance them, that is no longer required. You are only presented with a version, an adaptation, a mere SIMULACRUM. But do not comfort yourself by the NOTION that there is no harm in this. This is not some easy-read APOCALYPTIC fairy story, nor some latter day MORALITY play. The distorted TWISTED slant on REALITY gradually becomes its equivalent and EVENTUALLY replaces it. Just wake up and look around you. I want you to listen to this because it is important. Please show a chap a little courtesy, especially when he's in the middle of a confession. And do you know, the sickest, VILEST aspect to all this is the industry that has been set up solely to take your money and feed you all this worthless titillation and DISTRACTION. And I should know! You see, gents, as part of the very industry that titillates and distracts you I am partially responsible for your imminent descent into the fiery depths of HELL. For which I shall be REWARDED with lots and lots of your cash! Meet the enemy, gents, say hello to the opposition! It is TRUE, I promise you. I am part of a MASSIVE structure, a system so massive you could barely begin to COMPREHEND it, but it cushions you from the REALITY of your miserable pointless EXISTENCE and more importantly prevents you from QUESTIONING your own futility. It confirms on a daily basis the notion that you are POWERLESS, you have no value and it keeps you forever isolated from your fellow men. You are no THREAT anymore and we aim to keep it that way. Gentlemen, the greatest TYRANNIES exist without any visible tyrant and the greatest TYRANT of all has no face and no human form. Meanwhile, you are finding it harder and harder to even function like HUMAN BEINGS at all. Your FAITH is no LONGER in deities but only in things, you all seek ownership not ENLIGHTENMENT! The SECRET of human happiness! Sublime distraction! Dear Old DOCTOR FAUSTUS! He wouldn't stand a chance nowadays! Two minutes of ethical or THEOLOGICAL debate, a moment of doubt or MORAL UNCERTAINTY and pow! Too late! Back of the queue, Sir, behind the rest of us! Poor old sod! A person tells you a YOUNG GIRL has been killed, but you don't react to this, you no longer have that capacity. You don't respond on any HUMAN level whatsoever, aside from maybe the SENSATIONAL angle: was she PRETTY, was there anything SEXUAL? That's where this SATURATION of titillation ultimately leads you!! EVERYTHING is just debased and converted into titillation! Your precious titillation. Even something as tragic and heartbreaking as this! But that's all there is left. There is no understanding there, no EMPATHY, no awareness. A slight secret sense of RELIEF is in there too, somewhere, if you're HONEST. Thank God that it wasn't your daughter, eh? How lucky I am! God, everything in the world is great after all! Then that's it! It's ALL OVER. Just turn away. Turn the page, look what's on the TV later, choose another mindless SPECTACLE to pass before your weary, jaded eyes. Turn the page again, look at the tits of some young lady, just chase the nearest available DISTRACTION, that's all we can do. But our lives touch and connect, I GUARANTEE that someone here in this room knows the person who committed this TERRIBLE act tonight, maybe an acquaintance, maybe a good friend but the CONNECTION is there. It is a fair and logical assumption. But I doubt that matters much to anyone either. Let's FORGET about it, after all we've all come out tonight to enjoy ourselves, right? Yes, thank you for that, I really couldn't see that one coming! The meaningless DISTRACTION is talking back, so SHUT UP! Thank you. ONE DAY you will realise the TRUTH in what I'm saying, I guarantee it! But by then it will all be TOO LATE. Sit down! I'm not finished! So WHAT is the greatest spectacle, what is the most TITILLATING event do you think, a suicide or a HOMICIDE? It's a DIFFICULT one, isn't it, gents. What has the GREATER power to distract?

What do you think has the greater ENTERTAINMENT value? Come on, SHOUT out when you know the answer. SUICIDE or HOMICIDE? Simple choice. WHAT would you like to be FLEETINGLY diverted by? What would STIMULATE your taste buds more this evening? Don't worry if you don't know, we can come back to it later. I promised you a SPECIAL show this evening and I'm a man who keeps his PROMISES. Is that not right, Mister Langton? Thank you. You can't see him at the back but he's nodding his head. Yes, I do keep my promises. You see this EVENING I intend to try a little EXPERIMENT and involve us all in a SITUATION, if you will. An incident in which we can all be players. For this is the theatre of true DEMOCRACY, gentlemen, wherein we all play a part and work with each other. Just like the war. But in this SITUATION we are all going to be working on the same thing. Now, it strikes me that a lot of you gentlemen here tonight do not know who I am, you have no idea. Yes, thank you again, Sir. That is most sporting of you. Others, one or two ENLIGHTENED chaps might have guessed by now. Mmmmm, yes, one or two, maybe. PERHAPS? Perhaps not? But I imagine to most of you I am a complete STRANGER. You don't RECOGNISE me at all. Even though I have been known by SO MANY different names all the way down the YEARS, you still don't know who I am! AMAZING. I do confess, however, that I find this STATE OF AFFAIRS a little depressing. For a LONG, LONG time it didn't bother me, I suppose it actually WORKED to my advantage but recently. I have to admit, it has started to WORRY me. In fact it has worried me a great deal. You see, gentlemen, if forced to choose between NOTORIETY and OBSCURITY, what would be your choice? As I see it, notoriety suggests some EFFORT, some ACTION. To be NOTEWORTHY one must first do something of note. Anyone can be OBSCURE. Look at you, you are all obscure, are you not? UNLESS one of you is responsible for this

POOR GIRL'S demise, that of course would be very different. Instant NOTORIETY! IRONIC really, don't you think? I put it to you, gentleman, that to TRANSCEND this WHOLE CULT of TITILLATION, one needs only to become an OBJECT OF TITILLATION oneself. METEMPSYCHOSIS, gentlemen. By this means we recognise and accept this wretched PHENOMENON and at the same time we raise ourselves ABOVE and BEYOND it. (I'm not TALKING too fast for you, am I, Mr Langton? Oh good.) That, my friends is the CONCLUSION that I have reached too. You see, I have recently started to view my obscurity not as a POSITIVE thing, but as a sort of REFLECTION, a JUDGEMENT, if you like. My VERY EXISTENCE, remains, in common with my sense of PURPOSE, entirely SUBJECTIVE. You see, I'm not VISIBLE anymore. Well, not SUFFICIENTLY visible. I used to INVENT for myself all manner of CONSOLATIONS for this. I tried to turn it into some great VIRTUE, a means by which I might better achieve my aims. But I fear now that this process has failed me. It's a great shame that my FRIEND Sam could not make it this evening, he could certainly vouch for this. I have, in his terms, no PROFILE these days. Not that I ever did of course. I'm not NEWSWORTHY, nobody is interested and nobody gives a DAMN. Sit down and be quiet, it won't be much longer now. I am doomed to TITILLATE, AMUSE and DISTRACT quite anonymously. So, just HOW do we set ABOUT putting all this right? How do I become newsworthy again? I have devoted my ENTIRE life to my trade and BUSINESS, I have SACRIFICED everything and worked in DARKNESS for decades and DECADES. For NOTHING. So just how can I become newsworthy? How do I go about orchestrating a great VISIBLE climax to an otherwise largely INVISIBLE career? It's a tricky one, gents. How can we do this and remain TITILLATING? How do we make SENSATIONAL headlines? You are all going to help me, aren't you? It will not take much to CHANGE everything, even in your saturated, over-stimulated universe it requires just one SINGLE extraordinary act! Ah, but what an act it will be! I weary of MEDIOCRITY and OBSCURITY! I will become newsworthy and a subject of DISCUSSION and debate for years. I will reclaim my once LOFTY position and my NOTORIETY will be assured for ETERNITY! In a few MOMENTS, everything will be different; the reading of one man's LIFETIME will shift and change for ever. And all I will have to do is . . .

God, it was so hot that night.

When he speaks of the incident at the Grosvenor Place Oddfellows Club and Lodge, Detective Sergeant ******* tends to downplay his own role quite considerably. He will, however, with a humility that seems quite at odds with his professional demeanour, often declare that 'it was extremely fortunate' or 'jolly bloody lucky' that the police arrived on the scene when they did. 'Just the right place at the right time' is another of his favoured terms. This might suggest that he was the agent of some karmic or celestial retribution rather than the local constabulary.

Nightclub owners in his experience always knew their rights, they told you they knew their rights like most people said good morning. That evening, Tony Ashmore, the manager of Grosvenor Place Oddfellows Club and Lodge, had demonstrated this great and noble tradition and was most vociferous in declaiming his legal prowess. But it was just a polite word, they told him. Nothing to get all steamed up about.

There had been three of them, himself, young Steve Parkwood and that other one who got transferred to Cardiff. The call had come in just after 10 and they were on the premises within 20 minutes. A Fools Errand, they all agreed, a complete waste of their time. But the word had come down from the District Superintendent and no one could really argue with that. But it stunk of the old school tie. Alderman Hughes was kicking up a fuss because his mother had become 'disturbed and agitated' by all the obscene language being broadcast from the club in Grosvenor Place. The Mayor was a member of the same lodge as the Superintendent and one phone call and another phone call and another and suddenly *ner-ner ner-ner* and a car is on its way.

Caravan Hughes. He was another one for knowing his rights too, if memory serves. 'Good morning Mr Hughes, it seems that this mobile home on your forecourt has been parked so that it is partially restricting access on the pavement.' 'Bugger off! I know my rights . . .'

A polite word, that was all. Mr Ashmore was approached as he was making his way through the lobby, it was assumed that he'd prefer the matter to be discussed as privately as possible. But Ashmore didn't take too kindly to the intrusion and he got quite belligerent at one point. He claimed that the comedian who was currently on stage had not uttered a single profanity during his entire performance. This may well have been the case and subsequent investigations did support the claim but obscene language had been heard at approximately 9.55. Then Mr Ashmore started protesting that it was a private club for paying members and they were all consenting adults and basically he could do what he liked and that there had ever been any bother before. This may have been completely true but it was pointed out that because all the windows of the club had been opened for much-needed ventilation he was effectively producing a public performance and the privacy angle became somewhat debatable. Furthermore, despite the entertainment taking place indoors it could be argued that it was his negligence that was contributing to foul, coarse immoderate language being heard by people far away from the confines of his club. People who may not find such things amusing. Particularly children. Therefore he was personally responsible. After this, he put his case as best he could before posing what he justifiably felt to be a pertinent question of the evening. He asked why three policemen were wasting such valuable time on a relatively trivial matter when there was a murderer on the loose. Detective Sergeant ******* thought for a moment but declined to answer. Their exchange was finally concluded when it was suggested that Mr Ashmore might wish to discuss the intricacies of the matter with the Mayor around the time his licence was next due for renewal.

It was simply requested that the manager killed the power to the house PA system while all the windows were securely shut. It wasn't an unreasonable request and it had all the makings of a workable compromise. Minimum disruption and the Superintendent, Caravan and Caravan's mum would be satisfied with the result.

For the sake of discretion, the two uniformed officers remained in the lobby while ******* accompanied Ashmore into the Chaucer Room. They made their way to the side of the stage where the small two-channel mixing desk for the PA was located. As they got nearer Detective Sergeant ******* glanced at the stage hoping to catch the comedian's eye. It was at the precise moment that the comedian was reaching for something tucked into the rear of his trousers.

Time froze.

It is a moment divided by a moment divided by a moment.

He was seeing.

He was seeing what?

He was seeing what he was.

He was seeing what he was seeing?

Time thawed.

The man was reaching for a revolver of some sort.

God, no!

Now!

He hurled himself onto the stage with such force that in a single manoeuvre he had brought the comedian crashing to the floor. It was an impressive reaction and a particularly effective response but in his retelling of the event Detective Sergeant ******* managed to reduce it to a minor detail. *A bit of a tussle* being his most frequently used expression. As a result of the sheer force of the initial impact the gun clattered away harmlessly to the side of the stage where it was collected by Mr Ashmore. According to witnesses at the time, there wasn't even the slightest suggestion of a struggle, the comedian didn't even seem particularly surprised and as the Detective Sergeant remarked later it was almost as though he'd been expecting such a thing to happen to him.

There was actually quite a round of applause as ******* marched the older man out of the room. Quite a few members of the audience believed that it was all part of the show.

Oddly enough for someone who had been so loquacious during his performance, the comedian was reported to have said very little after he was apprehended. He was taken out to the car, read his rights and informed that at the very least he was looking at charges for being in possession of an unlicensed firearm, carrying a concealed weapon and maybe a few others if it could be proven that he intended to discharge the revolver. He nodded, quite amiably under the circumstances, but said nothing in response to this.

As they were about to leave Tony Ashmore rushed up to the car and tapped on the window. It seemed he was very keen to apologise for his earlier truculence. He was told that it didn't matter but he would be wise to keep his windows shut in the future. Particularly when the Mayor's mum needed her beauty sleep. Besides, at that moment he needed to go and reassure his customers; very few of whom appeared to have fully grasped what had happened on the stage. It was mutually agreed that this was probably all for the best and that very little purpose would be served by the matter being given any publicity. Then, referring back to their earlier exchange, Detective Sergeant ******* suggested that it might of passing interest to Mr Ashmore that less than an hour previously a man had actually been taken into custody in relation to a murder in the locality. No more could be said on the subject at this stage but the gentleman was continuing to assist with the enquiry. Then in his customary manner, ******* added that it was chiefly a result of good police work by Constable Parkwood, who'd spotted a car at various points throughout the day lingering at the scene of the crime and observed the driver acting in a suspicious manner. At this point Mr Ashmore said goodnight.

On the subject of subsequent events that evening, the recollections of Detective Sergeant ******* are fairly hazy after the conversation with Ashmore outside the club. He must have exchanged some words with the comedian, if they'd travelled in silence it would have been unusual and consequently made the trip memorable. They must have talked but the policeman has no memory whatsoever of what was actually said. He may well have asked the comedian what he was intending to do with his gun but, assuming there was a reply, ******* has not the slightest memory of it.

There is just the one thing.

The one thing that he has never been able to forget.

When they arrived back at Fort Hill Police Station, they were advised to use the rear entrance as word had seeped out about the earlier incident. Mr Eric Warne, various friends and family members were at that moment thronging around the front desk demanding to know if the man had been charged. ******* could appreciate their frustration but it was a scene that might easily have turned nasty.

Detective Sergeant ******* explained the situation to the comedian and a vacant cell was found for him while the policeman went to placate Mr Warne. Then, at very precise moment that the cell door was closed the comedian burst out laughing, not a chuckle, a titter or a giggle, not a polite or sarcastic laugh, but a really great guffawing hysterical laugh from deep way down in his chest. It didn't sound forced in any way, it was spontaneous and genuine. It was as though his confinement was the funniest thing in the world. He just laughed and laughed, you could hear him all over the station. Some claimed it made them feel nervous and unsettled or that there was something creepy about it and to this day, Detective Sergeant ******* can still recall with astonishing clarity the comedian's laugh.

It is something he will never forget.

In his confinement the comedian continued to laugh.

It was said that he laughed all night.

In the still of the dark dark hours, Barney Langton wakes and hears a sound. A memory stirs. Awake, asleep, awake, the sound is distant and comforting, growing nearer and nearer pulled by the long ago–far away, long ago–far away trains of the remote and once perfect childhood.

But now it sounds human. Familiar even.

So, limb from limb.

Flesh from flesh.

Slowly.

He moves very carefully and disentwines himself from the breathtaking line of his wife's naked back. In the moonlight he glimpses the subtle curve and arc of spine and shoulder and he can die tonight. His nostrils flare as he surrenders himself for a moment to their musky, lingering scent. A rare creation, a true collaboration, the heat of their moment; love's tangible witness. She moves slightly and is beautiful beyond words but she does not disturb.

He wanders over to the other side of the room and looks down at their son, who is smiling to himself and sleeping deeply.

Then the boy chuckles to himself again.

Barney smiles.

He is dreaming.